THE EVER-RUNNING MAN

Sharon McCone Mysteries
By Marcia Muller

VANISHING POINT
THE DANGEROUS HOUR
DEAD MIDNIGHT
LISTEN TO THE SILENCE
A WALK THROUGH THE FIRE
WHILE OTHER PEOPLE SLEEP
BOTH ENDS OF THE NIGHT
THE BROKEN PROMISE LAND
A WILD AND LONELY PLACE
TILL THE BUTCHERS CUT HIM DOWN
WOLF IN THE SHADOWS
PENNIES ON A DEAD WOMAN'S EYES
WHERE ECHOES LIVE
TROPHIES AND DEAD THINGS
THE SHAPE OF DREAD
THERE'S SOMETHING IN A SUNDAY
EYE OF THE STORM
THERE'S NOTHING TO BE AFRAID OF
DOUBLE (With Bill Pronzini)
LEAVE A MESSAGE FOR WILLIE
GAMES TO KEEP THE DARK AWAY
THE CHESHIRE CAT'S EYE
ASK THE CARDS A QUESTION
EDWIN OF THE IRON SHOES

Nonseries
CAPE PERDIDO
CYANIDE WELLS
POINT DECEPTION

THE EVER-RUNNING MAN

Marcia Muller

WARNER BOOKS

NEW YORK BOSTON

The events and characters in this book are fictitious. Certain real locations and public figures are mentioned, but all other characters and events described in the book are totally imaginary.

Warner Books
Hachette Book Group USA
237 Park Avenue
New York, NY 10017

Visit our Web site at www.HachetteBookGroupUSA.com.

Printed in the United States of America

First Edition: July 2007
10 9 8 7 6 5 4 3 2 1

Library of Congress Cataloging-in-Publication Data
Muller, Marcia.
The ever-running man / Marcia Muller. — 1st ed.
p. cm.
Summary: "The history of corruption may jeopardize Sharon McCone's marriage, but uncovering the secrets of a mysterious firm may be the only way she can save her husband's life, and her own"—Provided by publisher.
ISBN-13: 978-0-446-58242-1
ISBN-10: 0-446-58242-5
1. McCone, Sharon (Fictitious character)—Fiction. 2. Women private investigators—California—San Francisco—Fiction. 3. San Francisco (Calif.)—Fiction. I. Title.
PS3563.U397E935 2007
813'.54—dc22 2006100803

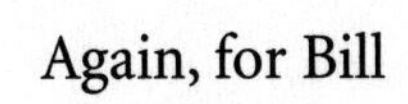
Again, for Bill

THE EVER-RUNNING MAN

Monday

✦

FEBRUARY 20

"Here's what we have on the ever-running man," Hy said.

He dropped the fat file on my desk and sat in one of the clients' chairs, stretching out his long legs and crossing them at the ankle.

I poked the file with my fingertip. It was at least three inches thick, with multicolored pages. "This is the job you mentioned last night at dinner?"

"Right."

"And why's he called 'the ever-running man'?"

"Long story. Maybe you should read the file, and then we'll talk."

I shook my head. "I'd prefer an overview from you first."

Momentarily he looked disconcerted, running his fingers through his thick, dark blond curls. A handsome man, my husband, with his hawk nose and luxuriant mustache and intelligent brown eyes. Normally self-assured, too. But he seldom dealt with me on a professional basis; I'd contracted a few times with Renshaw & Kessell International, the security firm in which he was a partner, but I'd reported to either Gage Renshaw or Dan Kessell. Sitting in my clients' chair and having me set the terms was something Hy wasn't altogether prepared for.

To put him at ease, I motioned to the file and said, "Facts, reports, other people's insights—they're static. Why don't you fill me in, make the situation come alive."

He nodded. He was primarily a hostage negotiator, not an investigator, but he understood the process. "Okay. You asked . . . ?"

"Why you call him the ever-running man."

He steepled his fingers under his chin. "Because every time anyone's seen him he's been running away, and because we've been chasing him for two years. It seems he's capable of running forever."

"And why are you chasing him?"

"He has a vendetta against RKI. As you know, we've got offices in most of the world's major cities. Some are large—New York, Tokyo, Paris, Chicago. Some're medium-sized—Atlanta, Toronto, Sydney, Munich. And others're staffed by one or two people who refer clients to the nearest large office and provide support for our operatives when they're working in the area. There's a complete list of them, along with contact information, in the file."

"And the ever-running man . . . ?"

Hy stood and began to pace, hands clasped behind his back. "It started two years ago last month. January seventeenth. The auto industry and allied businesses were cutting back on corporate security, and we'd downsized our Detroit area office in Farmington Hills. We had only three people working there. On the seventeenth, the office manager was putting in overtime. There was an explosion, and she was killed."

"The cause of the explosion?"

"Something to do with a leaking gas line—at least that's

what the police said. We weren't satisfied with their investigation, so we sent an operative back there to ask around. A woman who was working in an office across the street noticed a man running away from the building a few minutes before it blew, but it was dark and she couldn't see him very well."

"You took that information to the police, of course."

"And they said yeah, sure, thanks a lot. And back-burnered the case."

As Hy continued speaking, he unclasped his hands and began making the wide, swooping gestures that are characteristic of those who fly airplanes. I had never had that mannerism before I became a pilot, but now I caught myself employing it with increasing frequency. It gave me the illusion I could soar even when earthbound.

"Okay," he said. "We put it down as a one-time occurrence. But a month later there was another explosion in a small office in Houston. In the middle of the night, so nobody was killed, thank God, although a witness who was returning home late saw a male-sized figure running in the vicinity. The HPD said the explosion was deliberately rigged, and the FBI was called in, but they never came up with so much as a suspect."

"And I take it no terrorist organization claimed credit for it." In this post–September eleventh world, that was the logical assumption.

"No. The bomb wasn't much of one—simple black powder with a primitive timing device. Guess he was still learning how to build them."

"Obviously that wasn't the end of it."

"Far from."

I was surprised I hadn't an inkling of what seemed to be

a major problem, but I knew the reason Hy hadn't told me about the explosions before this: RKI's inflexible need-to-know rule. Even significant others or spouses didn't need to know about attacks on the firm's infrastructure. But why hadn't I read about the explosions in the papers or seen something on the news?

Well, of course. The media hadn't linked them, and individually they weren't much of a story. Explosions in distant places—unless they're massive or terrorist-related—rarely make the local newspapers.

Hy added, "The police reports're all in the file." He fell silent, staring out the window at the rain falling on San Francisco Bay.

I waited, letting him tell it in his own way and time.

"The next office he hit was Kansas City—again, no one on the premises, and again, someone seen running away. The KCPD techs lifted fingerprints, but they weren't in any of the databases. The FBI began taking more of a serious interest. Our people worked hard at minimizing information passed on to the media. Not a good thing for our clients to realize that their security firm's offices aren't immune to attack."

"And, again, the case was back-burnered."

"After a while, yes." Hy sat back down. "That's when we went on the defensive: closed the smaller offices that weren't worth policing, and put twenty-four-hour guards on those that were. For a while we thought he'd stopped, but the next year he went farther afield, to Mexico City. Guess he didn't want to risk another bombing on US soil so soon after Kansas City. The Mexico City PD's investigation wasn't much—they really didn't care about an attack on an American security firm. But the fingerprints they found matched those from Kansas City.

"After that the guy went underground for a few months, until the guard at our Miami office spotted someone sneaking out of the building and got the bomb squad there in time. No prints, no leads, and again we managed to control media coverage. Finally, last August, he hit our training camp. Blew up a bunch of the clunker cars we use for the new ops to practice evasionary driving."

I thought back to the previous summer. I'd been working a case in the Paso Robles area, and Hy had been spending an unusual amount of time at the training camp in the southern California desert near El Centro.

"You call in the police?"

"Hell, no. We don't even make the camp's existence public. The Imperial County Sheriff's Department knows it's there, but most of the locals think it's some secret government installation. Besides, as explosions go, it wasn't much of one."

"And since then?"

"Nothing. But I don't believe for one minute that he's quit. I feel like I'm sitting on a pile of dynamite, and so do Gage and Dan. This guy's targeted us for some reason, and . . ." Hy spread his hands. "So will you take on this job for us? Find the bastard?"

I asked the obvious: "Why, when this has been going on for two years, are you only asking me now?"

"Dan was determined we handle it ourselves; you know how he feels about outsiders. He was opposed to us hiring you the few times we did. And Gage claimed it was too big a case for you, until I pointed out some examples of big cases you've solved. Frankly, I think he's still pissed off at you for the way you outsmarted him down south years ago."

I smiled. Before Hy joined the firm he'd taken on a job for them to negotiate the return of a kidnapped executive, but had disappeared along with the ransom money. Renshaw had hired me to find him—buying into my claim I held a grudge against Hy—so he could recover the money and then kill him. Instead I'd rescued both Hy and the executive from the kidnappers. Gage hated to be conned—especially by a woman.

I asked, "So how'd you convince them I was the one for the job?"

"As I said, I used examples. And reminded them that you're an investigator, while none of us at RKI is; what we do is prevent crimes, and failing that, negotiate. We know now that we can't handle this ourselves, and as far as the cops and FBI are concerned the cases're cold. Besides, you're an outsider—fresh perspective."

"Okay," I said. "Do you have any idea why this guy has targeted RKI?"

"No, but these explosions have been rigged by someone who's very familiar with our operations. Maybe a disgruntled ex-employee who's getting information from an insider."

"Or he's an insider himself. In any case, I'd need a good cover story in order to visit your offices and training camp and talk with personnel. Otherwise, my connection to you would make it pretty clear what I'm doing there."

"Gage and Dan and I have talked about that. Your cover would be that you're my new wife and want to learn the business."

"A wife who just happens to own a detective agency."

"Look, McCone, we've always kept our professional and our private lives separate. I doubt anyone would make the connection. Besides, this agency is owned by Sharon *McCone*, not Sharon *Ripinsky*—which is what we'd call you. The staff at our office here in the city know you, of course, but you've seldom visited headquarters or any of the other locations."

"Still, somebody might recognize me. I've managed to keep my face off the TV and out of the papers for a while, but . . ."

"So we disguise you. Dye your hair blonde—"

"No, you don't!" My fingertips went protectively to where my black hair brushed my shoulders.

He shrugged. "Cross that bridge when we come to it."

"Not that particular bridge. We're *never* crossing it."

"Okay, okay." He held his hands up placatingly. "So you'll take it on?"

I considered. It struck me that we might be jeopardizing our marriage; neither Hy nor I responded well to authority, and in the investigator-client relationship both sides attempt to wield a fair amount of it. "Who would I report to?"

He smiled. "Knew you'd ask. Not me; I'd never subject you to that. You can take your pick—Gage or Dan."

"Gage, then." Better the one I'd had ample practice at manipulating.

"So it's a deal?"

"Deal. I'll have Ted draw up the contract. But I've got to warn you: since the job will take me away from day-to-day operations here and probably involve a fair amount of travel, I'm going to have to ask for more than the usual retainer."

"Retainer?" Hy widened his eyes, all innocence. "How, when your husband is in need, can you charge—"

"Retainer. Ten thousand will do for now."

He winced.

"Surely you didn't expect me to give a family discount?"

"I didn't, but I had to disabuse Gage and Dan of the idea."

"Well, I'm glad we're all on the same page now."

We both stood, and I went over and put my arms around

him. He was wearing his old leather flight jacket, and I pressed my nose into it, breathing in its familiar aroma.

"So you're off to San Diego?" I asked. RKI's world headquarters were located in an office park in nearby La Jolla.

"Yeah. I should be back here by Thursday, latest."

"You taking Two-Seven-Tango?" Our beautiful red-and-blue Cessna 172B.

"In this weather?" He gestured at the rain pelting down outside the big arching window of my office at the end of Pier 24½. The bay, and a lone tugboat churning by, looked dismal.

"It's a high ceiling," he added, "so I could fly, but I'm not a glutton for that kind of punishment. Southwest's five o'clock flight, a beer, and some of those stale pretzels'll suit me fine. Besides, you might need the plane when you start working on this."

"Good. I'd rather entrust you to the airlines, pretzels and all."

We kissed, and then he moved toward the door that opened onto the pier's catwalk. "Read that file tonight, will you?" he said.

"What else do I have to do?" My tone was somewhat edgy, and I tried to balance it with a smile.

"You could dream of how you're gonna spend RKI's money."

"Yeah. Dream of writing checks to contractors for the house renovation. I'd *better* read the file."

I let myself into the apartment and shut the door, set on the glass coffee table my briefcase and the pizza I'd bought after leaving the pier. The one-bedroom unit on the top floor of RKI's converted warehouse on Green Street at the base of Tel Hill was the firm's former hospitality suite, reserved for clients who had reason to fear for their safety. A few years ago a drive-by shooter had attempted to take out one of those clients, spraying the warehouse's brick façade with bullets and nearly hitting an innocent bystander. After that, Hy—who primarily worked out of San Francisco—had decided the company should shelter at-risk clients in a less conspicuous location: they'd bought a small apartment building in a nondescript neighborhood out in the Avenues as a safe house, and after that the Green Street apartment went unused. Except for now, when Hy and I occupied it while our house on Church Street was under renovation.

I turned on a table lamp, pulled the curtains shut against the February darkness. The light revealed a sterile living room: tan leather couch and chairs, white carpet and walls, motel art. The rest of the apartment was equally bland, and there was little to reflect Hy's or my personalities or lifestyle. Most of the furniture and breakable things from the Church Street house were in storage while contractors worked to make the small earthquake cottage more habitable for two people.

We both hated the apartment, and spent whatever time we could at Hy's ranch in the high desert country near the Nevada line or at Touchstone, our oceanside retreat in Mendocino County. But those places were too far away to commute from, either by plane or by car, on a daily basis. We'd been here since the first week of January, when renovations on the house began, and already we were chafing at our confinement—a confinement made more difficult by the building's oppressive security. If I spent too much time there, I felt as if I were under house arrest.

And I missed my cats.

Ralph and Alice were used to going outdoors, so we'd decided that cooping them up in a small apartment would result in chaos. In addition, Ralph had diabetes and required twice-daily insulin shots, which were administered by Michelle Curley, the teenager who lived next door, because—okay, I admit it—I'm afraid of needles. Finally we'd left the cats with said teenager, in familiar territory where they would be well cared for and free to come and go as they pleased. 'Chelle reported they were doing well, aside from a definite hostility toward the workmen at the house, and they certainly seemed fine every time I stopped over to visit them and consult with the contractor. Last Friday, I'd found them sitting on the fence between the adjoining yards; when I patted them, they'd given me brief, friendly glances before turning evil eyes upon our workers.

I opened the pizza box, contemplated its contents, and went to the small kitchen for a glass of wine. Came back, contemplated again, and decided to wait a while before I ate. My briefcase was fat with the file Hy had presented me with, but I felt no desire to take it out and read it. Only a restlessness that made me pace the floor as Hy had done in my office.

I needed to get away from these white walls and the motel-style watercolors of mountain lakes and meadows. Although I was usually content when alone, tonight I needed company. I went to the phone and dialed my friend and sometime operative Rae Kelleher. Only an answering machine at the Sea Cliff home she shared with her husband, my former brother-in-law, country music star Ricky Savage. Only machines at Hank Zahn's and Anne-Marie Altman's—my married attorney friends who, because he's a household slob and she's a household perfectionist, live in separate flats in the same building. Only a machine at the apartment that my office manager, Ted Smalley, shared with his life partner, Neal Osborn. Only a machine at . . .

Where *was* everybody?

I leaned against the wall by the living room window, which looked out onto the rear alley, and pulled back the curtains. The rain had stopped. A lone light shone in the building across the way, shielded by blinds. A cat slunk through the shadows. A couple of buildings away, a garbage can lid thumped, and moments later a man jogged along in a peculiar, uneven gait—probably one of the city's many scavengers who Dumpster-dived for the edible or useful.

I could go to a movie. No, too restless. Have dinner at one of the many restaurants in the neighborhood? Why, when the pizza—my favorite, Zia's Lotsa Pepperoni—didn't appeal? A drink at the brewpub around the corner that Hy and I occasionally visited? A walk? A drive?

No, no, and no.

Then I thought of my half sister, Robin Blackhawk. Robbie was in law school at UC–Berkeley, and for weeks she'd been trying to get me over there to see her redecorated apartment. I knew she studied hard on weeknights, but maybe she'd be willing to take a break and have dinner with me. Then I could come back and tackle the file.

Robbie was home, glad to hear from me, and said I should come right over, bring some wine, and she'd fix us exotic omelets. I put the pizza in the fridge, grabbed a chilled bottle of Deer Hill chardonnay, and left the apartment.

The guard on the desk in the lobby that night was Jimmy Banks, a student at USF who was putting himself through a graduate program in history by working part time at RKI. I liked Jimmy a lot, and had occasionally sat at the desk with him, discussing San Francisco history. I'm something of a local history buff, while Jimmy was just getting to know the city. He was especially fascinated by my tales of the wild days of the

Barbary Coast and the Gold Dust Saloon, which had stood on this lot before they knocked it down to build the warehouse.

Jimmy looked up from his textbook and waved at me as I went out the door. When I was in college, I'd also worked as a security guard, studying between rounds at various office buildings both here and in Oakland. At the time, I'd thought I was going to be a sociologist—although just what I'd do in the field was unclear. The security job had led me into investigation when I'd discovered that there's little need for sociologists who don't possess advanced degrees. Strange, where circumstance takes you. I hoped Jimmy would be as fortunate.

My old red MG sat across the street. RKI had an underground garage, but this parking space was so convenient that I hadn't bothered to put the car away in its slot. I was just taking my keys out when—

Whump!

The percussive blast threw me against the car. I felt heat on my face, and my ears rang. When I looked back across the street, I saw smoke billowing from RKI's building. The doors to the lobby had been torn off their hinges and were lying on the sidewalk, and glass rained down from the upstairs windows.

I scrambled around the MG, crouched in its shelter.

Another explosion, louder. It rocked the car, sending me off balance. I righted myself, peered over the hood, saw that its paint was blistering from the intense heat. Flames were shooting up from the building's roof. Through the ringing in my ears, I heard people shouting, feet slapping on the pavement, and the sound of a siren in the distance.

Another blast, this one quiet compared to the others, but it was the proverbial straw. I ducked down as the building's brick façade began to crumble.

Tuesday

✦

FEBRUARY 21

I turned away from the doctor just as Hy entered the reception area at S.F. General's emergency services. I shook my head and walked past him and outside. It was raining again. I tipped my head back and let the drops spatter down on my face.

It was after one in the morning. Jimmy Banks, the security guard whom I liked and had hoped would be as fortunate as I, was dead. The doctor had told me there had been no possibility of repairing the massive injuries he'd received as a result of the blasts at RKI's building.

Hy's footsteps approached from behind. He put his hands on my shoulders. "Good you came out here, McCone. I recognized a couple of reporters in the waiting room."

"I wasn't thinking of reporters."

"I know. Jimmy was a good kid, he didn't deserve this."

"Nobody does. You stopped off at Green Street?" I'd called Hy in La Jolla immediately after the explosion, and he and Dan Kessell had flown up in one of the company's jets.

"Yeah. The fire's out. Nothing's left but smoldering wreckage. Arson squad's got it cordoned off and they'll be on the job at first light. They tell me two people who were working overtime're probably also dead."

"Who?"

"Adkins and Shibuya. I don't think you knew either of them."

"No. Ripinsky, I think I saw him."

"Who?"

"The ever-running man. From the apartment window. Someone was running along the alley behind the building, maybe ten to twelve minutes before the explosions. I couldn't see him very well, and I thought he was a scavenger."

Hy turned me around, pulled me close. "Thank God you got out of there before it happened." He was tense, grim; I only felt numb.

"So what do we do now?" I asked. It was a pro forma question; I didn't really care. I kept flashing back to Jimmy's smile and wave as I walked out the door.

"Dan's reserved a room for us at the St. Francis, where he's staying." Hy released me but kept one arm around my shoulders, began moving us toward the parking lot. When I didn't speak, he said, "McCone?"

"I don't want to go to the St. Francis. I want to go home. But home's all torn up, and Touchstone and the ranch're too far away, and . . ." I stopped talking. I was already whining, and I didn't want to add whimpering to the mix.

"I know. Believe me, I know. But being together is the next best thing."

I thought of how close I'd come to never seeing him again. "No," I said. "It's the best. The absolute best."

Dan Kessell was stocky, all muscle in spite of his sixty-some years. His iron-gray hair was cut in an outdated flattop that he'd probably worn since he served in Vietnam, and his blue eyes were small and shrewd behind rimless glasses. Dan was a man of few words, weighing at great length what was said to him and sifting through his thoughts before he spoke. Sometimes his piercing gaze made me uncomfortable.

I didn't know much about Kessell's background, only that he had been Special Forces in 'Nam and then ended up operating an air charter service out of Bangkok. In strife-torn southeast Asia there had been fortunes to be made by the unscrupulous, and Dan had made his by transporting anyone and anything for exorbitant prices. And sending his pilots—one of them being Hy—on risky missions from which there was no assurance that they'd return.

It was on one of those missions that my husband had acquired enough nightmares to last three lifetimes: Dan, in exchange for a bribe from a Cambodian drug lord, had altered Hy's flight plan to a deserted village where his passengers—members of a rival drug operation—were slaughtered and he was forced to participate in the killing to save his own life.

I accepted Hy's reasons for later going into business with Dan. By then Kessell had become a quasi-respectable security pro and RKI was a large, profitable firm. A one-third partnership with generous compensation for what amounted to part-time work—before September 11, 2001, had made corporate and executive protection an extremely hot commodity—allowed Hy to indulge in various humanitarian and environmental projects of his own creation. However, I was always on my guard in Kessell's presence, always aware of the aura of corruption and danger that hung over him.

This morning, though, as he and Hy sat in my office, I felt a certain kinship with Dan. People had been needlessly killed; I would have been among them had I delayed in leaving the apartment last night. Kessell, Hy, and I were united against a common enemy.

There was a knock at the door, and a slender man in stylish slacks and a black leather jacket slipped inside and took a seat next to Kessell. He looked to be Eurasian, like one of my operatives, Derek Ford.

"My executive assistant, Brent Chavez," Kessell said. "Brent, this is Sharon McCone."

Not Eurasian—Latino, or part Latino, maybe with some Filipino blood thrown into the mix. In the melting pot that's California, often it's difficult to guess at a person's origins. I myself am one hundred percent Shoshone Indian, and when I tell people that, sometimes they ask why the Scotch-Irish name of McCone. I give them the short version: I'm adopted. The long story is too complicated to explain.

Chavez and I exchanged greetings, and Dan added, "Brent was in the city on company business yesterday, but fortunately he'd wrapped it up and gone to dinner a couple of hours before the explosion. Not as close a call as yours." He nodded at me.

It was late, nearing eleven. I felt unkempt, wearing the same jeans and sweater and underwear as yesterday. The hotel had supplied the necessities for the night, but I'd need to shop for some clothing later. Some of my clothes were bagged up in plastic against the construction-zone dust at the Church Street house, but they were more formal than my usual attire. I'd also need to call my doctor to get a replacement prescription for my birth control pills. And buy a new hairbrush, shampoo, conditioner, blow-dryer, deodorant . . . A briefcase, PDA . . . My God, the list was endless! This was going to be an expensive proposition until RKI's insurance paid off.

Fortunately, I'd left my laptop locked in the trunk of the MG, and nothing I had had at the apartment was irreplaceable.

Unlike Jimmy Banks's life.

Hy said, "I checked with the guard on the safe house, and nobody's staying there right now. McCone and I'll take one of the apartments. And I've already got our people working on setting up an interim operation on the top floor; our clients can't be left out in the cold because of this situation."

Dan frowned. "You sure it's secure? This guy—"

"Isn't going to wait around here to hit another target. He's long gone. That building's probably the safest place in the city."

"Okay, but watch your backs." Dan reached into his briefcase, pulled out a file, and slid it across the desk to me. "Replacements for the documents that were in the apartment."

"Thanks. What have the police told you about the explosion?"

"This one was different from the others. Before, he used a single charge consisting of ordinary black powder and a simple device for completing the electrical circuit. This time there were three bombs—one on the roof and two in the basement; they can't be sure yet, but they think these were C-4."

C-4: a form of plastic explosive.

Hy said, "You know, I blame the fuckin' Internet for this. Anybody can go online and learn how to construct explosive devices; they even give sources for the materials. We've got all this domestic spying and illegal wiretaps going on, but is anybody doing anything to stem the availability of that kind of information? No!"

To stop his rant, I asked Dan, "Have the feds arrived yet?"

"They're crawling over the site like ants."

"How will that affect my ability to pursue this case?"

He turned cold blue eyes on me. "We don't need the permission of those clowns to run a parallel investigation."

"I'm afraid 'those clowns' won't see it that way. My license—"

"We've got contacts at the Bureau. Hell, you've got a former agent on your staff. Besides, nobody can tell you not to do background on what's in that file." He gestured at the new one he'd given me.

I hesitated, then nodded. "Just see that you work your contacts. And I'll ask my operative Craig Morland to work his."

Annoyance flickered in those cold eyes; Kessell wasn't accustomed to anyone telling him what to do. Then they became as emotionless as before.

I glanced at Brent Chavez. His face was pale and tense, as if he were imagining a scenario in which he'd stayed late last night at Green Street. Or maybe he was attuned to Kessell's mood and hoping it wouldn't flare into unpleasantness.

Kessell stood and motioned to Chavez. "Come on; our pilot's standing by at SFO. We'll fly down south and monitor the situation from headquarters while Ripinsky sets up his operation here."

As the three of them left my office, Hy gave me a thumbs-up sign and winked.

I asked Kendra Williams, our assistant office manager—whom her boss, Ted Smalley, calls "the paragon of the paper clips"—to fetch me a sandwich when she came back from lunch. I fetched myself coffee from the urn in the conference room and asked Ted to keep holding off the media types—a few of whom knew my connection with Hy and had been sucking around the pier all morning—and field any phone calls. Then I settled in to read the file. It was after three by the time I finished. I got up, did a few stretching exercises, then went to the armchair by the window and curled up in it to contemplate the conundrum that was Renshaw & Kessell International.

The firm was a maverick in the world of corporate security. While they provided such routine services as security program design, preventive and defensive training for executives and other personnel, and risk analysis, their emphasis was more on what they called contingency services: crisis-management plans for extortions or kidnappings, ransom negotiation and delivery, and hostage recovery. Insurance companies that write large antiterrorist policies exercise the right to decide what firms will be called upon in case of a kidnapping or other hostile acts; their names are written into the policy, along with the ironclad stipulation that the FBI is to be called in immediately. Not always so with RKI.

Their risky and unorthodox methods more often than not turned out positively, but on occasion had proved fatal for both the hostage and the negotiator. While the other firms in their class mainly employed former CIA and FBI operatives, lawyers and accountants, many on RKI's staff had pasts even more murky and corrupt than Dan Kessell's. Most of their clients were legitimate companies with legitimate concerns and problems, but others had clandestine reasons for wanting a quick fix without notifying the FBI. For those reasons, they paid top dollar.

Gage Renshaw, the third principal in the firm and my old sparring partner, was even more of a puzzle than Dan Kessell. He'd been with the DEA, and had worked in Thailand with a select and low-profile task force called CENTAC; when

CENTAC was disbanded, Renshaw quit the DEA, disappeared for several years, then reappeared in San Diego and teamed up with Kessell.

Both men had returned to the States in possession of small fortunes. Gage's job while in Thailand had been to prevent drug trafficking, but in collaboration with Kessell and others of his ilk, he'd profited immensely from many illegal activities. As Hy had once told me, "Kessell would get at least one referral a week from Gage. Along with his official work, he was out there hustling and making contacts. People wanted to move stuff fast—firearms, gold, jewelry, artifacts, uncut stones, currency. Drugs, too, although Gage professed not to know about that. They wanted to move themselves and their families, and didn't care what it cost. And it cost plenty, because before Kessell gouged them, Renshaw had his hand out for his finder's fee."

Nice folks, my husband's partners. When I thought about them for any length of time, I wondered what he was doing with them.

I wondered what *I* was doing with them.

But then I remembered the hostages whose lives RKI had saved. The attacks on corporate personnel that they'd prevented. And the projects Hy funded with his proceeds from the firm: anything from the relocation of refugees to wetlands restoration.

Was it possible for so much good to come out of such evil? Or was every good deed tainted by the past?

God, McCone, stop trying to be a philosopher, and get your butt in gear.

Before I could stir from the chair, however, there was a knock on the door. Julia Rafael, one of my best all-around operatives, looked in at me. Her strong-featured face was strained, her large dark eyes filled with concern.

"Shar," she said, "I was watching CNN on the plane back from Seattle and found out about the explosion." She'd been up there tracking down a witness in a civil suit. "Are you okay?" she added.

I got up, motioned her inside. "Yeah, I'm okay. Thanks for asking."

"Do you and Hy have a place to stay? Sophia and I would be glad to have you with us; you could take Tonio's room and he could sleep with me."

Julia, who lived in a two-bedroom Mission district apartment with her sister and her young son, had the least to offer in a material way of any of my employees, yet she was willing to open her home to us. The others had offered too, but for them it had involved far less sacrifice. I blinked, afraid I might tear up.

"Thanks so much, Jules, but we've got an apartment available."

"What about stuff? All your stuff must've gotten blown up."

"It was." And I'd been obsessing about it all day. Ridiculous, in light of the enormity of what had happened, but it was my way of disconnecting from my deeper emotions so I could function. When in shock, focus on the small issues.

I looked at my watch. "Damn! I need to go to the store, but I've got to catch Mick before he goes home."

Julia sat down on one of the clients' chairs and took a notebook and pen from her jacket pocket. "Okay," she said, "what do you need?"

"You don't have to—"

"I'll put it on my credit card, and you can reimburse

me next expense report. Shampoo and all that stuff. What brand?"

"... Uh, Dove."

"A robe. Something pretty to cheer you up. Red, I think. Medium?"

"Yes."

"An outfit for tomorrow. Jeans and a sweater okay?"

"Yes."

"Underwear, a nightgown ... No, I doubt you wear a nightgown. Sizes, please."

As she quizzed me and I gave answers, I *did* tear up. And when she left the office carrying her list, I broke down and cried.

After I'd cried myself out, I buzzed my nephew, Mick Savage, who was head of our computer forensics department and my best researcher, and asked him to come to my office in ten minutes. Then I went to the restroom and washed my face and applied fresh makeup from the supply I keep there. I was at my desk and trying to look businesslike when Mick came in.

As he sat on one of the clients' chairs, Mick glanced at my face; a mixture of concern and surprise flickered in his eyes, but he didn't comment.

I broke the ice: "Okay, say it—I look like shit."

"You been crying?"

"Some."

He ran his fingers through his longish blond hair, and his mouth turned down. Mick was a grown man and—as his assistant Derek Ford was fond of saying—a technological genius, but in many ways he was still the kid who expected Aunt Sharon to be a rock at all times. The idea of me crying obviously unnerved him.

After a moment he said, "Well, I guess you're entitled. I mean, last night . . ."

"Was awful. Fortunately, our answering machine was blown up, so Ma can't leave messages on it. I've been taking calls from all sorts of people and family members—even Saskia and Elwood."

"Doesn't surpise me that your birth mother would call—but Elwood? How'd he even know about it?"

Elwood Farmer, my birth father, lived in his own little world on the Flathead Reservation in Montana. "I don't know, but he did express concern."

"The two of you have a strange relationship."

"Well, Elwood's a strange man, but we're working on the father-daughter connection. Anyway, my cellular's turned off, and Ted's holding my calls. I'm safe for a while."

Mick's anxious features—a handsome blending of his mother Charlene's and his father Ricky's—softened into a smile. "Grandma must be climbing the walls by now."

"More like hanging from the ceiling. But she knows I'm okay; Hy phoned and reassured her."

"Still, don't you think she'd like to hear that from you?"

"Yes, and she will—tonight, after I've had a decent meal and a couple of glasses of wine."

He nodded. "I know how you feel. I love Grandma, but . . ."

"Yeah, but." I paused. "How's your caseload coming along?"

"Finished the Aptech job, and Wells Vision is almost wrapped up."

"I've noticed nothing much has been coming in for you the past couple of weeks."

"It's February. All the white-collar criminals're in Hawaii or Mexico."

"Then you'll be free to take on some heavy-duty research for me."

"At your service."

"Okay, here's what I need; you can put Derek on it. A rundown on a long list of names of RKI employees and former employees. I'll ask Ted to copy the pertinent parts of the file and have them on Derek's desk first thing tomorrow."

"Shar, I can take care of it." Last summer I'd cut Mick out of a major investigation because his caseload was too heavy, and instead had used Derek. I suspected Mick still hadn't gotten over being excluded.

"No," I said, "I need you for something more important—and highly confidential."

He sat up straighter, waiting.

"The bombing last night wasn't the first RKI has experienced. There've been a series of them, and they've hired us to investigate."

"A *series* of bombings? God, you never said anything—"

"I didn't know about them. Remember RKI's mantra—"

"Need to know. Okay, who or what am I researching?"

"Three individuals: Dan Kessell, Gage Renshaw, and Hy. Deep background."

Mick's eyes widened. "You're investigating your own *husband*?"

"Mick, somebody's out to destroy RKI. I suspect whoever it is has a grudge against one of the partners. I need to find out everything there is to know about them."

"Why can't you just ask Hy if there's anything in his background?"

"Because I don't know what I'm looking for. And it could

be something he thinks so insignificant that he wouldn't mention it."

"But you're married. Don't you trust him?"

"I do. But people's memories are highly selective. Hy usually doesn't forget anything, but his recollections could be altered by the passage of time. I need facts."

"Does he know you're gonna do this?"

"We haven't discussed it but, yes, I think he realizes it's standard procedure."

Mick shook his head. "Jesus, if I ran deep background on Sweet Charlotte, she'd *kill* me." Charlotte Keim, my primary financial investigator, and Mick's live-in love.

I said, "Well, nobody's out to destroy her life, so you don't have to. But you'd do it in a heartbeat if she were in trouble and you thought you could help her."

That made him think. After a moment he nodded and asked, "Anything else?"

"That's all for now."

"I'll get going tonight, starting with Dan Kessell. I ran into him when he and his assistant and Hy were leaving this morning. There's something seriously creepy about the guy."

"Then find out what makes him that way. And thanks, Mick."

After he left my office, I folded my arms on the desk and put my head down on them, like we used to do during rest period in grade school. If only things were as simple now as they'd been back then, when the worst that could happen to you was being cornered at recess by the class bully and being humiliated in front of those who'd escaped her clutches. Now one had to worry about liars, vandals, crooks, abusers, rapists, kidnappers, murderers, terrorists, politicians . . .

The list was endless.

Wednesday

✦

FEBRUARY 22

"We've got a situation that's similar to the one last August," I said.

Patrick Neilan, a former accountant and the operative who assisted Charlotte Keim on cases involving financial matters, raised his eyebrows.

I explained, "A major job that'll require me to spend a lot of time in the field. I'll need you to coordinate things in the office again."

His freckled face flushed to complement his red hair, and his wide mouth turned up in pleasure. Patrick loved to organize information, make charts, and formulate theories. He wasn't bad in the field, either, but he preferred analytical work.

The waitress arrived with our breakfasts—bacon and scrambled eggs for him, toast and coffee for me. Usually when I go out for breakfast I stuff myself with all manner of cholesterol-laden things, but since the explosion I hadn't been hungry.

We were seated in a window booth at Miranda's, my favorite waterfront diner. After a long period of being in vogue, with lines of hungry customers spilling out onto the sidewalk, the place was undergoing a slump; I patronized it whenever I could, fearing it would close down. It didn't help that the personable owner, nicknamed Carmen Miranda from his days as a longshoreman who offloaded banana boats, had recently semiretired and turned the day-to-day operations over to his unpersonable son Steve.

After the waitress left, I watched Patrick pour ketchup over his eggs—an act that for me has a serious "ick" factor—and then said, "Ted will have a file on your desk by the time we get to the office. It's a thick one, so why don't you take the day off and read it at home? No interruptions that way."

"Great. My ex only bothers me at the office."

"What does she want now?"

"Increase in child support. The last time I picked up the kids, she saw my new car, so she figures she can extort more blood money from me. But you and I know the only reasons I could afford the car is that it's used and you cosigned the loan. And I know that very little of the money I give her goes to the kids, because they're always asking me to buy them things she's supposed to provide. Instead, I suspect it's going up the nose of the sleazy guy she's living with."

"This isn't her boss, the one she left you for?"

"No, he moved out a couple of months ago. This one's an unemployed musician."

I felt sorry for Patrick—more so because my agency had been instrumental in the ex getting her original judgment against him. I said, "Why don't you talk with Hank Zahn or Anne-Marie Altman? I'm sure they can help." Their firm specialized in family law.

"Can't afford to."

"Altman & Zahn and McCone Investigations have a professional courtesy agreement; they'll charge lower fees, extend credit, and dispense good advice to my employees and me—as I will to them."

His gloomy expression brightened, and I was glad of that. Patrick's friendly, open face had not been fashioned for frowns.

When Patrick and I arrived at the pier, I went to the restroom and threw up the coffee and the few bites of toast I'd managed to choke down.

Jesus, at this rate I'd starve to death! Hy and I had had dinner at a Thai restaurant out in the Avenues near RKI's safe house the night before, and we'd barely gotten back to the apartment before I vomited. And then I'd had to sit down and call Ma.

Her opening sally was, "Where have you been all day? Why wouldn't Ted let me talk with you?"

"I was very busy, Ma. And I had to shop." A white lie, but she highly approved of shopping.

Apparently not enough, though. "*Shop*? When you were almost blown to bits last night, you went *shopping*?"

"Everything I had at the apartment was destroyed. I couldn't go on wearing the same clothes forever." I fingered the belt of the beautiful red silk robe that had been among the numerous items Julia had delivered to me before I left the office. It was far nicer than anything I would have chosen for myself, and I suspected it had given her pleasure to pick it out. When I finally did get to the store, I'd buy her something just as nice, by way of a thank-you.

Ma sighed. "Oh, Sharon, I wish you'd get out of that line of work. It's so dangerous . . ."

"And then what would I do?"

"You've got a husband now; I'm sure Hy can support you."

"That's not the point." My tone was sharper than I'd intended. I softened it. "Investigating is what I *do*, Ma. I couldn't just sit around being supported. Besides, I don't think whoever bombed the building was after me."

"Who, then? Hy? Oh, my God, not *Hy*!"

"No. He wasn't even in San Francisco last night."

"Oh, Sharon, he leaves you alone so much . . ." Ma started to cry.

I rolled my eyes and took the glass of Alka-Seltzer that Hy was offering. Thought of Mick's statement: "I love Grandma, but . . ." Concentrated on the "love," rather than the "but."

"Don't cry, Ma. I'm all right, and Hy's all right. That's what matters."

"Oh, but . . ." A snuffling sound, like a pig after truffles.

I said, "Listen, it's late. Why don't you get some sleep, and I'll call you back tomorrow. Ask Melvin to make you some hot milk—"

"Sharon Ripinsky, I have *never* in my life drunk hot milk."

Okay, she's feeling feisty and insisting on calling me what she thinks should now be my name. That's good. Very good.

"A hot toddy then. That'll help you rest."

"Melvin, Sharon says you should make me a hot toddy."

In the background, my stepfather's voice said, "One hot toddy coming up."

An easygoing and loving man, Melvin Hunt. At one time I'd resented him for stealing Ma away from Pa. Now I blessed him.

By noon preliminary reports were coming in from Derek. He'd started on the lengthy list of present and former RKI employees who might have a grudge against the company. Among the former employees he'd isolated a few possibles, but most had settled into new lives, some had died, and a few —no surprise—were in prison. We discussed the possibles and agreed he should go deeper on them.

I knew I should eat lunch, but I was afraid I'd throw up again. When Hank Zahn appeared at the door with a bag from Red's Java House in hand, I actually cringed. Hank—one of my oldest friends from college days, when a bunch of us had shared a big, run-down house in Berkeley—was a tall, loose-jointed man whose head of curly hair had always resembled a Brillo pad, and did even more so now that it had gone completely gray. His eyes, behind horn-rimmed glasses, regarded me sternly.

"Ted says you haven't been eating."

"I've been eating. It just won't stay down."

"This will." He set the bag on the desk, pulled out paper-wrapped burgers, a large container of fries, and two Cokes.

"I don't think I can—"

"Just do it. If I'm wrong, I'll hold your hair back while you hurl."

"Oh, thanks. After all, what're friends for?"

"Right. As I recall, I did that for you a few times in college." He sat down and began unwrapping the food.

When he set my burger in front of me I eyed it warily, then felt a stab of hunger. Picked up a fry and bit into it.

"What brings you across the Embarcadero?" I asked. Initially, Hank's and Anne-Marie's law firm had occupied half of the office suite that was now my agency's. When we'd all needed more space because of our expanding businesses, they'd moved across the wide waterfront boulevard to Hills

Brothers Plaza. Our paths crossed frequently, and we also socialized, but I missed the daily contact with them.

Hank said, "I had a message from Patrick. When I returned the call, Ted told me you weren't doing well, so I thought I'd pop over for lunch and then see what Patrick needs."

"He'll appreciate that." I took a tentative bite of the burger. Pretty good.

"But you don't appreciate me interfering with food."

"I didn't say that." Another fry. Good.

"I don't blame you for feeling ragged. Another few minutes in that building—"

"Don't remind me." Another bite of burger, a sip of Coke. So far, no ominous rumblings in my stomach, no nausea.

"Still . . ." Hank let the word trail off, on his face the quietly waiting expression a therapist might employ.

"What d'you mean?"

"You've been in dicey situations before, and come through them pretty damn well."

I'd been about to take another bite of the burger, but now I set it down.

Finally I said, "This time is different. It's really unnerved me. I was hiding behind my car, watching an inferno that I missed being trapped in by less than a minute. Hank, the heat was so intense, it blistered the paint on my MG. And this guy who was on the desk, Jimmy Banks, he was around the same age as I was when I used to do security guard work during college. Ever since that night, I've been going on crying jags and throwing up, and I can't articulate my feelings, even to Hy, because I don't know what or why . . ."

And there I was, crying again.

Hank got up and came around the desk. Stood behind me,

arms circling my shoulders, cheek pressed against the top of my head.

"Post-traumatic stress, kid," he said. "And you're feeling your own mortality."

"The mortality concept isn't exactly foreign to me."

"But maybe it wasn't as real before."

"So why is it more real now?"

"Because your life has changed. You're married. You've made that ultimate commitment. In theory, since you and Hy have been together a long time, it shouldn't make a difference. But take it from one who knows: it does."

I closed my eyes, pressed my face into the sleeve of his corduroy jacket. Soon the tears stopped, and I felt something ease inside me.

After a moment, Hank released me and went back to his chair. I grabbed a tissue, wiped my face, then picked up the now-lukewarm burger.

Red's food had never tasted better.

"I'm drawing a blank on Dan Kessell," Mick said.

I looked up from the file I was once again going over and motioned him into the office. "What seems to be the problem?"

He perched on the edge of my desk. "Well, the facts as we know them are all there. Born and raised in Fresno, Special Forces in 'Nam, honorable discharge after his leg was shattered by machine gun fire and he spent months in a military hospital in the Philippines. But after that, the available information's sketchy. Nothing much on K Air, and he's barely mentioned or quoted in articles on RKI, other than as 'a partner.' "

"That's because he's always stayed in the background.

When, say, the *Wall Street Journal* does a story about the big guys in the corporate security field, Gage is the one they talk to. When something goes wrong, Gage is the spin doc."

"Makes me wonder why Kessell wants to stay out of the public eye. Like, does he have something to hide?"

"Good question. He claims he doesn't think fast on his feet, isn't articulate enough. And Gage, as you must have observed, is glib and can be charming when it's to his advantage."

"Do you believe Kessell's explanation?"

I frowned as I considered the question. "Now that I think about it, not really. What about personal details?"

"One marriage, to a Gina Benedetti, in Fresno two years before he went to 'Nam. It didn't survive the war. No children. Owns a condo in San Diego, a house—more like an estate—on Maui, various commercial real estate holdings, and a house in Timber Cove."

"Timber Cove? That's down the coast from Touchstone, in Sonoma County. Strange he never mentioned it."

"Maybe he just didn't mention it to you."

"No, I'm sure Hy would've told me if he knew."

Mick shrugged. "Well, there's nothing suspicious about owning property. He probably doesn't use it much, or rents it out to vacationers."

". . . Probably."

"So should I go deeper?"

"As deep as you can. I want to know more about what he did in the Special Forces, his wounds, and that hospital stay. And about K Air. Get the details on his pilot's license and ratings and where he learned to fly. There's got to be something. Also try to find out if the ex-wife is still living and, if so, get an address."

"I'm already on it, ma'am."

* * *

Within the hour Mick called on the intercom. Gina Benedetti Kessell had remarried shortly after she divorced Dan and moved to Albany, an East Bay town bordering Berkeley. She'd died of a heart attack two years ago, but her husband, Eliot Hines, still lived at the same Ramona Street address. The Hineses had one child, a daughter, who lived in Berkeley.

I looked at my watch. After four, and traffic would be heavy on the Bay Bridge, but if I could get an early evening appointment with Hines, I wouldn't mind the slow trip. And then I could pay a call on Robin, to prove to her that I was okay. We'd talked on the phone the morning after the explosion, and she'd sounded badly shaken.

I made my call to the Hines residence; Eliot was home and willing to talk with me as soon as I could get there. Then I dialed Robbie's cellular and left a message saying I'd be in the neighborhood and asking if she'd be free for dinner. After I checked in with Ted and went over a few minor matters, I went forth into the rush hour fray.

Traffic wasn't as horrendous as I'd expected, and I reached the Hines house around five-fifty. Set on a quiet tree-lined street a few blocks off bustling Solano Avenue, it was a pale yellow bungalow whose brick front walk was bordered by gnarled jade plants. The porch light was on against the gathering mist and darkness.

I rang the bell and in a moment a man whom I judged to be in his seventies opened the door and introduced himself as Eliot Hines. White-haired and stooped, with thick glasses and hands as gnarled as the jade plants, he let me into a tidy living room with a fireplace flanked by built-in bookshelves that overflowed with volumes. After offering me tea, which I refused, he motioned for me to be seated in one of a pair of platform rockers that faced the hearth. A Presto log burned there, throwing out very little warmth.

Hines claimed the other rocker and pulled an afghan over his knees. “How was the traffic?” he asked.

“Not too bad, thanks.” I took out my tape recorder, looked questioningly at him.

He nodded his agreement.

“I don’t get over the bridge much anymore,” he said. “After I retired and stopped commuting, Gina did the driving. She was quite a bit younger than me, and a much better driver. We used to go to the city for shopping, or to have dinner or catch a play or concert. Since she’s been gone, I haven’t seen the point in it.”

“I’m sorry for your loss.”

“Thanks.” He sighed. “I never thought she would be the first to go. You said on the phone that you’re looking for information about her former husband, Dan Kessell?”

“Yes. A matter of a relative needing to locate him.” One of my rules is to keep my reasons for asking questions simple—and conventional. “What can you tell me about him?”

“Well, he and Gina were high school sweethearts in Fresno. Married right after graduation—first love, and all that. Dan wanted to get on with the police force there, but he didn’t make the grade. Don’t exactly know why, and I’m not even sure Gina did. So he worked for one of the big food processors in the valley for a year or two, before he went into the military.”

“I take it the marriage wasn’t good.”

Hines nodded emphatically. “When he was sent to ’Nam, Gina was glad to see him go. He’d changed after he was rejected by the police department. Didn’t hurt her physically, but the drinking and the verbal abuse that went along with it were pretty terrible. She knew the marriage wouldn't last, so she went to Oakland and attended business college so she'd have a vocation to fall back on. That's when I met her, through mutual friends at a party."

A light came into Hines's eyes that hadn't been there before—old memories, warming him. "She was still married to Kessell, but had no intention of going back to him. I was divorced and living the high life in the city. If I must say so, I was considered quite a catch: I had a good job in management with PG&E, drove an expensive sports car, lived in a Tel Hill apartment with a bay view. Talk about having your choice of women! But when I met Gina, she changed all that, and I've never for a day regretted it."

"So she divorced Dan Kessell. Did she ever hear from him?"

"Not a word for many years. The divorce papers came back signed, and she thought that was it. But four or five years ago she ran into him on the street in downtown Oakland. She barely recognized him at first. They talked for a minute, and then he said he had to be someplace, and that was it."

"Do you remember what they talked about?"

"She never said. I sensed whatever it was had disturbed her, so I didn't press her." Hines thought for a moment. "You know, she might've told Cecily. They were pretty close at the time."

"Cecily?"

"Our daughter, Cecily Alfonso. She and her husband live up on the hill on San Antonio Street in Berkeley. They've been on vacation in the Caribbean, but they're getting back tonight. Why don't you phone her in the morning—but not too early. Give them time to settle in and start the laundry."

Thursday

✦

FEBRUARY 23

Hy and I were up early Thursday morning, he to meet with the RKI employees who were staffing the interim operation on the third floor of the building and I to go over the case with my staff members. As I was making coffee in the kitchen of the second-floor apartment in the safe house—much larger and better decorated than the one on Green Street—the phone rang. Gage Renshaw, calling from San Diego.

"Ripinsky says you've opted to report to me on this job. Any progress?"

"Nothing I care to discuss yet."

"I want a report e-mailed to me by close of business today."

Pushy bastard.

"Now, Gage, I'm planning to be in the field all day. Would you rather I did that, or wasted time in the office writing a report?"

"A verbal report, then. Five o'clock and no later."

Gage was as abrupt and commanding as ever, but I sensed something in his tone that I'd never heard before: he was unnerved. This last bombing had hit him hard, and his method of dealing with his emotions was to bully me—and probably everyone else he dealt with.

"You'll hear from me," I said. And didn't add, "When I have something to report and the time to do so."

The three-story building at Twenty-eighth Avenue and Balboa Street was nineteen-thirties vintage; its lobby had last been redecorated in the sixties. But the air of not-so-genteel neglect was pure façade. Near the water-stained acoustic-tiled ceiling were carefully placed surveillance cameras; the threadbare carpets covered motion sensors; and behind the cracked plaster wall opposite the garage entry was a high-tech command center from which every inch of the building could be monitored.

Jason Ng, the daytime supervisor, looked up from his bank of screens as I entered. "Morning, Ms. McCone," he said. "Everything all right up there? You need anything?"

"Everything's fine. Are you running a full surveillance on us?"

"Only up to the apartment door, ma'am. Mr. Ripinsky was specific about that."

"Good. Anyone else in the building besides the company people?"

"Two-A's occupied as of last night."

I glanced at the monitors, but he'd already pressed the controls so they'd swiveled away and I couldn't get a look at them.

"High-risk?" I asked.

"Nothing we can't handle. The party'll be gone tomorrow."

A smile for the boss's wife, but no information forthcoming.

Goddamn "need to know"!

* * *

My morning meetings were largely unproductive. Derek's backgrounding on the RKI employees was going slowly. Mick was working on further information on Kessell, getting started on Renshaw, and didn't want to be disturbed. Patrick was setting up his flow charts and entering information from the RKI file he'd read yesterday, but said they weren't worth looking at yet. My only small success was getting an appointment with Cecily Alfonso, Eliot and Gina Hines's daughter, for one p.m.

I'd had a message from Robin saying she was sorry she'd missed my call last night, so I got hold of her and we agreed to meet for lunch at her apartment on Cedar Street in Berkeley. She made the promised exotic omelets, and I admired the way she'd painted and furnished the studio. Seeing me whole and healthy eased her concern, although she did say as we parted—she to the law library, I to the Alfonso house—that I was to give her no more scares of that magnitude. I assured her that I'd try my best not to.

Cecily Alfonso's home on San Antonio Street in the lower Berkeley hills was set high above the street and screened by yew trees. I climbed a brick stairway to a door at the side and, after I pressed the bell, took in the expansive view of the Bay and the sunlit towers of downtown San Francisco. The recent rains had fled to southern California, where they were having mudslides, and the temperature had risen into the low seventies. People who claim California doesn't have seasons don't know what they're talking about; not only do we have a spring, summer, fall, and winter, but micro-seasons on a day-to-day basis.

The woman who answered the door was tall, blonde, and deeply tanned, wearing a long turquoise-and-pink dress whose thin fabric hung loose on her thin frame and swirled above her bare feet as she moved. Strange attire for February, but then this was Berkeley, where people are known for their individuality.

She identified herself as Cecily Alfonso and took me into a light-filled front room where plants—hibiscus and plumeria, I thought—bloomed by the windows and large paintings of tropical scenes dominated the walls. As we sat on floral-cushioned rattan chairs, she caught me looking at the ornate silver toe ring on her right foot and said, "We just got back from the Dominican Republic. My husband's extended family lives there, and every year we visit them for a month. I love it, and when we come back, I hate letting go. So I turn up the heat and wander around the house in my Island clothes for a couple of days. Then it's back to the old down jacket and sturdy shoes. And my job at the library."

"Your father didn't tell me you're a librarian."

"Oakland main branch. And don't get me started on the shortage of funds for our collections."

I nodded in understanding. Our state libraries were low on the legislative priority list and woefully underwritten. The worst example that had come to light in recent years was the near-closure of the public library in Salinas—the city where Nobel Prize–winner John Steinbeck had been born and raised.

"Tape recorder okay?" I asked.

"Fine."

I turned it on. "Your father said you might be able to tell me something about an accidental meeting your mother had with her first husband, Dan Kessell. It was four or five years ago."

Cecily Alfonso frowned, putting the tips of her fingers to her lips.

"Four or five years ago. That would have been . . . Of course. It was five years ago in August, the month I started at the main branch. Mom came over there and I gave her a tour, and then we went out for lunch in Chinatown. She called me the next day, very upset. After she left me, she ran into Dan, whom she hadn't seen since he left for Vietnam."

"What specifically upset her?" When Cecily didn't reply, I prompted, "Simply seeing a man she used to be married to after all that time? His appearance? Something he said?"

". . . I suppose all of those things. She did say that he acted hostile. Which, I suppose, would be normal for someone whose wife had divorce papers served on him while he was in the hospital recovering from war wounds."

"Did she repeat anything he said to her?"

Cecily hesitated again, her eyes on a brightly hued painting of flowers bordering a sand beach and blue sea.

"I'm sorry," she said after a moment, "but I can't remember. Mom could be . . . well, dramatic, and after I became an adult I kind of tuned her out."

"Dramatic in what way?"

"She blew every little thing out of proportion. If a man followed her down the sidewalk for more than two blocks, he was a stalker. If the UPS guy dropped a package on the porch, rather than setting it down neatly on the doormat, he had it in for us. If Dad missed his BART train and was late coming home, he'd been mugged or killed."

"Paranoid?"

"No, more like she needed drama in her life. I'm not sure she really believed any of it."

Interesting. She'd divorced Dan Kessell to rid her life of the drama of abuse, then gone on to manufacture various other over-the-top scenarios.

I asked, "Was she always like that?"

"As long as I can remember. Dad would make excuses for

her: 'Your mother is very nervous,' he'd say. 'Your mother is very high-strung.' " Cecily bit her lower lip. "That didn't make it any easier to live with."

"Did she ever seek professional help?"

"Once. I insisted."

"When?"

"About four years before she died."

"A year after she ran into her ex-husband."

"Right."

"Did it do any good?"

"No. It seemed to make her worse. She went to the therapist for two or three sessions and then she quit. After that she wouldn't leave the house except when she was with Dad. And even then . . . well, I don't think she enjoyed herself."

"What gave you that impression?"

"Because of something Dad once said. He's not the sort of person who communicates well about emotional things, so it surprised me, and I've always remembered it. He said that she couldn't enjoy herself because she was always looking over her shoulder."

Before I left Cecily Alfonso, I asked her to talk to her father about giving me permission to discuss her mother with the therapist she'd consulted. Then I left and drove down Solano Avenue, intending to take the freeway back toward the Bay Bridge and the city. But as I neared the on-ramps, an impulse made me turn east on Interstate 80, toward where it branched off to the Richmond Bridge and Highway 101 North.

The radio traffic reports warned of an accident and slowdown south of Santa Rosa, so at Petaluma I left the freeway, crossed town, and soon was in open country, where dairy and sheep ranches spread over the softly rounded hills. At Bodega Bay the weather turned foggy; the fishing village and tourist destination was relatively deserted, the saltwater taffy concessions and souvenir shops dark and closed, the extravagant kites outside one store hanging limp and damp. The weather worsened, and by the time I reached the hamlet of Jenner, where the Russian River meets the sea, visibility was poor. I pulled into the service station at the south end of town, bought a Coke, and called the office. After that point my cellular reception would be spotty to nonexistent, the high coastal ridge cutting off the signals.

Ted reported that it had been a quiet day. No new business, no important calls for me. I asked for Mick, but he'd gone out on an unspecified errand. When I spoke with Derek, he said he was making progress on his possibles list, but as yet had nothing useful. Patrick had finished with the flow charts, but he called them "nothing special" and said he'd gone back to working on a case for Charlotte.

Dull February afternoon.

Hy didn't answer his cellular. I called the apartment at the safe house and got the machine. Left a message telling him where I was and that I might continue on to Touchstone and spend the night there if driving conditions worsened. Then I went on, up the Jenner Grade—a series of extreme switchbacks that leave those who don't know the road white-knuckled and sweaty. The MG and I had been this way many a time, and we handled it like pros.

The mist worsened as dusk fell, and there was no southbound traffic. I switched on my fog lights. After a few miles, they picked out the weathered wooden cupolas and towers of Fort Ross—originally settled by Russian fur traders who had trekked down from Alaska in the early eighteen-hundreds, and now a historical monument. I slowed to a crawl once I was past the fort, enveloped in a thick, fast-blowing fog, and some minutes later picked out the lights of the little gas station and store south of Timber Cove.

The address for Dan Kessell's property was on Sandpiper Drive.

I went into the store, bought another Coke for politeness' sake, and asked for directions. The street, the clerk said, was in "a buncha little houses on the ocean side" a few miles north. "Turn left at the brown-shingled place with the big satellite dish," he advised me.

The brown-shingled place was hard to make out in the darkness, but the satellite dish loomed over its surroundings. I turned onto pavement that was ragged-edged and potholed, crept along looking for house numbers. Kessell's was one door away from where the road ended, its number fading on a mailbox that leaned in the same easterly direction as the wind-warped cypress on the bluff's edge. I made a Y-turn, allowing the MG's headlights to move slowly over the cottage.

Aluminum siding—had to be. Dark-green paint on wood couldn't possibly look that good after being battered by these strong sea winds. Small, perhaps four rooms, with a large window facing the bluff's edge. Propane tank to one side. Empty chain-link dog run to the other. Woodstove chimney protruding from the flat roof. A faint light shone at the house's rear.

I drove back along the street and left the MG in front of a dark house. In the distance I could see the lighted "Peace" sculpture on the bluff at Timber Cove Inn—a structure with an upraised hand that resembles a giant totem pole, created by the famed San Francisco sculptor Beniamino Bufano. I walked slowly, avoiding mud and potholes, glad that I'd dressed in my new black jeans and sweater that morning.

When I got to Kessell's cottage, I slipped along the side where the propane tank sat, toward the light at the back.

It seeped around a pair of blinds that had not been fully lowered. I went up on my toes, peered inside. Partial view of a small, tidy kitchen decorated with unfortunately garish blue tiles, and a sink drainer full of clean dishes.

Nothing interesting there. As I started around the house, looking for another window, I heard the rumble of a large vehicle approaching. I went the other way, realized it was a mistake when the vehicle's headlights and cab-top spots made me freeze by the propane tank. I threw up my arm to shelter my eyes.

"Excuse me, ma'am," a rough baritone voice said. "You lookin' for somebody?"

The driver of this monster vehicle, whoever he might be, had given me an out, since I didn't want Kessell to know I was backgrounding him. "Yes. My friend, Anne Altman. She doesn't seem to be home."

A bulky man stepped in front of the headlights, moving slowly and favoring his right leg. I couldn't make out his features, but he was wearing some kind of uniform. Private patrol. There are a lot of private patrol companies operating in the coastal area, where second homes are often left empty and vulnerable for months at a time. While they try to appear inconspicuous—no names or phone numbers on their neutral-colored vehicles—the spotlights on top and long antennas that allow them to monitor the police radios give them away.

"May I see some ID, ma'am?" The man's tone was nonconfrontational.

"Sure." I moved toward him, fumbling in my purse, and slipped out the falsified New Mexico driver's license that an informant—a convicted forger now almost gone straight—

had provided me. It said I was Nancy Estrada—a name that more or less fit with my Shoshone looks.

The man checked it with a flashlight. Now I could see his face—weathered and creased, with the deepest lines around his eyes and mouth. He studied the license, handed it back to me.

"Your friend doesn't live here," he said.

"No? I'm sure it's the address she gave me."

"No Altmans here."

"Whose place is this? Maybe the guy she's living with—"

"No woman living here. You'd best move on."

"This isn't Sand Dollar Drive?"

"Nope. Sandpiper. You got your sea creatures mixed up with your birds."

"Oh, God, I'm sorry! I feel so foolish . . ."

"No harm done, ma'am. You have a good evening." He touched the bill of his cap in a little salute and moved back toward the monster vehicle.

When I skirted it, angling for the MG, I spotted a big Doberman sitting in the truck bed; unmoving, it stared down at me. The door of the truck slammed and its engine started up, but the guard didn't turn around and follow me as I'd expected. Instead he kept going toward a secluded bluff-top home at the end of the road.

I debated waiting to see if anyone came back to the lighted kitchen in the green house, but decided against it. Many second-home owners leave a light on in the window, and the hell with electric company bills. Hy and I were not that extravagant, but we did leave a nightlight burning in the entryway at Touchstone, as well as lights around the property's perimeter that switched on at dusk.

Right now, those lights beckoned me.

Friday

✦

FEBRUARY 24

Past midnight, and I couldn't sleep. Normally the sound of the surf in Bootlegger's Cove below Touchstone lulled me, but tonight when I stepped out for some fresh air on the small deck beside the master bedroom, the crashing and booming of breakers heightened my restlessness.

I went back into the bedroom, locked the door, reset the security system. As with my mother, hot milk had never done the trick for me on a sleepless night, but a brandy might help . . .

As I went down the hall to the combined kitchen, living, and dining room, the house hummed with silence. While not nearly as large as the original structure that had stood on its foundations—which, coincidentally, had been destroyed in an explosion—it was larger than what I was used to. I skirted the pit fireplace that separated the sitting and dining areas from the kitchen, snapped on the overhead lights. The red indicator on the answering machine blinked at me; I'd forgotten to erase the messages that had accumulated during our two-week absence. Most had been the usual: wrong numbers, solicitors, friends down at the Sea Ranch hoping we'd come up soon and wanting to get together for dinner in Gualala. But two were from Gage Renshaw, who had apparently learned from the office or Hy that I was in residence. He was pissed off because I hadn't gotten back to him. I deleted his messages along with the others.

And then tensed, thinking I heard a sound in the guest wing. There were two bedrooms and baths there, reserved for the inevitable influx of friends and relatives, plus small offices for Hy and me.

I strained my ears. Another sound—faint, stealthy?

No, McCone, don't do this to yourself.

The security system on the gate and the property-line fence hadn't been breached. Neither had that of the house. As part of my routine precautions upon arrival, I'd checked the small stone cottage on the cliff's edge, where we used to stay before we built the house, and the shed where we kept an old pickup truck for the times when we flew here.

All was as we'd left it a couple of weeks ago.

So why the anxiety?

I took the brandy bottle from the cupboard, found a glass. Glanced toward the guest wing again. Set down the glass and went that way, switching on the hallway lights and looking into each room. No one there, nothing disturbed—

Except something was wrong.

It was in the air, the feeling of a violated space. Someone had been in the house in my absence. Someone who should not have been.

I checked the closets, the windows. Nothing out of place. Everything secure. When I went back down the hallway and stepped into the central room, my reflection in the dark seaward windows startled me.

That's what a violation of your personal space will do to you.

But who? And why?

I pulled the blinds against the foggy night, poured the brandy, and took it back to the bedroom, where we had a hot tub in an alcove with windows facing the sea. I got the jets going, pinned up my hair, and slipped out of my robe into the warm, soft water. Sipped brandy and leaned my head back against the tub's padded edge, telling myself that morning would be time enough to figure out how our security had been breached.

Tomorrow couldn't come soon enough.

"I found it," Garland Romanowski said as he stepped into the kitchen.

I looked up from the small round table where I was nursing a third cup of coffee. A big, gray-haired man in a plaid flannel shirt and none-too-clean jeans, Garland was the security specialist who had installed our system here at Touchstone. Hy, with paranoia born both of his past association with Renshaw and Kessell and his knowledge of the firm's inner workings, had insisted we not use any of their people; a friend who had installed my system in the city had recommended Garland as the best on the Mendocino Coast. Apparently he was very good; he'd arrived only half an hour before, and already he'd located the source of the trouble.

"So it *was* breached," I said.

"Yeah—and by somebody who knows what they're doing. There's this gizmo in one of the outside junction boxes. Looks like this." He held up three fingers in a configuration that I couldn't decipher. "The system's only weakness. If you disconnect it, the whole thing's disabled. But you gotta know where it is, and messing with it leaves signs, 'cause if you don't want anybody to know you got in, you gotta splice it afterwards. Wanna see?"

"I'll take your word for it." Understanding security systems has never been one of my strong points. "Any idea of where the person entered?"

"Probably the window of the smaller office. It's the closest to the junction box. But maybe not; that would be taking a chance, because it faces the highway."

"We're a long way from the highway, though." I paused, frowning. "But how did this person get onto the property? You checked the gate and the perimeter fencing and didn't spot anything."

"Well, there's the airstrip. But a plane landing on the bluff top is pretty conspicuous." Garland motioned at the windows facing the sea. "You got a cove down there where a small boat can be beached at low tide. And steps coming up to that platform on the edge of the cliff. I'd say that's a possible."

I sighed. "There's not much we can do about the airstrip. If somebody wants to land there, they will. What about the platform?"

"You might consider wiring it. I'd suggest weight and motion sensors hooked into a loud alarm that'll scare 'em off."

"What would that cost?"

"I'd have to work up an estimate. If we can wire it into the system on the little stone cottage, shouldn't be too much."

I pictured the checks Hy and I had been writing to the contractor for the house in the city. Pictured the checks we'd soon be writing to Garland. Finally said, "Work it up and e-mail it to me, please."

"Will do. Any idea what they were after?"

"No. As far as I can tell, nothing's missing or looks like it's been disturbed."

"Well, like I said, they knew what they were doing with the system. Probably knew how to make an inconspicuous search, too." He touched his index finger to the bill of his old Point Arena Pirates cap and started for the door.

"Garland," I called after him, "do you know any of the private patrol companies down Timber Cove way?"

"I know a couple of retired guys who patrol to supplement their Social Security. Why?"

I described the man whom I'd encountered the night before at Dan Kessell's place, his truck and his guard dog, too.

"Doesn't sound familiar. But I don't get down there all that often."

"Well, thanks. I'll look for that estimate."

After Garland's blue truck pulled away, I poured the rest of my coffee down the sink drain, rinsed the cup, and put it back into the cabinet. Then I went to the smaller office—mine, because in an effort to keep my professional and private lives separate, I seldom work at Touchstone—and stood in the doorway, looking around and trying to imagine an intruder slipping through the window, checking the file cabinet that contained little more than the architect's plans for the house, manuals and warranties for the appliances, and miscellaneous clippings. A number of phone books sat on the shelves, as well as books I'd brought up to read and decided to leave there, but they were greatly outnumbered by shells and pieces of driftwood I'd carried up from the cove. The table on which I set my laptop when I was in residence was bare except for a coffee mug full of pens and pencils, a scratch pad, and a photograph of Hy, Ricky, and Rae planting a cypress sapling in front of the house. Ricky stood by, arms folded, contemplating Rae, who, bent over, was placing the tree in the hole Hy had dug. Behind her, Hy raised the shovel, a fiendish look on his face as he mimed hitting her on the ass.

I smiled at the memory and went to Hy's office. It was more cluttered, as he liked to come up here alone and immerse himself in his charitable works. There was a fax machine, two four-drawer file cabinets, and an old tangerine-colored iMac that he professed to love so much he'd never part with it. I had a certain affection for the machine, too: one boring, rainy weekend when I was staying alone in the stone cottage on the cliff, I'd overcome my aversion to computers by playing with it.

Today the office felt strange; the aura of violation I'd sensed last night was very strong there. I checked the file cabinets, but the drawers were locked, and I couldn't find a key in the desk drawers; Hy probably kept it on his key ring. Then I turned the computer on and waited as it took its usual old-machine time to boot up. Finally the screen brightened to a sky-blue background, and icons appeared. Quite a few icons; Hy liked to keep most of his active files on the desktop. They were labeled cryptically, and I didn't know what the titles meant. I clicked on them—Mendocino Coast Coalition for Open Space, Hurricane Relief Fund, Olompali State Park Restoration Fund, among others—but all seemed innocuous and worthy causes.

Next I went to the listing of files on the hard drive, checked the dates they'd last been modified. The most recent was Sunday, two weeks past, before we'd left for the city. That didn't mean someone hadn't been looking at the files afterward; if the intruder hadn't made any alterations, I had no way of knowing whether he'd opened them or not. I clicked on the trash icon. Empty. Finally I logged on to the dial-up service—DSL still not being available on our part of the coast—typed in Hy's password, and waited for a connection. Checked his seldom-used AOL mailbox. Several messages, all of them looking like spam.

Your mortgage payment is due . . . Natural penis enlargement . . . Free stock tips . . . Swiss watches at bargain prices . . . She wants better sex! . . . A lonely housewife in your area . . . Viagra by mail . . . Custom-made caskets delivered to your door . . . Free stuff for completing survey . . . Contemplating a career change? . . . Sender unknown, no subject. I opened that last message.

YOU'RE TOAST, RIPINSKY!

I sped along the twists and turns of the coast highway, the iMac on the passenger seat. When I'd called Hy to tell him what I'd discovered, he asked me to bring the machine back to the city. "We'll get Mick to recover any files that might've been deleted," he said.

"Maybe he can find out where that nasty e-mail came from."

"You're taking it too seriously, McCone. I know a lot of people with . . . well, warped senses of humor. That's why I give them the AOL address, rather than my regular one." But there was an undertone of concern in his voice that I couldn't ignore.

At Timber Cove I detoured along Sandpiper Drive. No vehicle parked at the Kessell cottage, no smoke coming from the chimney, no dog in the fenced run. It wasn't the sort of place Dan Kessell would come for a vacation—he preferred expensive resorts with world-class golf courses—but it had occurred to me that he may have bought the place as an investment. Oceanfront property, being in limited supply, never depreciates in value; he might have had the idea of buying up the surrounding lots for future development as they came on the market. He'd done something similar with an old housing tract south of San Diego, turning it into a sprawling industrial park. Wouldn't you know that one of Dan's hobbies was disfiguring the landscape?

But it could be someone was living in the little house. Or at least coming and going, leaving a light on in the kitchen. I parked the MG and began knocking on doors.

The first three cottages I stopped at were closed up, obviously second homes. At the fourth, a voice, quavering and old, identifiable as neither male nor female, told me to go away. A woman at the fifth told me she wasn't buying anything and slammed the door in my face. But at one halfway between there and the highway, a big man with bloodhound jowls and wild, wispy hair that probably hadn't been in contact with a comb since 1992 greeted me pleasantly. Yes, he said, he knew the occupant of the green cottage. Not well, but he and Mr. Kessell got along.

"Mr. . . . Dan Kessell?"

"That's his name."

"Can you describe him for me?"

The man frowned, enhancing his canine appearance. "May I ask what this is about?"

I gave him one of my cards. "It's in regard to an inheritance."

The frown deepened. "You one of those heir hunters?"

"No, my client is a legal firm in San Francisco, Altman and Zahn. You can call them and verify that, if you like." Hank and Anne-Marie were used to covering for me. Part of our professional courtesy arrangement.

"No, that's all right. But you have to be careful these days, you know. So many breaches of personal privacy. Mr. Kessell is in his sixties. White hair, leathery face, stocky."

"What does he do for a living?"

"Private patrols for the second-homers. Home maintenance, too. Does well at it; there're a lot of moneyed people on this part of the coast and up in the hills, although you couldn't tell by looking at our little enclave." He snorted. "People complain that we, and that trailer encampment up the highway, are a blight on the coastline. They can't wait for all of us to die off so some fool can come in here and put up luxury homes. But we're not ready to croak just yet. Most of us have been here a long time—and we intend to stay."

"Has Mr. Kessell been here long?"

"Oh, my, yes. Before I came here, anyway, and that was in eighty-four."

"And he's here all the time?"

"As far as I know, the only time he goes anywhere is on Costco runs to Santa Rosa and hunting or fishing trips."

"Does he own a big truck, probably a GMC, and a Doberman?"

"Yes. Why? Have you seen him?"

"I just missed him as he was leaving yesterday. Mr. . . . ?"

"Bradshaw. Chuck."

"Mr. Bradshaw, thank you for your helpfulness. I'd like to ask you not to mention my visit to Mr. Kessell."

"Why on earth not? If the man's come into money . . ."

"I think I have the wrong Dan Kessell. Your neighbor doesn't fit his description."

"Well, that's too bad."

"Yes, it is. Thank you for your time."

On the way back to the MG, I tried to picture the property

search report Mick had given me. No owner's Social Security number, no identifying details except for the property location and the address where the tax bill was sent—and both had been the same. He'd merely hit on the wrong Dan Kessell.

But I didn't feel my coming up here was a waste of time. Not after what I'd found at Touchstone.

"Nothing to it," Mick said. "These ancient machines're as easy to crack open as a peanut shell."

Why, I wondered, were my nephew's similes always couched in terms of food?

"Crack away," Hy said, and left the office. He sounded annoyed. Probably because of Mick calling the iMac an ancient machine. For most of his life, my husband had been a confirmed PC user, until this bright-orange baby had lured him into the Apple camp. It was akin to being told your first love couldn't keep up with the younger, sexier numbers on the dance floor.

"Before you get started," I said to Mick, "I think you should know that one of the properties you came up with on Dan Kessell was a dud."

"Oh?"

"Timber Cove. Different Dan Kessell."

He frowned. "Interesting. Thing is, Kessell—spelled with two *l*s—is not all that common a name. And I found only two residential properties in California to which a Daniel Kessell holds title."

"A coincidence. It happens."

"Yeah." Mick turned his attention back to the iMac. "Well, let me see what I can do here. Shouldn't take long."

"That can wait till later," I said, taking Derek's chair and propping my feet on the shelf of his workstation. "First I need to know what you've come up with on Gage Renshaw."

Mick swiveled toward me. "Now, he is one interesting guy. Like Kessell, born and raised in Fresno, although I wasn't able to turn up any link between them."

"Dan's older than Gage; kids tend to associate with their peers."

"Right. I don't think Gage had many peers, though; he was a brilliant student, class valedictorian and, I gather from his lack of extracurricular activities, a loner. Received full scholarships to a number of colleges and chose USC, where he was prelaw. Started law school at Georgetown in D.C., but dropped out when he was recruited by the DEA."

"Why, I wonder?"

Mick shrugged. "Excitement, travel. Maybe the law bored him."

"Sounds like what I know of the man."

"You know about CENTAC?"

"Not a lot. They were an elite, high-security task force of the DEA that was suddenly disbanded. Almost everything about them is classified."

Mick smiled. "Yes, ma'am, but I'm working on getting it. The words 'elite' and 'high-security' suggest the kind of power their operatives had; most of them used it positively, but not Renshaw. Those stories Hy told you about his wheeling and dealing are accurate. I e-mailed a couple of people who would know, and they confirmed it. But that's not the part of Renshaw's story that interests me; it's the years after the task force was disbanded and he resigned from the DEA. There's no evidence he came back to the States, and no hint of where he was all that time."

I considered for a moment. "When did he reappear?"

"A year and three months after Dan Kessell established RKI—well, Kessell International, at that point. Renshaw turned up in San Diego, opened a bank account, and the next day, close to seven million dollars were wired to it from Credit Suisse."

"Some of which he used to buy into the company."

Mick shook his head. "Kessell gave Renshaw a fifty percent interest for one dollar. And here's another thing I find fascinating: the firm went from being Kessell International to Renshaw & Kessell International. Gage first."

I thought back to when Hy joined the firm. They'd solicited him with a one-third ownership, bonuses, and incentives. But at the time they'd badly needed someone who could negotiate in hostage and ransom situations—for which Hy had discovered a talent while flying for K Air in Thailand—and were willing to make concessions to bring him on board. But for Kessell to yield a one-half interest in what had then been a fledgling company without demanding any investment from Renshaw? What was that about?

I said to Mick, "I think Renshaw has something on Kessell. He's probably holding their dealings in Thailand over his head."

"But wouldn't that mean Kessell also has something on Renshaw?"

"Yeah. Except maybe Renshaw kept a video- or sound-taped record of their transactions."

"That sounds like a tactic Gage would employ."

I considered for a moment, then said, "Why don't you put that iMac on hold, or turn it over to Derek when he gets back from lunch. Keep digging on Renshaw and Kessell."

* * *

By one that afternoon, Gage Renshaw had left five messages for me—each sounding more irate than the one before. I ignored them and consulted with Patrick—giving him information to plug in to his charts—and caught up on agency business.

Kendra had a problem with the UPS guy; twice now he'd tossed packages into the locked enclosure that served as the pier's mail room, damaging their contents. She'd heard he was going through a divorce, but that was no excuse, and would I authorize her to complain to his employer?

Hell, yes!

Ted reported that there was a new program that would allow him to process employee expense reports more efficiently, and would it be okay to purchase it?

Of course.

At four-thirty, Cecily Alfonso called to say that her mother's former therapist, Wendy Benjamin, had agreed to talk with me, but that it would have to be on the weekend. I phoned Ms. Benjamin, and we agreed to meet at noon on Sunday at a restaurant on Fourth Street in Berkeley. "I'll treat you to brunch in exchange for wrecking your day off," she said. "This is a busy week, and that's the first opportunity I'll have to come up for air." I agreed and put it on my calendar.

Gage called again at five. "Where's that report, McCone?" he growled.

"I don't have anything written yet, but I can give you a verbal rundown on the investigation." I turned to the computer and opened the file Derek had sent me on the former RKI employees. None of the possibles had checked out as being in the vicinity at the time of any of the explosions. After I read it to Gage, I said, "Of course, this is preliminary information—"

"That's *all* you've accomplished in four days?"

There was no way I'd tell Gage that I'd been deep-backgrounding Kessell and him. It was a line of investigation he'd be sure to resent and, if he did have anything to hide, it would put him on his guard.

"Not all. I've been working my contacts and interviewing people."

"More like sitting on your butt at Touchstone."

"There was a security problem, and I had to run up there."

"Oh? What kind of security problem?"

"Nothing major. It's fixed."

"I told Ripinsky he was a fool not to use our people for that place."

"Yes, I know you did."

"So when do I get that report?"

"How about if I fly down there on Monday? I want to take a look around headquarters and the training camp."

"Sounds good."

"I'll see you then." Quickly I broke the connection and left the office.

On the catwalk, I ran into Julia. In her tentative manner—which I attributed to a horrible past that made her expect rejection at every turn—she asked if we could have a drink over at Gordon Biersch, a brewpub on the other side of the Embarcadero.

I agreed, even though I was eager to get home. Julia's life was problematic, and I hoped she wasn't about to lay one of her crises in my lap. But it turned out that she only wanted to know if the items she'd bought me were okay, and if there was anything else I needed. I reassured her that all was well, and we chatted for a while, mostly about her son, Tonio, who had started music classes after school and was showing a talent for the guitar. When we parted, I felt almost happy.

But not for long: that evening I had to ask my husband questions that would transport him back into his painful past.

"What do you know about Renshaw's whereabouts between the time he resigned from the DEA and when he became a partner with Kessell?"

Hy steepled his fingers under his chin and stared into the fireplace. We were seated in matching black leather chairs in front of the hearth at the safe house apartment. The night had come on cold and rainy, and after dinner he'd made a fire. Normally the flames would have warmed and cheered me, but I had a bad feeling about the turn this conversation might take.

After a moment he said, "Nothing."

"But you knew him when he was in Thailand."

"Everybody knew Gage."

"When I met him, he said you'd been friends."

"Did he? Then Gage has a strange definition of friendship. And, as I recall, at that first meeting he hired you to locate me so he could take me out."

"He said you *had* been friends."

"More like drinking buddies."

"Did you know him from Fresno?" Hy had been born there, although his parents divorced when he was ten and he'd moved to Mono County with his mother and her new husband. Still, he'd spent time in the valley with his crop duster father until, as happens so often in that occupation, a plane crash had claimed Joe Ripinsky's life.

"Our paths never crossed."

"What about Kessell? He's from Fresno, too."

"Nope. He's a lot older than me, and probably was long gone when I was just a kid."

"So you met Renshaw . . . ?"

"Through a mutual friend in Bangkok."

"And Kessell?"

"When I arrived there. I answered a help-wanted ad in one of the flying magazines, and Dan hired me on the phone, paid my way over."

"So you flew for Kessell and drank with Renshaw and then . . . ?"

"What is this, McCone?"

"You know I've got to get more background on the two of them. When someone's the target of a vendetta, you look into the victim's past."

"That's not the whole of it."

"What d'you mean?"

"You're looking into my past, too. I know you've got to, but it makes me damned uncomfortable. I don't even like to *think* about those years."

"I know. We've talked about what happened then, and I hoped we wouldn't ever have to discuss it again. Let me take another tack: what was Renshaw's relationship with Kessell back then?"

Hy frowned thoughtfully. "Closer than with most people. Sure, neither of them would hesitate to use the other to make a profit, but they seemed more of a team."

The phone rang. I got up and answered it. Mick.

"Sorry to bother you at home, but I just got this information on Dan Kessell. He lived near the Fresno airport as a kid, and apparently the proximity made him want to fly. He traded maintenance jobs for lessons, and got his license the day he became of age. Holds a commercial license, instrument rating—and just about everything else. I talked with the owner of the flying school there, a guy who also hung around because his father was part owner of a crop-dusting service—"

"What's this guy's name?" I asked.

"Ben Galt. You want his number?"

"Please."

He gave it to me and added, "He's the one who told me about Dan living near the airport. I got the other stuff through public records. Galt says Kessell was a natural pilot, could handle any emergency, like the time—"

"Mick," I said, "I'll talk to you after I read your report. Now, here's something else you could look into: where did Kessell get the money to start K Air? If you don't have the time, put Keim on it."

"Will do."

I set the receiver down and remained standing, my back to Hy for a moment before I returned to my chair.

"Who was that?" he asked.

"Mick. Nothing important."

"You sounded kind of abrupt with him."

"I'm tired, that's all." I massaged my temples.

"Well, as you were saying . . . ?"

I couldn't for the life of me pick up the thread of the conversation because I was preoccupied with what Mick had told me.

"Ripinsky—" I began.

"Yes?"

Coincidence, that's all. Something that could easily be checked out.

I said, "Nothing. Let's not talk about this anymore tonight."

Saturday

✦

FEBRUARY 25

"I need to use Two-Seven-Tango today," I told Hy. The morning had dawned brilliantly clear—perfect flying weather.

"Fine with me. I've got no plans except for monitoring the interim operation upstairs, sitting around and reading, and maybe watching a couple of old movies."

Old Westerns—his passion. "Great. I should be back by dinnertime. Maybe we could go to—"

"How about I make my famous chili?"

"That would be great. Do we have—"

"I bought the ingredients yesterday. It'll be simmering when you come home."

"You, too?"

He smiled, and his eyes gleamed as they moved slowly over me. "You bet, McCone. Me, too."

Damn, I was glad I'd picked up that new prescription for my birth control pills!

The San Joaquin Valley spread out below me, close to sixty miles wide between the Coastal Range and the Sierra Nevada. The land was geometrically laid out, brown plowed fields interspersed among green ones where winter crops grew. The valley is one of the richest agricultural areas in the US, the crops that spring from its soil grossing billions of dollars a year, and the city of Fresno is the sixth largest in the state. Soon I could see the dual runways of Chandler Executive Airport two miles to the west. Chandler is non-towered, so I contacted the UNICOM on 123.0, announced my position, and set my course at a forty-five-degree angle to the field. Traffic was heavy today—a lot of people practicing touch-and-goes—and I slipped into the pattern behind a Piper Cub and in front of a Cessna 150.

Then I was on the ground and taxiing toward the visitor tie-downs. Chandler is a small airport, compared to Fresno-Yosemite International, with no landing or parking fees, and I spotted Galt Aviation easily. When I stepped down from the plane, a warm breeze ruffled my hair; it must have been well over sixty degrees there. I shed my suede jacket—a beloved possession that I'd had on the night of the bombing—and, after I secured Two-Seven-Tango, hurried toward the low cinder-block building that housed the flight school. I'd phoned Ben Galt earlier, using the story that I was trying to track down Dan Kessell because he'd inherited money.

Galt looked to be in his sixties: wiry and agile, with a concave chest and a slouch that made his body mimic a question mark. His face was wrinkled and suntanned, and bright blue eyes inspected me from under the bill of a baseball cap advertising the flight service. When I shook his hand, it felt stiff and gnarled. He took me inside, insisted on pouring me a cup of muddy-looking coffee, and seated me on one of the battered armchairs next to a counter; behind it a dark-haired man was talking loudly on the phone.

"Look, mister, that information's available online. Look it

up . . . No, that's *not* what I'm here for . . . Hey, we've got *students* with more brains than you!"

He banged the phone down, and a couple of pilots who were hangar-flying over by the soft-drink machine gave him looks and shook their heads.

Galt muttered, "Good help is hard to find." Then he called to the man, "Hey, dummy, go easy on the callers, will you?"

"Screw them, if they don't have the smarts to find out the pattern altitude on their own."

"You lose the airport customers, we lose customers, and your ass is grass."

Dummy didn't answer.

Galt said to me, "Unfortunately, he's my grandson and my daughter would give me hell if I fired him."

I nodded sympathetically, although secretly I sided with Dummy. Such information as pattern altitude, fuel availability, and airport communications and services is easily accessible—both on the Internet and from printed sources; calling ahead is the lazy pilot's method.

Getting down to business, I said, "I understand your father operated a crop-dusting service here."

"Yes. Galt Aviation used to be Galt Crop Dusting. My father got his CFI and began instructing when I was five or six, but maintained the original name; when he retired and turned the business over to me, I changed it. We still do crop-dusting, but the bulk of our business is with renters and student pilots."

"You told one of my operatives that you knew Dan Kessell."

"Yeah. Kessell was a couple of grades behind me in school. He did maintenance work for my dad—mopping the floors, that kind of stuff—in return for lessons."

"You also said that he was a natural pilot." I'd read the story Galt had told Mick in the report he'd e-mailed me, but I wanted to hear it for myself.

"He surely was. The second time he went out solo—after only eleven hours—he had an engine out. He maintained total control, brought the plane down on one of the farm roads—straight along the center stripe. Could you have done that after eleven hours?"

"No."

"Me neither."

"Kessell left town a couple of years after high school to go into the military," I said. "By then he had most of his ratings."

"Right. Instrument, commercial, multi-engine. He'd even started flying helicopters."

"I wonder why he went into the Special Forces."

"Probably because of their elite image. Dan was always into image—he used to say you could get more women showing up at the fuel pumps in a Citabria than in a Cessna. Not that he had the money for either back then."

Well, he does now.

"Have you seen Kessell since he left Fresno?"

"Sure. He flies in here in an old Piper a few times a year, has family—a sister—in the area. He may own a security firm and all, but he's the same old Dan, right up to the flight jacket that's as beat-up as his plane."

"This sister—do you know her name?"

He thought. "Elise. I don't know her married name, but I do know that she's living in the old family home on Wolfe Road. White clapboard, picket fence, rose garden out front. You can't miss it."

I hesitated, wondering exactly what I hoped to find out

about Kessell. Maybe I'd only flown down as an excuse to take to the skies and clear my head. Certainly I'd done thinking on the trip, allowing my mind to range freely over the facts of the case.

Well, what harm could there be in talking with the sister?

I asked Galt, "Is there a rental car service on the field?"

"I can call Enterprise for you."

"Thanks. I'd appreciate that."

When Galt came back from telephoning, I said in as offhand a fashion as I could muster, "By the way, did you ever know a crop duster named Ripinsky?"

He smiled. "Joe Ripinsky? Of course. He was my father's partner, till he got stupid and messed with some high-tension wires." After a pause, he added, "Funny you should mention Joe: he was the one who taught Dan Kessell to fly."

The house on Wolfe Road that Ben Galt had described to me was larger than I'd imagined, an old two-story farmhouse in the middle of an eighties-style, low-rise housing tract that had been built after the surrounding acreage was sold off to developers. The name on the mailbox next to the gate of the white picket fence was Carver. In summer the rose bushes would crowd up against the fence, their branches heavy with blossoms, but now they were freshly pruned and stubby, new growth just beginning to show.

I was halfway up the walk when a white pickup drove by and turned into a driveway to the right of the house. By the time I went back down the walk and followed, it was pulled up near a side door, and a woman with long gray hair had the truck's tailgate down and was struggling with a couple of plastic grocery sacks. She looked over her shoulder at me, round face red with exertion.

"Elise Carver?" I asked.

"Yes." She tugged at the bag, and it split, a cantaloupe rolling along the bed of the truck and coming to rest under the window of the cab. "Damn cheap bags!" she exclaimed. "And the kids they hire to bag 'em cram 'em way too full."

"Let me help you with that." Before she could protest, I climbed into the truck bed, rescued the cantaloupe, and got back down again. Then I hefted another sack and looked questioningly at the house.

Elise Carver frowned. "Who are you?"

"Sharon McCone, a private investigator from San Francisco. I'd give you one of my cards, but . . ." I nodded at the cantaloupe and sack.

"And you're investigating what?"

"I'm trying to locate Dan Kessell. He *is* your brother?"

"What d'you want him for?"

"It's nothing important. An insurance matter."

"Danny being sued?"

"Oh, no. He's a witness to an accident, and I need to have him sign a form. Strictly routine."

Elise Carver's freckled face registered uncertainty. "I don't know if I should talk with you."

"As I said, it's routine."

"But how do I know that? I don't want to get Danny into any trouble."

"He wasn't involved in the accident, if that's what you're afraid of."

"I'm not afraid of anything, I just don't know—"

My arms were getting tired from holding the heavy sack and melon. "Look," I said, "at least let me help you with the groceries and then, if you don't want to talk to me, I'll go."

". . . Okay." She nodded and dug a key ring out of the

pocket of jeans that stretched tightly over her ample hips and thighs.

We went inside, through a mudroom containing a washer and dryer, and into a kitchen that was a far cry from what one would have expected in an old farmhouse: granite countertops, steel-topped center block, richly toned wooden cabinetry, all the latest appliances. Carver indicated where I should set the sack and melon and put hers down beside them. Then she said, "Wait here," and went out to the truck for the remaining groceries.

When she came back, I asked, "Weekly shop?"

"No. Big family dinner tomorrow. My sons and daughters-in-law and all seven grandkids."

"May I help you put this away?" I motioned at the sacks.

"No, it'll keep. Now, what is it you want with Danny?"

"A few months ago he was witness to an accident at Oakland Airport's North Field—a couple of student pilots collided while taxiing. The insurance company that I contract with needs his signature on a form, so the settlement money can be released, but we haven't been able to locate him at any of his addresses."

"That's Danny. Here today, gone tomorrow." She ran her fingers through her thick hair, tugging at where it was wind-tangled. "I don't know if I can help you, though. Danny's kind of a mysterious character."

"Oh? How so?"

She motioned to a small table in an alcove overlooking the backyard. "Please, sit down. Would you care for some coffee?"

"No, thanks. But you go ahead."

She wrinkled her nose. "I can't take the stuff after about ten in the morning. Don't understand this coffee culture we've gotten into in this country. It's always go for coffee, come over for coffee. I tell you, if it wasn't for the caffeine it'd be pretty vile stuff."

"I know what you mean. So your brother is mysterious . . . ?"

"Yeah. We were never close, even while we were growing up, and then he got married to a friend of mine. I didn't like the way he treated her one bit, and I let him know it. Then when he told me he was going into the military and leaving my friend here to fend for herself, I let him have it with both barrels. After that I didn't hear from him until about six, seven years ago, when he showed up, all smiles, with a big box of candy and some fancy wine. He'd flown here in his own plane."

"And you reconciled?"

"To a point. Danny shows up every six months or so. Never any advance warning. Always brings expensive presents. He's owner of some security company, says the work is highly confidential. I don't have a name for the company, or an address or phone number for him. He tells me he moves around a lot."

Probably doesn't want you intruding on his day-to-day life. That's the Dan Kessell I know, but . . .

"Mrs. Carver, what kind of plane does your brother fly?"

"Oh, some little two-seater. Looks kind of grungy. I think it's a wonder it flies at all, but he says it's a classic."

And it doesn't attract attention at Chandler Field, where one of the RKI jets would.

Carver said, "I'm sorry I can't help you more. Danny . . . he's strange, secretive. Always was, even as a kid. The only thing he was ever open about was flying. He loved to fly. Purely *loved* it."

Kessell's love affair with flying seemed to have cooled

down; Hy had told me he kept several pilots on call for when he wanted to use the company's aircraft, but rarely took the controls.

When I got back to the plane, I took my briefcase from where it rested on the passenger-side floor, set it on the seat, and opened it. It was an old one I'd had lying around the office, and the catches stuck. I made a mental note to buy a new one next week; maybe I'd splurge and get something really nice, although the lack of longevity of my briefcases was an issue. In recent years, I'd had one stolen, one drowned by a burst water pipe, and one blown up. Maybe I should carry my files in a paper bag . . .

The original RKI file had expanded into two. I took out the latter and paged through it to the information on Dan Kessell, found Mick's report on when and where he'd gotten his pilot's licenses. The date of the last—commercial—was the year Hy would have been two years old.

Yes, Kessell had been long gone from Fresno before Hy could have had any recollection of him. But hadn't he and Kessell ever discussed the coincidence that Hy's father had been Dan's flight instructor? It wasn't as if his last name were Smith; Ripinsky was far from common.

Had Kessell failed to connect the two? Doubtful. Not bothered to mention it? Maybe. Had he mentioned it, and Hy later forgot? Impossible. Hy seldom forgot anything.

All right, then. Had Hy simply failed to mention it to me because he thought it irrelevant? Withheld the information from me for some private reason of his own? Lied to me?

No, he hadn't lied.

Not yet.

* * *

"Taste," Hy said, holding out the spoon he'd been stirring the chili with.

I tasted. "Good. Great, actually. One of your better batches."

"I think so, too." He set the spoon down and sipped his beer. "So how was your day?"

"Profitable."

"You were working?"

"Yes. As a matter of fact, I went to your old hometown."

"Fresno?" Something flickered in his eyes.

"Uh-huh."

He set down his beer, leaned against the counter, and crossed his arms over his chest. "I don't suppose I should ask you what you were after there. Since we decided you wouldn't report to me."

On the defensive.

"No, but I have to ask you something: why didn't you tell me your father taught Dan Kessell to fly?"

Hy looked away at the pot of bubbling chili on the stove. He moved over there, lowered the burner's heat.

"Ripinsky?"

"I didn't know that," he said, facing away from me.

"Oh, come on, Ripinsky. Kessell didn't hire a pilot named Ripinsky who just happened to have been born in Fresno, and not make the connection."

"If he did, he didn't mention it."

"Why wouldn't he?"

"Maybe he didn't think it a very interesting coincidence."

"Coincidences are *always* interesting. He must've said something."

"Nothing that I recall, but I met Dan a long time ago. It could've slipped my mind."

"Nothing significant slips that mind of yours."

"What, are you accusing me of withholding the information from you?"

"No, but—"

"Because it sure sounds that way." Silence. Then: "Well, I guess the honeymoon's over."

"What the hell does that mean?"

"Take it any way you want to."

We locked angry eyes. Before I could reply, the damned phone rang.

I snatched up the receiver. "Hello!"

Gage Renshaw. At first I thought he was going to remind me that I was to fly down there on Monday, but then I heard the tension in his voice as he asked, "Is Ripinsky there?"

"Yes, but if it's about the ever-running man, you can talk to me."

"He's changed his MO. Dan's been shot. The two of you had better get down here."

"When? Where?"

"Tonight, outside his condo."

"How bad is it?"

"Bad. Head wound. Bullet's lodged . . . ah, hell, somewhere. How do I know? They're operating on him now."

"And you think it was the ever-running man." Hy was reaching for the phone. I shoved his hand away.

"Who else?" Renshaw said. "Perp was seen running away by one of the neighbors."

"Okay, we'll be there as soon as we can."

"I'll send the jet—faster than your plane or the airlines."

"We'll be waiting to hear its ETA."

I hung up and faced Hy with the latest bad news.

Sunday

✦

FEBRUARY 26

I woke to sunlight filtering through the mini-blinds and slanting across the foot of the bed in the safe house apartment. At the last minute I'd decided against flying to San Diego with Hy; in a second call advising us of the company jet's ETA, Renshaw had said that Kessell was still in surgery and would be unable to talk with anyone until the following day at the earliest. Since it now seemed that he was the ever-running man's central target, I was eager to keep my noon appointment with Wendy Benjamin, Kessell's first wife's therapist. I'd go to San Diego when I could speak with Kessell—if he survived what sounded like a long and complicated surgery.

I got up and drank a couple of cups of coffee while reading the Sunday *Chronicle*. Slow news day, lots of ads. Sometimes I thought that most of the copy in the paper was written by Macy's advertising department. A review of a new movie that might be worth seeing, a feature article on the latest computer scams, the comics—that was it for me. I stuffed the paper in the wood basket next to the fireplace and went to get dressed.

Deciding what to wear was no problem; I'd never had so

few clothes in my closet. I laid out a new pair of jeans and a red turtleneck—both courtesy of Julia's shopping spree—before I took my shower. Styled my hair with the blow-dryer and brush she'd bought me. Applied a minimal amount of makeup rescued from the office restroom, and grabbed my suede jacket, then decided against it. It was warmish here and would be even warmer in Berkeley.

Before I left, the phone rang. I let it go on the machine. Hy, saying that Kessell had survived the surgery, but was still unconscious and on the critical list. Normally I would have snatched up the receiver, eager to talk with him, but I was running late. Plenty of time to talk later.

When I was in college I never ventured into the area around Berkeley's Fourth Street. It was then filled with grimy old buildings and warehouses, many of them unoccupied and falling into ruins. But one day the developers discovered the place, and now it's a vibrant mixture of restaurants, boutiques, a major independent bookstore, and antique shops, with the occasional thrift store to attract those on a tighter budget. Even the few remaining auto body shops cater more to new Volvos and BMWs than to old VWs and Chevys.

I had difficulty finding a parking space; everybody seemed to be out enjoying the fine weather. Couples strolled along hand in hand, stopping to peer into the shop windows or read the menus posted outside restaurants. Others walked purposefully, intent on errands. Dogs were leashed to tables in the outdoor dining areas of cafes. I finally wedged the MG into an iffy corner space and told myself nobody gets a ticket in Berkeley on Sunday. Then I headed toward George's Extraordinaire, where I found Wendy Benjamin seated as she'd said she would be at an umbrella-covered table on the patio.

Benjamin was a large woman, nearly six feet, and, while heavy, she carried her weight well. Her hair, a dark brown with purplish highlights, was cut short in a style that softened her severe features. As she rose and shook my hand, her keen gray eyes appraised me.

"You don't look like you sounded on the phone," she said.

"How did I sound?"

"Older. Very professional. I expected you to show up in a tailored business suit and heels. Frankly, I was surprised you agreed to meet me on a Sunday."

As we sat down, I said, "I'm not sure the individual you describe is anyone I'd want to be."

"Maybe not. But the impression you convey makes one place confidence in you, sight unseen. Your telephone persona suggests high professional standards."

Psychobabble. But why not? She's a shrink.

"The eggs Florentine here are wonderful," she added.

Even though I normally would have welcomed a suggestion from a person who frequented the restaurant, I resisted and ordered a cheese-and-mushroom omelet.

Wendy Benjamin's eyes acknowledged my response: I wasn't someone to be analyzed or manipulated.

After the waiter left, she said in an apologetic voice, "I hope I didn't offend you. I've made comparing people's voices on the phone with their actual selves into something of a hobby. When I talk with someone, I jot down impressions, then correct them after we've met."

"And what have you found?"

"Most people sound very different than they really are. One man, the property manager of the building where I rent office space, sounded as if he should be a TV newscaster: very deep, charismatic, sexy voice. When I met him—well, he was a total train wreck. Bald, very obese, bad complexion, horrible breath and posture. You, on the other hand, *are* very professional. And I suspect you're older than your years. As for appearing more casual, I assume you're something of a chameleon. You dress in the manner that the situation calls for."

I spread my arms. "Brunch in Berkeley on a Sunday."

She toasted me with one of the glasses of orange juice the waiter had set in front of us.

I considered taking out my recorder, but sensed this woman wouldn't allow its use. "So," I said, "Gina Hines."

"You realize I'm only speaking with you because Gina is dead and her husband requested I cooperate. And Gina and I didn't have a long-standing relationship."

"You're covered on the confidentiality issue. If you'd like me to sign a release—"

She dismissed my suggestion with a quick hand gesture. "Not necessary. As a matter of fact, Gina was an interesting case. She only came to me for three sessions, and I wish I'd had more time to break down her barriers."

"What kind of barriers?"

"Well, when her daughter made the first appointment for her, she described her as someone who needed to manufacture great drama in her life. But the woman who came to that session was not overly dramatic. In fact, she was afraid. So afraid she did not want to leave her house."

"Afraid of what?"

"That was what I worked on. The usual labels—agoraphobia, fear of crowds, for instance—did not apply. The fear was real, but it took three sessions before I even touched upon it. And then, I caught only a glimpse."

"And that was . . . ?"

"She mentioned a former husband, and a meeting with him on the street. When I began probing, she cut me off. Left the session with twenty minutes to go, and never scheduled another."

"What did she say about the meeting?"

"I consulted my notes this morning, to be clear on this. All she said was 'I destroyed his life, and now he's going to destroy mine.' "

"She didn't give you any further explanation?"

"No, that's when she bolted from my office."

When I returned to the apartment, there was another message on the machine from Hy, saying Kessell's condition remained the same. His tone was curt and curiously formal. There was also a message from Ma, pleading that I call her. Much as I appreciated her concern, I simply couldn't face another long, semi-hysterical conversation. The cheese-and-mushroom omelet at George's Extraordinaire had been terrible, my stomach was threatening to rebel, and my head was throbbing. I found a bottle of aspirin in the medicine cabinet, popped three, and lay down on the bed. Soon I was asleep.

Phone ringing. Somewhere . . .

I propped myself up on my elbows, reached for the extension, but the call had already gone on the machine. By the time I got to the living room, Hy's voice was saying, "So that's it—"

I picked up. "I'm here. Sorry, I was asleep."

His voice was grim. "Dan just died."

"Jesus. Complications from surgery?"

"Yeah. His heart gave out."

"I'm so sorry."

"Bullshit, McCone. You're no sorrier than I am. Neither of us liked the man."

I ran my hand over my forehead; the headache I'd had earlier was again pounding. "Still . . ."

"Save your emotions for something that really matters," Hy said. "And what matters is this: Dan may have been the ever-running man's primary target."

"Or he may not have. Why the bombings as a lead-in to the shooting? Why not use a bomb on Dan's condo instead? Why the change in MO?"

". . . I don't know. Can you come down here?"

"Of course."

I should feel as if something's just ended. Why do I feel as if it's just begun?

Monday

✦

FEBRUARY 27

The officer at the SDPD in charge of Dan Kessell's case was Gary Viner, an old friend of my dead brother Joey. I'd consulted professionally with Gary a few times before, and he maintained the pretense that he'd lusted after me since the days when I was a high-school cheerleader. The sight of my lace-edged panties when I turned cartwheels really got to him, he claimed, ignoring the fact that our cheerleading undergarments had been plain and unrevealing.

Today as he ushered me into his office, Gary's manner was somber—no cartwheel jokes. He looked older than his years, his sandy hair thinning and deep lines carved around his mouth and into his high forehead. He motioned me to one of the visitors' chairs, sat down at his desk, and folded his hands on a file that lay there.

"It's good to see you," he said.

"You, too. How've you been?"

He shrugged. "Hanging in there."

"What does that mean?"

"Oh . . ." He sighed. "The usual cop trouble. My wife left me, got custody of the kids, moved home to Idaho."

"Oh, I'm sorry."

Another shrug. "Takes a certain kind of woman to be a cop's wife. Ann isn't that kind. She's better off. The kids, too."

"And you?"

"I'll make it through." A pause. "I still think of Joey. How he didn't make it through. But my problems are ordinary compared to what his must've been. So I remind myself of that and go on."

At least something good has come out of Joey's drug- and booze-soaked death.

"Joey wasn't very strong," I said. "You are."

"Thanks." He straightened, took his hands off the file and opened it. "Dan Kessell. Partner in Renshaw & Kessell International. Shot at close range with a thirty-eight-caliber handgun at approximately nine p.m. on Saturday night. Bullet was removed during surgery. No weapon present at the scene. Died at eleven-thirteen p.m. yesterday, of cardiac arrest after extensive surgery. What's your interest in the case?"

"I've been working for RKI on a series of bombings at their offices."

"I heard about the bombings after Kessell was shot. My people're talking to the FBI and gathering information on the various incidents, but I'd appreciate it if you'd fill me in."

I did, as completely as I could without my files.

Gary said, "I figured RKI might've brought you in on it, now that you're married to one of the partners. Congratulations, by the way."

"Thank you. How'd you—?"

"There was a mention of it in the *Union*."

Oh, hell! That was Ma's work.

At the time, I'd thought it a quaint social gesture, but now it made me feel vulnerable. How many people paid attention to such items? Not a lot, unless they knew you, or you were a celebrity.

I said, "Well, I've worked for RKI before. And I'm not reporting to my husband. If my involvement isn't already public knowledge I'd like to keep it under wraps."

Gary nodded. "No one's going to hear about it from me. Let me ask you this, though: do you think the bombings and Kessell's shooting are related? I mean, the change in MO . . ."

"I've wondered about that, too. And I have no conclusions at the moment."

"Well, if you come to any, let me know."

"Are your people finished with the crime scene?"

"It's still sealed. Why?"

"I'd like to take a look at the condo. I'll probably need Kessell's lawyer's okay, but if it's all right with you . . ."

"Sure. Just stay clear of the patio; it's the actual crime scene." Gary glanced at his watch and stood. "I've got a meeting in five minutes, but you're welcome to stay here and review the file. Just leave it on the desk and shut the door when you're done."

"I appreciate your letting me see what you have."

He went to the door and paused with his hand on the knob. "Let's just say it's in memory of Joey. Seeing what his death did to your family and his former friends has kept me from eating my gun on a lot of lonely nights."

He opened the door and went out, then turned and added with a bittersweet smile, "Hope you're still turning those cartwheels, McCone."

* * *

The information in the SDPD file was sketchy. In spite of it being a Saturday, Dan Kessell had put in a full day in his office at RKI headquarters in La Jolla, then drove home, left his car in his garage, and walked a few blocks to Alex's, a popular restaurant, for dinner with a client. The client, James Hoffman, security chief of Motoscope, a national software firm, had told the police that he'd requested the meeting because he was concerned about RKI's ability to oversee their executive protection program after the bombings in San Francisco and other cities. Hoffman had been reassured by his conversation with Kessell, and the two parted at eight-twenty in front of the restaurant, Kessell walking off in the direction of his condo, while Hoffman waited for the valet to bring his car around. The parking attendant, maître d', and waiters at the restaurant confirmed that the men's conversation had been low-key and businesslike, and they had parted amicably.

A neighbor of Hoffman's in suburban Del Mar had seen him arrive home at around five to nine—a reasonable driving time on a Saturday evening—and spoke with him as he got out of his car. However, the time frame between Kessell's departure from the restaurant and arrival at his deluxe condominium complex near Harbor Drive was inconsistent with the distance. Even a slow walker—and, according to my observations, Kessell's stride was always brisk—could have traveled the distance in ten minutes. But he had not arrived outside the courtyard entrance to his unit until around nine-fifteen, when a neighbor who was coming back from walking his dog heard what he thought was a shot and encountered a man running out through the wrought-iron front gates. The neighbor thought the intruder had come from Kessell's unit, went back to investigate, and found Kessell slumped on his patio, blood seeping from a head wound. Kessell's cell phone was clipped to his belt and the neighbor used it to call 911. The police had canvassed all residents of the complex but only one man said he had heard the shot; he also mentioned he'd heard loud voices coming from Kessell's patio shortly beforehand. The police were talking to employees of any establishments Kessell might have stopped into along his route home, but so far had come up with no witnesses.

Searches of Kessell's condominium and office at RKI were ongoing.

Autopsy results were pending.

What a morning. I'd spent most of the time since I arrived down here at eleven waiting to see Gary, reading this fairly useless file—and being reminded of Joey's death.

Just when you think the hurt is starting to heal, it flares up, and you know it'll always be with you.

I looked up at the clock on the wall—two p.m., time to get moving; I had an appointment with Kessell's lawyer at three.

Madison Crawford, Kessell's personal attorney, had his offices on top of the Shelton Towers, one of San Diego's newest downtown high-rises. While outside the day was bright and sunny—the rains having blown southeast into Mexico and the mudslides drying up and being cleared—the inside of the office felt gloomy. The walls were light gray and hung with black-and-white photographs that recalled Ansel Adams's work. The furnishings were black leather, the thick-piled carpeting a darker gray that complemented the walls. A receptionist in a gray dress—regulation color, perhaps?—spoke into her phone and told me Mr. Crawford would be out momentarily. When he emerged from his office to greet me, I saw that Crawford was gray, too—hair, eyes, suit. The only things that saved him from blending into his surroundings were his maroon tie and ruddy complexion.

He took me into his private office, and we went through the usual rituals: Coffee? No, thanks. Drink? No, thanks. My condolences on Dan's death. He was a long-time client and will be missed.

Finally, down to business. I said, "I spoke with the SDPD officer in charge of Dan's case, and he said it would be okay with them if I took a look at the condo. May I have your permission as well?"

"I have no problem with that. In fact, they called to say they finished there half an hour ago. The private patio out front is still a sealed crime scene, but you can enter the condo through the garage at the back."

"Thank you. Is it possible you could allow me access this afternoon?"

"Certainly." He buzzed the receptionist. "Sylvia, when Ms. McCone leaves, would you please give her the keys and garage-door opener to Mr. Kessell's residence . . . Thanks." He hung up, smiled at me, and said, "All set. I'd appreciate it if you'd return the keys and opener by close of business tomorrow."

"I'm sure I can have them here before then. Isn't it unusual for an attorney to have keys and a garage-door opener to his client's home?"

"Yes, it is. Dan only gave them to me a week ago. It surprised me, because he was a very private man. When I asked him why he wanted me to have them, he was vague, said 'In case something happens to me.' "

"So he may have been afraid someone wanted to kill him."

"That's possible."

"Did you tell this to the police?"

". . . No. I only just remembered it."

"I'd advise that you do so. Mr. Crawford, I assume you drew up a will for Dan?"

He nodded. "A trust, a will, the usual."

"Can you give me any idea of who will benefit from it?"

"I'm sorry. Until it's probated—"

"I understand. Have you notified the next of kin?"

He frowned. "As far as I know, Dan had no relatives."

"Actually, he has a sister in Fresno—Elise Carver—whom he visited occasionally. Nephews, nieces; grandnephews and -nieces, too."

"That's news to me. They're not mentioned in his will. But I should have the sister's address, so I can notify her of his death."

I gave it to him, and he copied it down. I asked, "Can you at least give me a general idea of who will benefit from his death? Seeing as it was a homicide . . ."

"Well, I wouldn't be violating ethical standards if I told you that much of the estate goes to various charities."

"*Much* of the estate? Are there any bequests to individuals?"

"I've revealed all I can, Ms. McCone."

"Let me suggest a name: Gage Renshaw."

Crawford's eyes remained impassive, but the corner of his mouth twitched before he said, "I cannot reveal—"

"Try this one: Hy Ripinsky."

He compressed his lips to control another twitch. Then he said, "I've given you all the time I can afford, Ms. McCone. Sylvia will give you the keys and remote on your way out."

* * *

En route to Kessell's condo, I considered the probable bequests to Renshaw and Hy. In the case of large firms like RKI, keyman life-insurance policies are usually taken out on partners to compensate for their potential loss. Did the three of them own such policies? I'd assumed so. But individual bequests from one partner to another? That was unusual.

The complex where Kessell had lived was a two-story Spanish-style building, well landscaped, and spread over an entire block on the edge of downtown, within walking distance of the Gaslight Quarter. I left my rental car at the curb and went to the massive wrought-iron gates. They were locked, with an intercom system for guests and a key-card mechanism for residents. Through them I could see an expansive courtyard full of brightly colored plantings; the units looked to be large, and each was fronted by a high wall and a smaller version of the main gate. I identified Kessell's unit at the left rear corner by the yellow crime-scene tape that stretched across the gate.

I walked along the sidewalk to the driveway at the side of the building. When I located the garage for the unit, I depressed the remote's button; the door rose, and I saw Kessell's white Jaguar in one of the slots. The rest of the garage was spotless, not so much as a box or a tool stored there, and the garbage can and recycle bin were empty. I searched the Jaguar's interior and trunk. The glove box contained only the registration slip, which showed it belonged to RKI. The rest of the car was so clean that it must have recently been detailed.

Now for the interior of the condo. A door led from the garage into a laundry room. The washer and dryer looked as if they'd never been used and the cabinets above the appliances were empty. Kessell had been strictly a laundry-and-dry-cleaner man.

Into the kitchen. It made even an indifferent cook like me envious. State of the art, as was Kessell's sister's kitchen in her old farmhouse in Fresno. Unlike Elise's, however, it looked as if it was seldom used.

First I did a quick walk-through. The condo was enormous. Lower floor: living room, formal dining room, multimedia room—all with gas fireplaces—office, half bath. Upstairs were a master bedroom suite with a bathroom that put our luxurious one at Touchstone to shame, two guest rooms with individual baths, and a fully furnished exercise room. No wonder Dan had been in such good shape.

My work was cut out for me. I went back downstairs and looked out the front window. The private patio where Dan had died was more like a yard: flagstone area with teak furnishings, small swimming pool with attached spa, plantings in redwood containers.

He'd had a nice life, what with this condo and the house on Maui. Even for a partner in RKI. Even with his real estate developments, of which he'd divested himself as soon as they became profitable.

Maybe I could find the secret to his success.

All I learned from the living room was that Dan had had a penchant for Asian art. Jade figurines, intricately painted Chinese vases, and lacquered boxes were displayed on the tabletops and in glass-fronted cases. Original prints and paintings, all by Asian artists, were arranged on the walls.

The formal dining room was uninteresting. Just a rosewood table and chairs for eight, and a cabinet where Imari ware was displayed.

The kitchen told me Kessell favored microwaveable Lean Cuisine, diet ginger ale, Grape-Nuts, nonfat milk, and Bushmills Irish whiskey. If he'd ever entertained in that elegant dining room, he must have had the meal catered.

Multimedia room: Kessell listened to jazz on a surround-sound system and watched DVDs on a big-screen plasma TV—mainly action films or war movies, with the occasional horror film thrown into the mix. No surprises there.

Office: desk drawers empty of anything but supplies. Cabinet with files on household insurance, paid bills, deed to this house and the one on Maui. No papers for the beat-up Piper he flew to Fresno on his visits to his sister. That wasn't unusual, though; the company probably owned and insured it, as it did Hy's and my plane. Bank account statements, but no canceled checks. I left them alone, knowing the police would have gone over them.

A workstation had a printer on its lower shelf, but there was no computer or discs. Probably the SDPD had taken them.

Upstairs: the guest rooms were as impersonal as a room at the Hilton.

Exercise room: lots of expensive equipment. Instruments of torture, I call them.

Master bedroom: interesting in terms of what *wasn't* there. No personal photographs, nothing out of place, no condoms in the nightstand or bathroom. Yet Hy had told me Dan always had a woman or two, and someone like him would have been very concerned about safe sex.

No handgun. That was strange; people like Kessell—and Hy—slept with a weapon within easy reach. I'm comfortable with firearms and a damn good marksman, but the first time I realized how close to hand Hy kept his .45, I'd been unnerved. Now I was used to it. I couldn't imagine Kessell not having a weapon handy. Of course, the police might well have appropriated it.

I turned my attention to the closet: lots of expensively tailored suits and formal wear. Casual wear, all designer labels. Dress shoes and athletic shoes, and several pairs of fleece-lined slippers. A brown flight jacket, its leather smelling like a newly purchased car . . .

. . . He's the same old Dan, right up to the flight jacket that's as beat-up as his plane.

The same old Dan, as his friends and relatives used to know in the old days in Fresno?

I didn't think so. It must be an act he put on for his sister.

I gave the entire condo another going-over, checking the obvious and not-so-obvious hiding places, and found nothing. Then I left, locking the inner door to the garage, and went around the complex to the main gate, where I pressed the buzzer for the neighbor who had found Dan shot and bleeding in his own front patio. A man's voice, high-pitched and nervous, answered and said yes, he was Wynn Daley. When I identified myself and asked if we could talk about Mr. Kessell's death, he was reluctant at first.

"I've already told my story to the police—several times."

"I've seen their reports, but I'd really appreciate it if I could hear it directly from you."

"Who exactly are you working for?"

"Renshaw & Kessell International. They hold keyman insurance on Mr. Kessell's life."

". . . I see. The problem is, this whole episode has upset me—"

"If you're concerned about having me come into your

home, we could meet in the courtyard." I'd noticed there were little tables and chairs scattered among the plantings.

"Well . . . I was thinking of taking Shan for a walk. I could bring him along, and we could talk for a few minutes."

"That would be fine. Thank you, Mr. Daley." He probably wanted his dog along for protection.

He buzzed me in and I waited next to a pink camellia bush that was just coming into flower. In a couple of minutes, a man came out of one of the nearby units, leading—no, being led by—a five- or six-pound furball that was all pink tongue, wagging tail, and dark eyes that glittered through a fringe of hair. It yipped with excitement when it saw me. So much for protection.

When I looked from the dog to the man, I blinked in recognition. I'd seen him for years in TV commercials; he always played the beleaguered husband, the office klutz, the guy with the hangover, or the man who was bested by a woman at anything from getting the dishes clean to using power tools. Most recently—

"Mr. Tacquerito!" I exclaimed, then immediately regretted it. The ad was an extremely stupid one in which he pranced around in a giant frying pan wearing a taco suit and grinning like a fool.

Professional pride has no bounds, however. Wynn Daley beamed at me. "At your service."

Shan yipped and jumped up on me, licking my hand. He was a happy dog. His owner might have a preposterous résumé, but jobs like that bought a lot of kibble, to say nothing of an expensive condominium to call home.

Mr. Tacquerito led me to a table in the shade of a palm tree and we sat, Shan on my right foot. I'm more of a cat person, but I like dogs on an individual basis, and this one had decided—rightly so—that he was admitted to the club.

"What is it you want to know?" Daley asked me.

"I'd like you to tell me what you experienced the night Mr. Kessell was shot, and then I may have some questions of my own."

"Fair enough." He proceeded to give a version of what I'd read in the police reports.

"Did you get much of a look at the man who ran past you?"

"No. It was dark, and he was moving fast."

"Did you actually see him come through Mr. Kessell's gate?"

"Well, no. But I saw Mr. Kessell's gate standing open, and I assumed that that was where he'd been."

"What about the main gate? It's always locked, isn't it?"

"Oh, yes. The complex has very good security."

"But the person was able to get in that way."

"The gate closes slowly, in case someone's entering with parcels or whatever. He could've followed Mr. Kessell in."

I nodded, recalling how slowly it had closed behind me when Daley had buzzed me in. "Okay, how long before the man ran by you did you hear the shot?"

"Around the time I was putting my key card into the slot."

"Did anyone else in the complex come outside in response to it?"

"No. People here . . . well, they keep to themselves."

A nice way of saying they didn't want to get involved. Turning your back on your neighbor has spread like a contagion through our nation's large cities.

* * *

After Wynn Daley and I finished talking, I tried to reach the neighbor who had heard the loud voices coming from Kessell's patio shortly before the shot, but no one was home. I considered questioning some of the other residents of the complex, but decided against it. People were only beginning to return home from work, and soon it would be the dinner hour; it's been my experience that when you disturb someone at that time they're bound to be cranky and uncooperative. But I didn't want to return to RKI's condo in La Jolla; I didn't like it any more than the apartments at Green Street or the San Francisco safe house, and Hy had said he'd be working late at headquarters. Instead I headed to the one place in the city where I could make some phone calls, think in private, and then perhaps talk through my confusion with someone close to me.

It always gave me a strange feeling to return to the old, rambling house on Mead Avenue where I'd grown up. For one thing, it was now in much better shape than it had ever been when I lived there—with a new roof, paint job, and landscaped yard. For another, I would never be anything more than a visitor there—although one who was welcome to appear unannounced at any time.

Several years ago Ma had filed for divorce from my father and moved in with her . . . well, "boyfriend" is too undignified a term for the very dignified Melvin Hunt, but that's what it amounted to until their wedding ten months later. After her departure Pa pretty much let the place go—if it's possible to let a place go when it's practically been falling down for decades. When he died, the house was sold for a pittance, but proved too much of a challenge for the new owners; it came on the market again, and my brother John—his own little house in Lemon Grove having become too confining for him and his two growing boys—decided to buy it.

John's motorcycle was parked in the driveway, right behind a Mr. Paint truck. Mr. Paint—the contracting firm he'd founded—had grown, and my brother hardly ever wielded a roller or brush or sprayer anymore, but while he complained as much as I've been known to do about being desk-bound, he was secretly pleased with his success. And despite his efforts to keep up his working-class image, I knew that a sporty new Honda convertible resided in the garage at the end of the driveway.

I went to the side door, rang the bell twice in quick succession, and let myself in with the key John had given me. The kitchen was a mess, as usual—typical all-male household problem. I avoided a slick-looking patch of some unidentifiable substance on the floor, and headed for the door to the hallway. John came through it at the same time, and we bumped into each other. After he gave me a big bear hug, I stepped back and surveyed him; his blond hair was tousled, his face cheerful, and he looked trim and fit.

"Quiet here," I said. "Where're Nate and Matt?"

"Over at their mother's."

John's former wife, Karen, and her husband lived only a mile or so away, and the boys alternated between the two households. The arrangement worked well for everyone—especially the boys because, I suspected, they could easily sneak in the occasional unauthorized night away from home. Both parents were aware of their teenage transgressions, but they were also aware that the boys' sins were small, compared to the scrapes John and Joey had gotten into at their age. As yet neither parent had been obliged to post bail.

I looked around the kitchen, frowning. "I take it Krista's

off on a buying trip?" Krista was John's girlfriend, a fashion buyer for an exclusive chain of boutiques. She traveled a lot, but she kept him and the boys in line when in town.

"How'd you know?" he asked.

"She'd never tolerate that mess." I waved my hand at the dirty plates, takeout containers, and smudged glasses.

"Oh, yeah." He shrugged. "I was gonna clean it up. She's not due back till next weekend."

"How can you live with it? That stuff in the sink *smells*."

He sniffed. "It does, now that you mention it. How about we clean it up together?"

"How about I go make some phone calls while you clean it up? Then we can have a drink and talk; there're a few things I want to run by you."

"What about dinner?"

"What do you have on hand?"

"Not much, but we could order a pizza."

I noted the two pizza boxes stuffed in the garbage can. "How about we go out for a real meal?"

"Are you down here on business?"

"Yes."

"As long as we can put it on your expense account."

"Whatever." I threw up my hands in surrender and went into the family room overlooking the backyard and the lush greenery of the finger canyon that ran behind the house. When I took my phone from my purse, I could hear John clattering around in the kitchen. Nothing like the prospect of a good dinner on somebody else to energize him.

Around seven o'clock, after I completed my calls, I went out onto the expansive redwood deck that—so far as I knew—was the only improvement the interim owners had made on the property, and stood by the railing looking out at the finger canyon. It was so overgrown with palms and oaks and eucalypti and madrone and vines that I could barely see the houses on the opposite side. Somewhere down there were the steps that Pa had set into the slope so we kids could climb down to the treehouse he'd constructed in a sturdy oak. The last time I'd seen the little structure, it had been only a platform, and now I wondered if it had deteriorated completely. All my life I'd taken the canyon for granted, but now it struck me as strange to be standing at the edge of a veritable jungle in the midst of a large city, white noise from the freeways blending with the birdcalls and the rustling of wind in the leaves.

My call to the agency hadn't been particularly productive. Ted, with whom I'd talked first, had reported that all was under control. Next I'd spoken with Patrick, who sounded bored and grumpy; no one assigned to the RKI case was giving him reports, so he had nothing to plug into his charts. Would I please speak with them?

Derek was still in the office, so I started with him. He'd found a couple of suspicious circumstances with former RKI employees and was going into the field to interview them in the morning. I didn't waste time on the details; he'd already e-mailed them to me. Mick was gone for the day, but he'd told Derek he was making headway on the backgrounding of RKI's partners, and had uncovered some things he felt were better to report to me in person.

"What things?" I asked.

"He didn't say."

"When does he plan to do this?"

"When you get back here, I guess."

"I'll get hold of him. Thanks, Derek."

Mick wasn't available at any of his numbers, nor was Keim. Probably out stuffing their faces at some chic new restaurant. Keim had a friend who was a food reviewer for the *Chron*, and she and Mick were often invited along on her incognito excursions. I left irritable and demanding messages on their machine and cellulars. Then I returned several calls to clients and one to the Church Street house contractor who wanted my permission to order a part for the bathroom plumbing system. I didn't know what the hell it was, but I figured if he said we needed it, we did. He then subjected me to a long-winded description of how the job was going, which I interpreted as meaning progressing very well.

Now John came up behind me, handed me a glass of white wine. "Kitchen's clean," he said.

I took the glass. "Thanks. That'll make Krista happy."

"I'm thinking I ought to marry the woman, or at least talk her into moving in here. She's good for me—and the boys."

"Well, why don't you ask her?"

"The letter K."

"What?"

"Karen. And after we divorced there was Kelly, then Kate, and then Kathy. The letter K could spell a problem for me."

"I hardly think—"

My phone rang. I went inside where I'd left it and picked up.

"McCone." Hy. There was an urgency in his voice.

"What's wrong?"

"There's been another bombing."

"Damn! Where, this time?"

"Chicago."

"When?"

"Nine o'clock, their time. I've been trying to reach you for fifteen minutes. One person was killed, five others injured. I need you back there."

"I'll get the first flight out."

"Thanks. Things're really starting to fall apart here."

"How so?"

"I'm monitoring a major situation with one of our South American clients and may have to go down there, as well as keeping in hourly touch with a couple of our operatives in the Middle East. And a lot of the employees here at headquarters're really upset about the Green Street bombing and Dan's murder and aren't functioning too well."

"Can't Gage calm them down? He's good at that."

"Well, that's another problem, McCone: Gage."

"What about him?"

"I don't know where the hell he is. Haven't seen him since he left the hospital after Dan died Sunday night. He didn't go home; the current live-in girlfriend said she hasn't seen him and he hasn't called. His cellular's out of service range. He's not at any of our branch offices or the training camp. And he hasn't checked in at the office."

"Has he ever done this before?"

"No. I think something may have happened to him."

One down. Maybe two.

One left to go—my husband.

"McCone?"

"Okay, you handle things here. Don't worry about the situation in Chicago. I'll deal with it."

Tuesday

✦

FEBRUARY 28

My flight from San Diego connected with a red-eye out of Los Angeles that put me into Chicago O'Hare only twenty minutes late. Bob Cleary, head of RKI's operations there, had informed me that no flight had ever arrived at or departed O'Hare on time since 1952, and I wasn't so sure he was joking. As we landed, I saw a light dusting of snow on the ground and was worried that I'd freeze in my suede jacket. I almost did while wheeling my bag to the cab stand, but there were plenty of taxis waiting.

Cleary had made me an early-arrival reservation at the downtown Sheraton, a towering structure on the Chicago River near where it empties into Lake Michigan and a few blocks' walking distance from their ravaged offices. When I got to the hotel, I found my room was ready as promised. I showered and dressed in the black Ellen Tracy pantsuit that before leaving San Francisco for San Diego I'd rescued from the closet at the Church Street house where I'd stored my more "grown-up" clothes—an item that had cost a fortune but was so classic, wrinkle-resistant, and well made that it would get me through any occasion for the rest of my life.

Then I sat for a while in front of the room's window, staring out at the brownish-green water of the river and the wide Michigan Avenue Bridge leading over to Wacker Drive. In the distance, the lake lay gray, placid, and seemingly endless.

I'd slept some on the LA–Chicago flight, but mostly I'd spent the time reading Derek's e-mailed reports, thinking about the investigation, and probably muddying the waters more than clearing them. In the end several possibilities had occurred to me, none of them conclusive: to begin with, the ever-running man was an extremely busy individual. He had blown up RKI's San Francisco building a week ago Monday, shot Dan Kessell on Saturday, and bombed the office in Chicago yesterday. Either he was a version of Superman or there was more than one person involved in the vendetta against the company.

And then there was the possibility that Dan's death might have had nothing to do with RKI's troubles. An angry spouse of a cheating wife, a disgruntled friend, someone he owed money to—there were any number of other explanations. And since Kessell had so zealously guarded his private life, there was no way of knowing without further intensive digging.

Exactly how had the shooter gotten through the locked gate at the condo complex? Yes, it closed slowly, but a man with Dan's past was always watching his back; he would not have allowed a stranger to enter behind him—much less someone who held a grudge against him. But what if the killer had come up behind him with the murder weapon? Forced him inside? That would make sense.

I turned my attention from the dead to the alive—namely, Gage Renshaw. I knew him better than I knew Dan, had seen him at various quasi-social business functions, but seldom with the same woman; Hy had told me that so far as he knew, Gage had never been married, and he moved women in and out of his house on a six-month basis. The latest was named Paulina Morales, but otherwise neither of us knew anything about her.

And then there were Renshaw's missing years in Southeast Asia. Gage was impulsive, dangerous, and downright strange. There could be any number of reasons why he'd dropped out of sight Sunday night. Perhaps he'd gone off on an investigative tangent of his own, but that didn't feel like something he would do; Gage hired people like me to find out things.

I looked at my watch. Nearly nine, when I was supposed to meet Bob Cleary for breakfast in the hotel coffee shop. I wished I had time to call Mick to discuss the information that he had for me. But he wanted to talk in person, rather than on the phone or by e-mailing a report. That didn't sound good.

I grabbed my bag and headed down to the coffee shop.

It was apparent that Bob Cleary hadn't slept all night. Yellowish-green circles that resembled recovering bruises stood out under his reddened eyes, and his thinning gray hair looked as if he'd recently washed it but hadn't bothered with a blow-dryer; comb-tooth tracks revealed his pink scalp. He sat across from me and toyed with a cup of coffee. I played with an English muffin, spilled my own coffee onto the table. Said, "Sorry. Long day yesterday, and now jet lag's catching up with me."

"I thought maybe you'd catch a few winks after getting to the hotel."

"No. Rush hour traffic made it a long trip in, and when I'm on an investigation I'm too wired to rest much."

"Know what you mean. I'm mainly an administrator now, but when I was with the DEA—forget sleep."

I regarded him, placed him at around Renshaw's age, in his early fifties.

"You know Gage Renshaw while you were with the agency?"

"Some. In D.C. before he went overseas. He was the one who recruited me for RKI when he joined up with Kessell."

"An odd duck, isn't he?"

"More of a son of a bitch."

His frankness startled me. I covered my surprise and said, "Well, Mr. Cleary, we're on the same page. Tell me about Gage Renshaw."

Renshaw, Cleary said, would do absolutely anything for money. "As long as I've known him he's had no loyalty to the DEA, no loyalty to any organization or individual—except to himself."

While in Washington he had passed on confidential information to the highest bidder. His connections had spread like tentacles from the criminal underclass to the highest levels of the bureaucracy. "And some said even higher," Cleary added. "Congress, minor officials in the White House—who knows?"

"So he sold information about . . . ?"

"How investigations were proceeding. Who was—or wasn't—about to be indicted. Who was sleeping with whose wife or mistress. What was the drug of choice of the powerful, and who their suppliers were."

"And he got away with that?"

"Gage was clever. There were rumors, but no proof."

"Did he deal in drugs himself?"

"No way."

"You think he did drugs?"

Cleary shook his head. "Nope. Money is Gage's drug—and I mean that literally. The more he gets, the more he wants. In Washington the rumors got so persistent that the agency was afraid he might become an embarrassment, or create a major scandal for the administration. That's why they shipped him off to Thailand. Figured things were so corrupt there that he *couldn't* embarrass them."

"But they assigned him to CENTAC—"

"Yes. Because a special force like that needs people of Gage's . . . ingenuity. And he did well for them."

I said, "One thing that bothers me—if you knew all of this about Renshaw, how come you allowed him to recruit you for RKI?"

"Because he made me an offer I couldn't refuse."

"And why did he do that?"

"He knew my record with the agency. And he knew that I was aware of his." Cleary smiled ruefully. "In short, Ms. McCone, I was the kind of man he needed. And I had the goods on him."

"A touch of blackmail on your part?"

"Not really. Gage was the one who approached me. Could you have refused?"

"I don't know. I've never been made that kind of offer."

But Kessell made that kind of offer to Gage when he sold him the partnership in RKI for a dollar. And both were extremely generous with Hy when they brought him on board.

My God, what is Hy mixed up in?

And, by extension, what am I?

Cleary borrowed a heavy coat for me from a woman he knew on hotel security and we walked over to the site of the bombing, along the broad river walk bordered by newish, expensive-looking condos and apartment buildings. The air was bitterly cold, wind off the lake gusting along the river and between the buildings. As we started to turn left at a large, multi-tiered fountain whose cascades sheeted noisily down, there was a hissing sound, and a high arc of spray shot into the air all the way to the opposite shore. Given the temperature and the windchill factor, I wouldn't have been surprised if it had frozen and hung there.

"Water cannon," Bob said, seeing my startled expression. "Goes off at regular intervals."

"Why?"

"Damned if I know. It just does. I never thought about it."

We walked down a side street and turned right into what seemed to be an area of converted factories and warehouses similar to where RKI had had its building in San Francisco. Exclusive shops, galleries, professional offices, and a grocery store whose window display of exotic breads made me wish I'd finished my English muffin occupied the street level.

We turned a corner and I spotted a police barricade. Sawhorses and tape blocked both the street and the sidewalk on either side, and emergency vehicles stood beyond it; police and fire department personnel moved about. Cleary and I pushed our way through a bunch of rubberneckers, and he showed his ID to an officer who guarded the perimeter. The officer raised the tape and let us inside.

The familiar stench of fire, chemicals, and charred and water-soaked debris took me back to Green Street on the night of the explosion there. My stomach lurched and sweat popped out on my forehead; I closed my eyes, breathed through my mouth. When I opened them and looked up, I took an involuntary step backward, bumping into Cleary.

At the hotel, he'd described the extent of the destruction, but it still hadn't prepared me for this. Between two scorched and sooty three-story brick buildings was a gaping space mounded with blackened rubble. The street and opposite sidewalk were puddled and littered with glass, bricks, twisted metal, and other unidentifiable pieces of what had once been a building. Several windows in nearby structures had been blown out. Even mouth-breathing didn't keep the stench from me; it must have filtered in through my pores. Cleary steadied me as a man in a black trench coat came toward us. I made myself focus on him.

The man introduced himself to me as Special Agent Lloyd Zyzek of the FBI; he and Cleary had already met, and he'd been told I was on my way. He explained what they knew about the blast. It sounded similar to the Green Street explosion, with three charges set. As in San Francisco, the guard in the lobby had been killed; five other employees had suffered serious injuries. Because the explosion had happened at nine in the evening, there were few people on the street and only three had been hit by falling glass and debris. One of the adjoining buildings was under renovation and vacant; the employees in the other had all gone home by then. People in the block backing up to the RKI offices and others nearby reported being shaken up by the noise and reverberations, but not hurt.

"We immediately assumed this was a terrorist bombing," Zyzek said. "At least until we made the connection to the other RKI blasts. We'll try to dispel that notion in our statements to the press; people're very nervous about terrorism these days, and we don't want to fuel public anxiety."

"Is the fire mostly out?" I asked.

"We've got some hot spots still, but yeah."

"Any idea of what type of bomb he used?" I asked.

"From what we've recovered, we suspect plastic, like in your San Francisco bombing. Timing device was probably simple, remote-controlled. Given the info on the Web these days, any idiot could've put them together."

But this guy's not any idiot.

Zyzek added, "So far we haven't found enough to see if there's a signature on them."

People who manufacture bombs frequently leave what is called a signature on the device. Nothing so obvious as their names or initials, but some repetitive and largely unintentional detail that tells the experts which bombs were made by the same individual. I made a mental note to check with police in the other cities where RKI's offices had been blown up about a possible signature. There had been nothing about that in the reports I'd read. If they were reluctant to release the information to me, I'd use my contacts at SFPD.

I asked Zyzek, "Any sightings of suspicious individuals?"

"No one's come forward with any information so far."

"Well, thanks for sharing what you've got." I looked at Cleary. "I guess I'd better get back to the hotel and start interviewing your people." He'd arranged for the employees who had already left the premises last night to meet with me in one of the Sheraton's conference rooms in staggered shifts, beginning at eleven.

"I'll walk you back."

"That's okay; you've had a long night, and have more important things to do." I handed my card to Zyzek. "Will you call me on my cellular number if you find out anything else?"

He nodded. "I surely will."

I turned and walked toward the barricade. The rubberneckers were still there, joined now by a couple of media types. A woman with a microphone came at me, and I dodged, hid my face from the probing lens of a minicam. Felt one of those little psychic tugs you sometimes get when someone's watching you, and turned to my right.

A man, slipping around a lamppost, moving away fast.

I shrugged off the insistent hand of the woman with the microphone, and went after the man. He sped up, running across the street. My view of him was momentarily blocked by a truck.

By the time I reached the corner, he'd disappeared. I looked straight ahead, then to the right and to the left, but saw no one resembling him.

My second glimpse of the ever-running man?

Minutes later, I leaned against the railing of the river walk in front of my hotel and tried to remember what I'd noticed about the man. The ripples on the brownish-green water soothed me, and soon I closed my eyes and called up his image.

Medium height. Fat? Thin? Hard to tell because of the loose navy blue jacket he wore. Hair? Gray. No, not gray. His head was covered by a gray baseball cap, its bill pulled low on his forehead.

Hats like that usually bore some kind of logo—team, equipment company, university. This one had . . . nothing. A man who didn't want to call attention to himself.

The lower part of his face: Nose? Shadowed by the cap's bill. Lips? Thin, or maybe pulled tight by exertion. Mustache? No. Beard? Chin hidden by the upturned collar of the jacket.

Pants: standard American uniform—blue denim jeans. Shoes: more standard uniform—dirty white, probably cross trainers.

He could have been Everyman.

But . . . something. Something . . .

The way he moved. Peculiar uneven gait when he started running.

The same way the man in the alley behind RKI's San Francisco building had moved.

I'd recognize that gait if I saw him running again.

It had begun to snow in the late afternoon, and the 9:45 flight from O'Hare to San Francisco was delayed an hour. I hadn't even lain down on the bed in my hotel room, much less *in* it, and I must have looked so exhausted at check-in that the sympathetic airline clerk bumped me up to the nearly empty first-class cabin. I croaked a thank-you to her; my throat actually hurt from asking questions all day.

Once on the plane, I accepted a pre-takeoff glass of wine, hoping it would put me to sleep. By the time we were airborne, I was as alert as if I'd slept for a week. I said yes to another glass of wine, tilted my seat back, and sipped contemplatively.

Too contemplatively. My mind went into overdrive. Finally, after fifteen minutes, I gave up and took out my recorder and headset. Began reviewing the three tapes of interviews with RKI employees that I'd made at the Sheraton that afternoon.

After all, San Francisco time was two hours earlier than Chicago's. I'd have plenty of opportunity to rest in my own bed.

Sure I would. Given the way my sleep cycles operated, by the time I was through with this investigation, I'd have bags under my eyes the size of steamer trunks.

Tape number one, comments worth noting:

I saw a pair of men loitering on the sidewalk in front of

the building yesterday when I went to lunch at twelve-thirty. Didn't think much of it, though, because I assumed they were workers from the renovation project next door taking a smoke break... They were wearing parkas and jeans and work boots... The parkas, I think, were olive drab. Other than that I didn't pay much attention to them because I was hungry and in a hurry... Wait, here's something strange: the work boots looked new, weren't even dusty.

There was a guy from Adams Electric going around checking the wiring that morning... Yes, I'm sure he was from them. He had on a uniform and a visitor badge and would've had to present his ID to the guard in the lobby and be shown in by the person who ordered the work done... That would be Mr. Wilson, head of maintenance.

I never ordered any electrical work—although if I had, it would have been from Adams—and I didn't bring anyone up from the lobby... No, not yesterday, or any day this month... Uniforms like their employees wear can be bought at any outfitter's, and the lobby guard that morning, Toni Goodman, really isn't one of our more observant employees... Certainly I'll send her in to talk with you.

Yes, I'm sure it was an Adams Electric uniform. And he had ID... Well, I didn't examine it with a microscope, if that's what you mean, but it certainly looked genuine. I had him sign the log, and called up to Mr. Wilson's office... No, I didn't speak with him, but his secretary said he'd be right down... No, I don't remember him coming down, but a few minutes later the guy was gone, so somebody must've let him through the locked door... The log? I suppose it was destroyed in the explosion, and

I don't remember the name the guy signed. God, I'm glad my shift ended at noon that day! Just thinking about sitting there and then—boom! It gives me the shivers.

Yes, I'm Mr. Wilson's secretary, but I didn't receive any call from reception about an Adams Electric employee . . . Yes, I was away from my desk for a while that morning—I'm pregnant, have morning sickness. When I leave the desk, Dana in the next cubicle picks up for me.

She's always in the bathroom hurling and I'm always picking up for her. I really get tired of it. She knew what she was getting into when she decided to have a kid. Why can't she be pregnant and still do her job? . . . Okay, I admit it, I did pick up, but I was in a rotten mood and I'd had it with her. I said Wilson would be down and then didn't pass on the message to either of them. I thought maybe if she got in trouble she'd shape up . . . I suppose the electrician could've slipped in behind an employee who was coming into the building. I myself would've let him, seeing as he had on a uniform from a firm we often deal with.

Tape number two, comments worth noting:

The problem is, Bob Cleary rides people too hard, especially those in my division . . . Right, we monitor the executive protection program, twenty-four seven. Keep track of where every client is at every minute. That's why four of the injured people were my coworkers—the department's staffed round the clock. The irony is, two of them shouldn't've even been there; they were working unnecessary overtime at Cleary's insistence—and they were both people for whom he's expressed a personal dislike.

* * *

Cleary's an asshole, and I don't mind if this gets back to him . . . Why's he an asshole? He runs the offices like his own little fiefdom. If you're in favor, you're in for good treatment, a raise, a promotion. If you're not, it means overtime, heavy workloads, and he bad-mouths you. He'll say something negative or potentially damaging about anybody who gets on his wrong side . . . No, he never spoke about Renshaw, Kessell, or Ripinsky to me, but he did to Dave Markowski.

Kessell, Cleary didn't talk about him. Ripinsky, all he would say is that he was a very dangerous man . . . No, he left it at that. No details. But Renshaw, he hated *Renshaw. I don't know why . . . Corruption? Well, sure Renshaw's corrupt, but so's Cleary. He's got some sweet deals going . . . I don't know the details, but Ken Manning might be able to tell you.*

Sweet deals? Well, I wouldn't exactly put it that way. I mean, it's nothing exceptional: padding the expense accounts, overbilling clients to make the office's profitability look better to headquarters. Penny-ante stuff, nothing that every single one of our managers isn't doing. If you ask me, the partners should hire a first-class auditor to look into how they're being screwed.

Tape number three, comments worth noting:

I left at eight-thirty. There were several people on the street . . . Well, one in particular I noticed. He was standing under an awning of a store on the opposite side, looking toward our building. When I got close to him, he turned toward the window behind him. At the time I didn't think much of it; it's a lingerie store, and you know how guys are . . . He was pretty nondescript. Wore a dark jacket, jeans, and a baseball cap . . . Light-colored cap, maybe beige. I never really saw his face.

For a top security firm, the security in the building was a joke. Eric Simms, the personnel manager, hired the lamest people to staff the front desk and surveillance cameras. This Toni Goodman, for instance, she has half a brain cell. Big tits, though. I'd say Simms is screwing her.

I am not *"screwing her"! She is my* fiancée, *for God's sake! And I do not hire "lame people." Who told you this? . . . Confidentiality? Bullshit!*

All I know is the executives we're supposed to be protecting are out there in the cold with no lifeline since the explosion. Bob Cleary and I are trying to set up an emergency operation in an empty storefront we've gotten hold of, but it's not coming together fast enough. Maybe that's what the bomber wanted—to leave the people depending on us hanging out to dry and then go after them.

Maybe it's not RKI he's out to get, but one of our clients . . . Well, some of them're major; I can give you a list . . . The other bombings could be a smoke screen . . . Yeah, I know that's one hell of an extreme action, but look at Oklahoma City, Nine-eleven. Look at the terrorist crap that's happened in England and God knows where else. Sometimes I can't believe the lengths people will go to assert their beliefs.

With all these encouraging and cheerful comments on my mind, I finally drifted off into a fitful sleep.

Wednesday

✦

MARCH 1

The insistent ring of the bedside phone woke me from a nightmare in which glass and bricks and steel beams were raining down on me. I flailed around in the tangled sheets, threw a pillow to the floor, and sat up, my heart pounding. There was a digital clock on the nightstand; the numbers read 8:25. The phone rang again, then switched over to the machine in the living room; I couldn't make out who the caller was.

After a moment I got up and grabbed the pretty silk robe Julia had picked out for me. Pulled it on as I went to the living room. Murky gray light filtered around the mini-blinds—another foggy San Francisco day, but no sound of rain, thank God. The light on the machine flashed reproachfully at me.

My flight from Chicago had gotten in after one in the morning. I'd taken a cab to the safe house, had a soak in the apartment's deep tub, and crawled into bed, not expecting to sleep. But I had—a full five hours' worth.

Now I pressed the play button on the machine. Hy.

"McCone, what's happening? I tried your cell several times yesterday, but it was turned off. If you check this machine for messages, call me."

I'd turned the phone on after landing at O'Hare yesterday, but switched it off again when I met Bob Cleary for breakfast, and also left it off while I interviewed RKI's employees. After that . . . well, weariness and another long plane flight had prevented me from even thinking about it.

I called the RKI condo in La Jolla where Hy was staying. Another machine. When I dialed his cellular, he picked up on the first ring.

"Where are you?" he asked.

"San Francisco, the safe house. I got in very late. Where are you?"

"Headquarters. Been here all night. That situation in South America that I mentioned is defused, and I'm about to head back to the condo to get some sleep. You certainly made a quick trip. What did you find out back there?"

I summarized the high points for him, then added, "I think you should have an audit conducted of your branch offices' expense reports and billing. According to what one person told me, Bob Cleary pads expenses and overbills clients. And apparently he's not the only manager who does that."

"Shit. I wonder why Dan didn't pick up on it? He was a good administrator." Pause. "Well, an audit'll be necessary anyway, now that he's dead."

"Has Renshaw surfaced?"

"No. I'm kind of overwhelmed here, might've caved in entirely if I didn't know you were handling things back in Chicago. Dan's assistant—you met him, Brent Chavez—has been out sick, but he's due back tomorrow. He'll be a big help, even though he's relatively new to the operation."

"Well, it's good you'll have *some* support there."

"You sound as tired as I feel."

"I'm okay. You're the one who needs rest."

"Yeah, I know. I'm practically out the door."

"Oh, Ripinsky, before you go, there're a couple of things I want to ask you: I know the company owns our plane and the Citations and the Jet Rangers, but do they have title to a beat-up old Piper that Dan occasionally flew?"

"Never heard of it. We reviewed the aircraft inventory a year ago, sold off a couple that weren't necessary, and there wasn't anything like that on the list. Why?"

Interesting. Instead of answering his question, I asked, "Also, do you and Dan and Gage have keyman insurance on your lives?"

"Gage and I do. Dan didn't. Couldn't get it without exorbitant premiums. Bad heart."

"But he was still flying. Wouldn't his FAA medical review have shown that?" Licensed pilots with commercial ratings are required to have medical exams with certain agency-approved doctors every year.

"I never knew Dan to pilot, at least not since I've been with the firm. He always took the right seat. Besides, you and I know there're a lot of people flying who shouldn't be. And a lot of docs who can be fooled or bought. Why the interest in the keyman policies?"

I explained what I suspected about the individual bequests in Dan's will.

"Yeah, that was how we decided to deal with the problem; he'd will us money in the amount of our insurance. Look, in Gage's absence I guess you'll be reporting to me. That okay?"

"Has to be. Let's just try not to wreck our marriage."

"I couldn't wreck *anything* at the moment. I'm dead on my feet."

"Sleep well, Ripinsky."

"I will—but hopefully not till I get to the condo."

* * *

I was grinding coffee beans when the phone rang again. This time it was Mick.

"How'd it go in Chicago?" he asked.

"Inconclusive. But I think I spotted our perp near the bombed-out building."

"See him clearly?"

"More clearly than any of the other witnesses have. He made a mistake revisiting the scene."

"I thought they only did that on TV or in mystery novels."

"Well, the concept has to have some basis in fact. I understand you want to talk with me in person about what you've come up with on the background checks."

"Yeah, I do. Face to face, in private." His tone had become subdued, cautious.

"Why not come here, then. I'll make breakfast."

"Oh, God, please don't do that!" Mick has a low opinion of my culinary expertise, and in the case of breakfast, he's probably right.

"Coffee, then."

"Coffee's good. And Shar . . ."

"What?"

"Even though it's early, you might want to make it Irish coffee."

Mick said, "I'll start at the beginning of my deep-backgrounding on Renshaw." He was sitting in the other leather chair in front of the fireplace, his right foot tapping the floor the way it always does when he's nervous.

"I'm assuming that what you came up with on Gage leads to something on Hy."

"Uh . . . well . . ."

"Just get on with it."

He nodded, took a sip of coffee, and made a face. "Shar—"

"I know: my coffee takes the enamel off your teeth. If I'd thought of that I'd've suggested we meet at Starbucks for a latte."

My tone had been sharper than I'd intended. Mick blinked, but clearly understood why. "Sorry. It's just that I don't know how—"

"As you said, start at the beginning."

"Okay, when we last talked, the trail on Renshaw ended when CENTAC was disbanded and he quit the DEA. I remembered you once told me that he'd disappeared into Thailand."

"Did I? Oh, right—when I first met Renshaw, I asked the investigator I trained under about him, and that was what he told me."

"Well, he didn't disappear into Thailand. I can't tell you how I accessed this information or from whom. You'd probably fire me on the spot if I did. But Renshaw was in the Middle East, arranging for shipments of illegal arms and explosives, and making a fortune. He was based in Azad."

Arab emirate, formerly progressive, but now embroiled in a bitter civil war. Hank and Anne-Marie's adopted daughter, Habiba Hamid, was the granddaughter of the now-deceased San Francisco consul from that country.

I said, "I suppose in those days it was one of the safer places to live over there."

"Right."

I could feel the tension rising in the three feet between Mick and me. "Go on."

"Shar, I don't want to upset you . . ."

And then I remembered a story Hy had once told me, could practically hear his voice: "*One of our hotdog pilots, name of Ralston, got his ass thrown in jail in Qatar. The son of a bitch was importing alcohol into an Arab country on the side . . . When he got caught, it was a potential life sentence. Dan and I flew in, delivered a load of pipe fittings to the oil fields, spread a lot of US dollars around to the jailers. When we left we had Ralston in the skin of the plane.*"

Meaning dressed in thermals and hidden in the space between the plane's outer body and inner cabin. Hy had told me K Air frequently delivered supplies to the Middle East oil fields. And Qatar was very near Azad.

But what *else* had they delivered?

Mick saw my expression and realized I'd figured out what he'd come to tell me.

"Illegal arms and explosives," I said flatly.

He nodded and stood. Set a file on the table between us. "I'll leave this for you to read."

"You bastard!" I yelled.

Hy jerked awake and sat up in the king-size bed in RKI's La Jolla condo. I'd entered quietly, and he'd been sleeping so deeply he had no inkling I was there. Out of habit, he slid his hand under the other pillow for his .45, then withdrew it quickly when he recognized my voice.

"What . . . ?" He raised his arm, shielded his eyes from the overhead light I'd turned on. Because operatives frequently used the condo to sleep at odd hours, the windows were fitted with black blinds that made it appear to be the middle of the night—even now, at three in the afternoon.

"Try illegal arms and explosives. Renshaw directing sales from Azad. You and Dan flying into Qatar and God knows what other places. Compared to that, the massacre of those Cambodians you were involved in sounds like a mercy killing!"

He stared at me. Shook his head.

I added, "A lot of things about your past I can accept. If you'd told me about this when you supposedly came clean, I would've accepted it, too. But not now. Not years later, when I find out you withheld the truth from me!"

"Shar, calm down—"

I took Mick's report—that I'd read so many times on my flight down I had it memorized—and flung it at him. It smacked his forehead and fell to the floor.

"Read this, you son of a bitch! And then explain why you hid a major detail of your criminal career from me. Tell me about the other stuff you've withheld. And *then* try to convince me why I should trust another word out of your mouth. *Or* remain married to you!"

I whirled and left the room.

I heard him jump out of bed and follow me, but I kept going across the living room and wrenched the front door open.

"Where'll you be?" he called.

"I don't know. You can reach me on my cellular when—and if—you come up with what you consider a convincing enough story."

I went home. Well, not exactly home—John's house. When I let myself in, I found he wasn't there; neither were the boys. I left my purse and carry-on bag in the kitchen and went to the family room. Opened the door to the deck and stepped outside.

Quiet, warmish late afternoon. Wind rustling through the

trees and plants in the canyon. Somewhere far away a dog barked and, closer by, another answered. Then all was still again.

I walked across to the deck's railing. There was a new little gate near the place where Pa had built the steps that led into the canyon. I went through it, found the moss-slicked top stone, and felt my way down, batting away the encroaching vegetation. Nobody had come this way in a long time. John's boys were into iPods and text messaging, not treehouses.

It was still there, though, nestled in the branches of a giant oak. The oak had prospered, and so had the treehouse. Someone—presumably the interim owners of the house, who'd had kids—had rebuilt it. Not well, but it was whole again, with wooden footholds nailed to the tree's trunk. As it was, I scarcely needed them; the little structure was set low, and I'd grown tall since the days when I played there. I climbed up, sat down cross-legged on the floor, and recalled the last time I'd been there.

A wild, grief-soaked night years ago, when I'd been told that a body had been discovered in a burned-out adobe in nearby San Ysidro—a body whose description matched Hy's. I'd assumed the worst. So I came here, to my childhood refuge, to vent my sorrow and rage.

This afternoon I felt only rage.

Yes, I'd always known, as one of the RKI employees in Chicago had remarked, that Hy was a very dangerous man. He'd done things he wasn't proud of. He'd killed several people—but only to save his own life. And for years he'd suffered before he made an uneasy peace with his actions.

I was not one to preach. I wasn't proud of some of the things I'd done. I'd killed, too—but only to save my own life and those of people I cared about. And, like Hy, I still had the occasional painful flashback or nightmare.

But we'd admitted all the bad stuff to each other years ago. Or so I'd thought. I'd regarded our relationship as one based on mutual trust and honesty.

But now I'd found out Hy had sold arms and explosives to warring factions in troubled nations. Weapons and devices that could kill thousands and thousands of innocent people. Perhaps even materials for weapons of mass destruction. Mythical as they'd turned out to be in Iraq, they did exist elsewhere.

He must have thought it monstrous, because he hadn't admitted it to me. He hadn't trusted me enough to forgive him and go on loving him.

I put my hands to my face. They were sweating and shaking. Anger rose like bile in my throat.

When I took my hands away and looked up, the first thing I saw was a loose board on one side of the treehouse. I crawled over there, pulled it free, began to smash at the other boards. When I had destroyed that wall, I took on another. Then I began punching shingles from the roof.

It must have been late when I finished my one-woman demolition derby, because dusk had crept into the canyon, but I couldn't tell the time. In my frenzy I'd somehow broken my watch. Only the roof beams and corner studs and part of one wall remained.

I lay on my back, looking up through the branches of the oak. My hands were bloodied, my rage spent. It felt as if another, irrational woman had taken possession of my body after I'd read Mick's report. Why? Had Hy really done something so terrible in withholding a shameful chapter of his past? Didn't we all have places like that where we didn't want to go, much less take someone else to?

I recalled my conversation with Hank the day he'd brought me lunch and comforted me about the Green Street explosion.

"You've been in dicey situations before, and come through them pretty damn well."

"This time is different. It's really unnerved me . . . Ever since that night, I've been going on crying jags and throwing up, and I can't articulate my feelings, even to Hy, because I don't know what or why . . ."

"Post-traumatic stress, kid. And you're feeling your own mortality."

"The mortality concept isn't exactly foreign to me."

"But maybe it wasn't as real before."

"So why is it more real now?"

"Because your life has changed. You're married. You've made that ultimate commitment. In theory, since you and Hy have been together a long time, it shouldn't make a difference. But take it from one who knows: it does."

Well, of course. Ever since I accepted this case, I'd been walking through an emotional minefield—worrying about what it might do to my marriage, traumatized by nearly being blown up in the Green Street explosion, viewing the destruction in Chicago. And the mine I'd stepped on was the file Mick had handed me that morning.

Well, I couldn't put the pieces of the treehouse back together. But maybe I could mend the pieces of my marriage.

Thursday

✦

MARCH 2

I woke to the alarm in my old bedroom, which John had turned into a guest room. Seven o'clock, and my head hurt. He and I had taken the boys out for burgers the night before, then sat up very late, drinking and talking. Hy didn't call my cellular, and I finally turned it off when I crawled into bed at one-thirty.

I'd confided to John what I'd found out about Hy, although not the havoc I'd wreaked upon the treehouse; in retrospect, it seemed like a childish tantrum, and I hoped if he discovered it, he'd assume it was the work of teenage vandals. John counseled that I proceed cautiously, hear Hy out before making any judgments. This coming from my brother, who had once been the hottest-headed bar fighter in San Diego County.

"But the evidence is all there in Mick's report," I said. "And we know he's got great sources and checks everything twice. K Air was importing illegal arms, explosives, and God knows what else into the Middle East."

"They may have been, but unless you can get access to their records you can't know for sure if Hy made those trips, or knew what he was transporting."

"Hy would've been captain on those flights; he was senior

pilot, and even Kessell took the right seat when they flew together. The captain always knows what's aboard. Besides, the records were probably destroyed years ago."

"Well, I still think you should give him the benefit of the doubt, listen to what the man has to say."

"I'll listen to him, yes. But how am I going to tell if it's a lie?"

"Shar, has Hy ever actually lied to you?"

That gave me pause. "No. What he employs is silence. When we were first together, he was totally mum about his past, but he made no secret that there were things in it that he didn't want to talk about. When he was ready—when he was sure of our relationship—he explained everything. Or so I thought."

"But you say he told you the story of flying into Qatar and rescuing that hotdog pilot in an offhand way."

"Yes."

"And when you were working on that case involving the bombing of the Azadi consulate, did he ever say anything about Renshaw having lived in Azad?"

". . . No. But that could mean he didn't want to open up that particular can of worms."

"Then why would he have talked about Qatar?"

"Slip of the tongue, because the story was interesting."

John shook his head. "Guys like Ripinsky don't make slips. They've got too much to lose."

Too much to lose—me, our life together.

John added, "Just think about it."

"I'll think about it." I drank more wine, even though I knew I'd regret it in the morning.

And now I did regret it. My eyeballs felt as if they'd been sandpapered and there was a dull pounding in the vicinity of my sinuses that had nothing to do with allergens. But as I lay in bed, listening to John and the boys get ready for work and school, I made a decision.

I was going to see this case through. I'd signed a contract, accepted a retainer, and was committed to delivering a solution. Since Renshaw had not yet reappeared, I'd report to my husband—in a professional, unemotional manner.

Until the case was concluded we would not speak any more about the arms dealing. Then I'd hear him out and decide if I could live with whatever he told me.

I took my cellular off the nightstand, turned it on, and listened again to my voice mail messages. They'd all come in yesterday, when the phone was in my purse in John's kitchen and I was in the canyon wrecking the treehouse; after that I hadn't been in any shape to return the calls.

Mick: "Shar, are you okay? Let me know. Also, I've come up with stuff on Kessell's tour of duty with the Special Forces, and his hospital stay in the Philippines. Still can't get any leads on where he got the bucks to start his aviation service."

Ted: "Thought I'd phone in my daily report. Everything's under control here."

Derek: "One of those field interviews I conducted with the former RKI employees turned up something suspect. I've e-mailed the file to you, but I'd really like to discuss it. Right now I'm starting to check over that ancient iMac of Hy's."

Gary Viner: "Hey, Shar, I've got the autopsy and ballistics reports on the Kessell case. Give me a call when you get a chance."

Nothing from Hy.

He and I had always had a strange psychic connection; we often knew where the other was or what the other was thinking or feeling without being told. Now the connection was broken.

I called the condominium, got the machine. Called his cellular, and he answered.

"It's me," I said.

"McCone, I was hoping you'd call."

"I thought you were going to call me."

"I wanted to give you time to cool off."

Or you needed time to work on an explanation.

"I've cooled. There are things we need to discuss. Where are you?"

"Headquarters."

"Let's make an appointment."

"We could have lunch—"

"No, in your office. When?"

Long pause. "An hour and a half?"

"Good. I'll see you then."

My God, I thought, I just made a formal appointment to meet with my own *husband.*

"McCone, let me explain—"

"No." Hy had gotten up and started around his desk toward me, but now I waved him away and sat down in one of the chairs facing the desk. "This isn't the time for that. We're in the middle of an investigation. It has to take top priority."

He backed up, sank into his chair. He was haggard and hadn't shaved very well; in fact, he looked worse than I felt—and even with the help of aspirin, coffee, and some breakfast I wasn't in top form.

I got down to business and explained that I would continue with the investigation and report to him, but any personal discussions would have to wait till it was wrapped up. "Those are my terms," I ended. "Can you live with them?"

"At this point I'll live with any terms you offer me."

"Good." I glanced at the drugstore watch that I'd bought on the way here to replace the one I'd broken in my treehouse rampage and stood up. "First I'm going to speak with Renshaw's live-in girlfriend. Later on, maybe I'll want one of the company choppers available to fly me to the training camp."

He nodded. "And then?"

"I'll report back to you." I turned and left his office before I could weaken and move around the desk to hold him.

"McCone," he called after me, "take care of yourself."

". . . You, too, Ripinsky."

I didn't leave the building right away, but borrowed an empty office and started returning calls. Ted said everything was still under control, and turned me over to Derek. Derek said his suspicious lead on the former RKI employee had turned out to be false—which I had concluded would be the case when I'd earlier read his e-mailed report. He also told me he'd need more time with the iMac, because it was temperamental and recovering a file that had been deleted was proving difficult.

After I assured Mick that I was all right, he told me the gist of Kessell's service in the Special Forces: he'd been in a unit operating out of Long Hai for a year and three months when he took a round of machine gun fire that shattered his tibia. His hospital stay in the Philippines extended to six months, because he needed extensive therapy in order to walk again. Mick had tried to track down the doctors who treated him as well as other hospital personnel, but several were deceased, and he hadn't been able to locate the others or the surgeon. Nor had he any leads as to how Kessell had gotten the funds to start his aviation service.

"I'll keep going till I get something," he promised.

"Also try to find out anything you can about K Air. And Kessell's life in Thailand."

"Will do."

Mick was like a mole—he wouldn't stop burrowing.

I then spoke with Patrick, who said the reports from the other operatives were finally coming in and he was noting information on his flow charts. "But it's insane, Shar. Nothing relates. I've got scribbles in the margins and arrows running every which way, and I can't make any sense of it."

"Well, keep at it, and we'll go over the charts when I get back there."

He sighed. "I wish human beings' actions were more like the numbers I dealt with back when I was an accountant."

Gary Viner was out of his office.

In the lobby, I stopped at the security checkpoint and asked the guard if I could speak with Kessell's former assistant, Brent Chavez, who had sat in on my meeting with Hy and Dan in San Francisco. She buzzed him and then directed me to his office.

Today Chavez looked tired, and I remembered that Hy had told me he'd been out sick. He rose from his chair and extended his hand, then motioned for me to sit.

"How are you feeling?" I asked.

"Better, thank you. There's been this flu bug going around, but at least it's a mild one. How can I help you?"

"I thought I'd bring you up to speed on my investigation." I gave him a brief summary. "And now I'd like to talk about Dan Kessell. You've worked for him how long?"

"I started last fall."

"And before that?"

"Well, I took a couple of years off after I graduated from Stanford's MBA program."

"Stanford. That's impressive. You must've had a lot of job offers. Why sign on with RKI?"

He flushed. "I hate to admit it, but I grew up on TV crime shows, read thrillers too. I thought it was going to be exciting. And it has been, to some extent, at least when we've got a situation or two going. Otherwise, my work is pretty routine."

"What kind of boss was Dan Kessell?"

He hesitated, considering. "Polite, but distant. You do your job, I'll do mine. We never talked about anything but the work at hand."

"He ride you hard if you made a mistake?"

"No, he just said everybody made mistakes, and I should fix it."

"You seem to be an honest, straightforward individual with a clean past. How does it feel working for a corporation that's—"

"Not honest and straightforward? At first it was weird. I mean, some of these people're pretty scary. Then when I realized Mr. Ripinsky is trying to change the culture here, I accepted it as a temporary problem."

"How is he trying to change the culture?"

"Well, he got more involved in the hiring and firing decisions. Weeded out the really hard cases and brought in more legitimate professionals. I feel that he's intent on reining in excess, getting things under control."

"What about Mr. Renshaw?"

Chavez shook his head. "I can't figure him out at all, and I'm not sure I want to."

"Back to Mr. Ripinsky—he's primarily a hostage negotiator. How come he's now involved in personnel decisions?"

"You don't talk about his work?"

"No more than we talk about mine."

Chavez looked confused.

"Need to know, Mr. Chavez," I said, "need to know."

"Company policy, yeah. But it's strange—the two of you and Mr. Kessell and Mr. Renshaw seem to be the only ones who observe it."

"Oh?"

"All the employees talk to their spouses or significant others about what's happening. I mean, how can you be in a relationship and maintain that kind of secrecy?"

"Well, Mr. Ripinsky and I are both in positions where confidentiality is important. But this investigation takes priority over confidentiality. How would you like to be my second eyes and ears around headquarters?"

"In what way?"

"Find out what people are saying about the situation, which outsiders they've been talking to."

"I can do that. I haven't been here long enough to have gotten close to people, but they accept me enough to talk frankly in my presence."

"Thanks, Mr. Chavez. I'll be in touch, and don't hesitate to call me."

As I drove from La Jolla to the Point Loma area of San Diego where Gage lived with his girlfriend, Paulina Morales, I wondered how Hy and I had managed to separate our work and personal lives so thoroughly. Was it professionalism, or something deeper—perhaps a flaw in both our personalities?

I began going back over all the things we'd told each other during our years together, and finally came to his explanation of how he'd honed his hostage-negotiator skills. It had begun when a passenger on a K Air charter had attempted to take over a flight he was piloting from Bangkok to New Delhi.

"I talked him down, made him hand over his weapon," he'd said, "even though we had to communicate in a bastardized version of Thai and English. It was like I'd been doing it my whole life. After that, I read up on the techniques, and when one of our other pilots had a hijacking attempt, I was able to resolve the situation via radio. After Dan and Gage formed RKI, they called me in for a few special situations and, except for the one when you had to come and rescue me, they always turned out right. It's like this ability I have for languages." Hy spoke four languages fluently—English, Spanish, Russian, and French—and could get along in Thai, Japanese, and Cantonese.

I pulled my attention back to the present, and turned onto Sunset Cliffs Avenue at the upper tip of Point Loma, the peninsula that extends south of downtown San Diego. Aptly named—the cliffs face due west, and the evening light show is spectacular. Renshaw's starkly modern house was one that commanded an especially good view of the Pacific; as I parked in front, I thought of all those ill-gotten gains that had purchased it.

I'd called ahead to ask Paulina Morales if she'd heard from Gage. No, she said, she hadn't, and she was really worried. Would I come over and talk with her? Of course I would.

When she answered the door, I saw that she was very young and very scared. Also very beautiful. Even with her black hair straggling from a ponytail, dark shadows under her eyes, and wearing clothes that she'd obviously slept in, she was striking. Like all of Gage's women.

She took me to the back of the house, through the kitchen to where a breakfast room overlooked the sea. "Coffee," she said, "do you want some?"

"Do you?"

"No. It'll only make me more nervous."

"Then neither do I."

We sat opposite each other at the table. Paulina clasped her hands between her knees.

I said, "Nothing from Gage since I called?"

She shook her head. "I don't know what to do. Yesterday the real estate agent came here. She showed me papers he had faxed her, authorizing her to sell the house."

"Where were they faxed from?"

"I didn't notice. I was so shocked. This woman, she went through the house like the police, told me to put away stuff, clean it up, and get ready to show it. She said she'd be back this afternoon with the sign, and hold an open house on the weekend."

"Did she give you a card?"

"Yes." She got up, went into the kitchen, and brought it back to me.

SUZANNE RICHARDSON, SOTHEBY'S. Dealers in high-end properties.

I said, "I'll talk with her, see what the situation is."

Paulina had started to cry—quietly, the tears sliding down her face to the corners of her mouth. She licked them away. "I don't know what to do. I gave up my apartment and my job when I moved in with Gage. He said he'd take care of me."

He's taken care of you, all right.

She spread her hands out on the table; I put mine over them, to still their trembling.

She added, "A notice came for him today from the bank. I know I shouldn't've opened it, but I did. It confirmed a transfer of all his money to some bank I've never heard of."

"May I see it?"

Again she went to the kitchen, returned with the letter.

Credit Suisse. Kessell's murder had prompted Renshaw to

liquidate his assets and disappear. Once again. Probably he was afraid of something in their mutual past that would come out in the investigation of Dan's death.

Paulina's large dark eyes were teary and dazed. "What am I going to do?"

"For the moment, nothing but rest and take care of yourself. After that—well, we'll figure out something. Now, tell me everything you know about Gage."

She didn't know much.

She'd met him four months ago at an exclusive men's clothing store downtown where she worked as a salesperson; he bought some ties and asked her to lunch at an expensive restaurant. That afternoon, she called in sick and went home with him; she never again returned to work.

Gage gave her a generous allowance; she hadn't had so much money of her own in all her life. He bought her a little Toyota sports car and gave her a gas company credit card on which he paid the bill. He didn't ask for any explanations of how she spent the allowance or the amount of the gas charges.

He never talked about his past except to say he'd had a bad childhood and, though she snooped through the entire house, she'd found nothing revealing.

He never talked about his work, except to say it was confidential.

She'd never heard of RKI.

What did they talk about? I asked.

Movies. Food. Wine. Travel to exotic places, but they hadn't gone to any of them yet.

"Mostly," she said, "we stayed home and fucked. I started feeling like a prisoner here. He didn't like any of my friends, so I couldn't invite them over, and they all work, so I couldn't see them in the daytime when he was gone. I started taking long drives in the car just to get out of here."

"Not a good life, for someone of—what's your age?"

"Eighteen. I turned eighteen two days before I met him."

And I was willing to bet Gage asked her how old she was before he mentioned lunch. No way he would ever get involved with jailbait.

But the difference between eighteen years and seventeen years three hundred and sixty-four days is negligible. When a woman's that young, it's easy for a man like Gage to first control, then use, and finally dump her. And chances were she wouldn't make a fuss afterward.

We'll see about that, Renshaw.

Suzanne Richardson of Sotheby's downtown office was the perfect picture of a high-end real estate agent: beautifully dressed in a taupe suit, with a dark brown silk blouse and low-heeled shoes to match. Conservative gold jewelry, light blonde hair in a short, pert style. Icy demeanor because I wasn't a possible source of a commission.

I gave her one of my cards and said I was working for Renshaw & Kessell International. Told her there was some concern because the advice of one of the partners was needed to head off a crisis, and I had discovered that Gage Renshaw had left town and listed his house with her. Did she have an address for him?

Richardson extracted a file from one of the many on her desk, consulted it, and said, "No, I don't. Nor a phone number. I faxed the necessary papers to him, and he returned them."

"When was this?"

"Last Monday afternoon, around two."

"May I have the fax number? Perhaps we can get in touch with him there."

"Well, he said it wouldn't be valid after seven that evening. He was in transit. I sent copies of the documents back to him shortly after six."

"I'd like to have the number anyway."

She looked conflicted, then shrugged and read it off to me.

I asked, "How are you supposed to get in touch with him when you have an offer on the house?"

"He said he would call in on a three-day basis. If the offer is acceptable to him, I have his power of attorney to complete the transaction and collect the funds."

"And what kind of an offer is he hoping for?"

"Three point nine million. Cash. He was emphatic that he would not take back paper."

"Ms. Richardson, when he calls in next, would you let me know?"

"Certainly. And I'll tell him you're anxious to hear from him."

"No, please don't do that. As I said, it's a crisis, but it may be resolved by the time he calls, and I don't want him unduly concerned. Just see if you can get his phone number. His partner can take it from there."

"I called the number, and the recorded greeting said it belongs to an Office Stop in San Mateo," I told Hy. "I looked them up; they're one of those places that offer services like copying, faxing, and shipping." We were once again seated across from each other at his desk at RKI headquarters.

"San Mateo. He was there at six in the evening, when he signed and faxed the real-estate agent copies of the documents."

"Yes, San Mateo, near SFO. From there he could have flown anywhere. He left the hospital immediately after Dan died. That gave him time to drive north. He contacted his bank and had all his liquid assets transferred to Credit Suisse—where he's probably had an account since he was in Thailand or maybe even D.C. Then he arranged for the sale of his house. What does that suggest to you? Is he the one behind the bombings? Did he kill Dan?"

Hy considered, shook his head. "Gage isn't a killer. I think he was afraid of something damaging that might come out after Dan's death, and once again he's reinventing his life."

"Yeah. You know what that thing might be?"

He shook his head.

"You sure, Ripinsky?"

Irritation flickered in his eyes, but he didn't respond to the accusatory nature of the question. "I'm sure."

"It might be something for which he could still be prosecuted."

"Might."

"What about the arms dealing? What agency or country would have jurisdiction over that?"

". . . I don't know. Probably there's some statute of limitations that would've run out by now."

Hy's expression was remote; he didn't like the direction this conversation was going. Neither did I. We were straying too close to the personal minefield between us.

"Okay," I said, "I'm out of here."

"To where?"

"San Francisco. I want to consult with my staff before visiting your training camp." I stood, turned to leave.

Once again, he called, "Take care of yourself, McCone."

This time I didn't hesitate when I said, "You, too, Ripinsky."

Friday

✦

MARCH 3

The morning had dawned gray and foggy—the way I felt. I called Patrick, Derek, and Mick into my office, where we sat in a circle on the floor, Patrick's flow charts spread out before us.

His description of them had been accurate: scribbled notes clogged the margins; arrows pointed in all directions; there were crossouts and question marks. Patrick went over the high points—if they could be called that. His earlier assessment had been right. Nothing made any sense.

When he was finished, I asked Mick and Derek, "Anything else to report?"

Derek said, "That iMac of Hy's—I recovered three deleted files. One was a letter to the executive director of the Spaulding Foundation." He handed me a printout.

The Spaulding Foundation: an environmental organization set up and funded by a bequest in the will of Hy's late wife, Julie Spaulding. Hy was chairman of the board. The letter had to do with how he thought a recent endowment should be allocated, but it wasn't very cogent, and there were a number of typos. He must have been feeling muddleheaded when he wrote it, and given up. I looked at the date and time when the file was opened: oh, yes, definitely muddleheaded; the night before he started the letter we'd consumed a fair quantity of champagne while relaxing in the hot tub.

"This doesn't have anything to do with the break-in," I said. "What else?"

"Another letter. Similar."

I took the paper from him, scanned it. Hy had apparently started afresh, then given up. "You can get rid of both of these."

"This other one is more interesting. It's titled 'Dr. Richard Tyne.' Backgrounding on his education from grade school through medical school, internship, residency, and military service."

I studied the sheets he handed me. Born, Fort Wayne, Indiana. Tyne would be sixty-five by now. Attended elementary and middle school there. The family moved to Indianapolis shortly before he started high school. He'd attended Purdue University for his undergraduate and medical degrees. Internship and residency at South Bend Memorial Hospital. Upon finishing his residency he joined the navy and was assigned to their hospital at Subic Bay in the Philippines.

I looked up at Mick, raising an eyebrow. He nodded. "Tyne was Dan Kessell's surgeon after his leg was shot up in Vietnam. I still haven't been able to locate him."

Seemed Hy had been investigating his own partner's background. Another thing he'd kept from me.

I said, "Try again. Find out everything you can about Dr. Tyne."

"Why don't you ask Hy—" Seeing my frown, Mick switched tacks.

"I'll get on it."

* * *

After the others had left my office, I wondered why I *didn't* just ask Hy about the Tyne file. My hand strayed to the phone, but then I pulled it away. Truth was, I was afraid.

If he denied having started an investigation about the physician who had performed surgery on Kessell in the Philippines, or—worse—refused to explain, it would result in a confrontation that might very well end both my investigation and our marriage. I'd stick to my decision to carry this job through without further personal complications.

Okay, next step. I called Gary Viner in San Diego. Today he was in his office.

"Autopsy and ballistics reports were as we expected," he told me. "Single shot, from a thirty-eight, close range, powder burns on the left side of the victim's head. Actual cause of death was a heart attack after extensive surgery. He probably would've been brain-damaged if he'd survived."

"Up-close and personal shooting."

"Right. He was probably off his guard, because he had a fairly high blood-alcohol level. We located a cocktail lounge on the route between the restaurant and his home, where he stopped off that night. Kessell was something of a regular there, so the waitress remembered him. He had two martinis, and that was on top of wine with dinner. I could read you the details of the reports, but why don't I just send the files."

"Thanks. I'd appreciate having both for the record. By the way, did your people find a firearm in Kessell's condo?"

A pause. "A forty-five in the bedside table. And a three-five-seven Magnum in the room with the TV. Neither had been recently fired, and we're holding them."

Gary added, "I see there was another bombing in Chicago. It was all over the news here. The press is speculating that RKI is a target of terrorists, and that it won't be long before they strike in La Jolla. People're on edge and paranoid as hell. The FBI and ATF have been sniffing around here about a possible connection to Kessell's death, and I'm damned annoyed with them. Frankly, if they hadn't pissed me off so much I probably wouldn't be giving you access to those files."

"I spoke with the FBI agent in charge of the Chicago bombing when I was there the day after. He seemed cooperative, although he hasn't contacted me with any further developments. I also interviewed a number of RKI employees. Nothing conclusive, but it doesn't feel like a terrorist attack to me."

"No?"

"No. I still think it's a personal vendetta being carried on by one, or maybe two, people."

"Interesting. Did you find out anything at Kessell's condo that I should know?"

"The neighbor verified what he told your people. The contents of the condo gave me no leads whatsoever. Do I have your permission to keep pursuing this?"

"McCone, we need all the help we can get. Just report anything pertinent."

"I'll do that. By the way, did you contact the sister?"

"Yeah, she and her husband're flying down soon to make funeral arrangements and talk with the lawyer. I smelled greed there."

"They're going to be disappointed; they weren't mentioned in Kessell's will. In fact, his attorney didn't even know the sister existed."

"Well, that's life—as I know only too well."

"Yeah, Gary, that's life."

* * *

I moved to my comfortable old armchair by the arching window overlooking the bay and began jotting down notes on a legal pad. Sort of a to-do list. After a while I ran out of ideas, but felt satisfied with what I had. I got up, buzzed Patrick.

"Here's something you can do to help me," I said. "Call the investigators in each of the RKI bombings, and ask if there was a signature on any of the bombs."

"Say what?"

I explained about signatures, adding, "If they're not willing to talk with you, transfer them to me."

"Will do."

"Thanks." I hung up, buzzed Craig.

Craig told me he'd been working his contacts at the FBI, but with little success—which he interpreted to mean they were as baffled with the case as the local police departments and we were.

"Well, keep at it, please."

Next I dialed an acquaintance, Warren Keane, who was head of parking garage security at SFO. Last night Hy had given me the license plate number of Renshaw's new Lexus, which was owned by the company. I asked Keane if he and his staff would be on the alert for it and give me a call with its location. He said he'd get on it right away.

Suzanne Richardson, at Sotheby's in San Diego, was out of the office, and didn't answer her cellular.

Paulina Morales didn't answer the phone at Renshaw's house and she must have turned off the machine.

Again I settled down in the armchair with my now-voluminous case file, paging through it, looking for something, anything, I'd missed. An hour or so later when Keane called back, I'd found nothing.

"Your client's car is parked on level three of the short-term garage," Warren told me. "United terminal. You want the exact location?"

"Yes, please." RKI was going to have to retrieve the car.

He read it off to me, then added. "Ticket was on the dashboard. Not smart, but lots of people are careless that way. Date and time stamp show he arrived at 7:25 last Monday night."

"Thanks, Warren. I owe you one."

"I'll remember to collect."

Okay, I thought, short-term parking. Normally that would indicate a swift return. But not when the person's liquidating his assets and moving funds to Credit Suisse. He used short-term parking because he was in a hurry and didn't plan to return to the car. Maybe he'd left the ticket on the dashboard in the hope someone would steal it.

United terminal. That limited the search, except they had so many flights departing SFO . . .

I paged through my file to the basic background information on Renshaw. No other residence, except for the Point Loma house—unless he had one in another country that wasn't covered by the databases we used. No help there.

After a few moments, I picked up the phone and speed-dialed my travel agent, Toni Alexander, who knows everything about airline schedules.

"Seven twenty-five last Monday night," she said. "Lots of United flights departing at that time, but not as many two hours later. Given the time it takes to check in and pass through security, he probably would've boarded at nine or nine-thirty."

I could hear keys tapping in the background. Toni asked, "You thinking national or international?"

"Probably international."

Click, click, click.

"That narrows it down to three choices: Tokyo; LA, connecting to Sydney; New York, connecting to Zurich."

"Any way of checking to see if a Gage Renshaw was on those flights?"

"For me? No trouble. My best connections are at United. But you've got to promise me: take a really expensive trip with that new husband of yours soon. I could use the commission."

I was catching up on paperwork, after going over some routine matters with Ted, when Patrick buzzed me.

"The cops in all the cities where there were bombings were cooperative. There was a signature, and they all match. But it's one they've never seen before, doesn't indicate any known bomber. I'll send you the report."

"Thanks, Patrick."

"Okay if I leave early? I've got an appointment over at Altman & Zahn, about the child support and custody."

"More than okay. Good luck."

I looked at my watch. Four o'clock, and I'd never once thought about lunch. The idea of dinner wasn't appealing, even though by now I should be hungry.

The phone buzzed. Ted.

"Toni Alexander on line two."

"Shar? Your guy was on the Tokyo flight."

Tokyo. And from there he could vanish into Asia, drawing on his Swiss bank account for the rest of his life. Gage knew only too well how to disappear.

"Listen," Toni added, "I have a great deal at a luxury resort that's just opened on Moorea. You and Hy—"

"Thanks so much for the information. I'll get back to you about a trip."

The phone buzzed again. Mick.

"Shar, do you want Sweet Charlotte and me to cancel our weekend plans?"

"What plans?"

"The trip to Big Sur—remember?"

Oh, hell! It had been scheduled for weeks. Mick planned to propose marriage; he'd even bought an engagement ring.

"I take it you've found nothing on Richard Tyne or K Air?"

". . . I haven't started yet."

"Why not? It's been hours."

"A glitch with my computer. Derek and I just now got it up and running."

I knew all too well about computer glitches; they could stump even my nephew, the genius.

"We can cancel and go later," Mick added.

"No, go. This is your special weekend. Besides, I like Charlotte, and I want her in the family."

Our general contractor had called earlier, wanting to show me the progress that had been made on the house, so after I left the pier I drove over to Church Street. As I parked in the driveway, I felt a rush of nostalgia, as if I were visiting an old home after I'd been gone a long time. Even the neighboring houses seemed visions from my distant past.

Jim Keys, who had also been the general contractor on the renovations at the RKI safe house, greeted me at the front door and led me back past empty rooms and through the kitchen. Although the front portion of the house wasn't being affected by the add-on, we'd stored the furnishings so the hardwood floors could be refinished and the walls re-painted.

The room that had once been my bedroom now had a large hole in one corner of the floor; Jim pointed it out, and led me toward an oak spiral staircase that descended to the space behind the garage that soon would be a bedroom and bathroom.

"Watch your step," he cautioned. "The railing and posts aren't being delivered from the woodworker till next week."

Once downstairs, I was surprised at how much had been done since I'd last visited. The Sheetrock was in place and partially mudded; electrical switches and plugs, minus the plates, were in the proper places; the bathroom fixtures were installed, and its floor was partially tiled. At first the project had gone slowly, mainly because hard-packed dirt that reached almost to the floor joists of the kitchen, bathroom, and bedroom upstairs needed to be removed—dirt that was shoveled there when the earthquake cottage was raised up to make room for the garage. Then there had been some structural problems. But now all was moving swiftly toward completion.

"Floor refinishing guys for upstairs come Monday," Jim said. "We've already got your lights, closet doors, and hardware for down here. Painters're scheduled for Thursday. Carpet company for down here the next Monday, blinds for the windows and final detail work that next Tuesday. After that we'll schedule the walk-through, and if it's all to your liking, you'll be ready to move in."

And who will I be moving in with? The Hy I've always known and loved? A stranger I happen to be married to? Or by myself?

Jim frowned. "Anything wrong?"

"Oh, no. It looks great. I'm just kind of distracted today."

"No wonder. I heard about RKI's buildings being blown up. You think it's terrorists?"

"I don't know what to think at this point, but it's been a difficult time. Thanks for the tour, Jim. I guess I'll go next door and visit my cats now."

Ralph and Allie were perched on the fence, staring malevolently at the house. When I came outside, they saw me and blinked. Then Ralph jumped down and hit the ground, running to be patted. Allie followed more slowly, reluctant to show she'd missed me; after all, *I* was the one who'd deserted them.

Apparently the cats' expectation was that we were going into *their* house. When I headed for the Curleys', they hesitated, then trotted after me. At least they were getting some exercise for a change; in our last phone conversation 'Chelle had told me that they spent most of their time on the fence, moving only their heads, tails, and eyeballs.

Nobody came to the door, but I found 'Chelle in the backyard, cutting flowers. She was a skinny, spiky-haired fifteen-year-old with a fake diamond stud in her nose and several earrings in either lobe. No visible tattoos, but she'd once informed me she had a spider on her butt. She did pet-sitting for people all over the neighborhood and saved her money—not for a college fund, but because she wanted to buy real estate. "Land," she was fond of saying, "that's where it's at." I wouldn't have been surprised if she swung her first deal before high-school graduation.

"You see what they've done at your place?" she asked. "Awesome."

"It sure is."

"Makes me think I should buy a broken-down house—not that yours was—and rehab it."

"You have those kinds of skills?"

"No, but I know a couple of guys I could subcontract the job to."

I thought back to when I was her age. My biggest ambition was to become head cheerleader.

I said, "Then go for it."

"I think I will. There's this place a few blocks over, it's falling down. By the time I've got the money, they'll be thanking me for taking it off their hands."

We talked a little more, mostly about the cats, and then I left her to her dreams.

Saturday

✦

MARCH 4

Michelle Curley had her dreams, I had my nightmares.

On the clifftop platform at Touchstone, waves thundering below, inundating the beach. Water pouring into the sea caves where bootleggers once stashed the Canadian whiskey they smuggled in by boat. Undermining the cliffs, making the land up here vulnerable.

But the geologist who inspected the caves and the land told us we would be fine unless we wanted to live here for a thousand years!

The waves threw spray so high it touched my face. The land beneath me began to tremble. And then the earth and the platform split apart, and I was falling into a chasm . . .

I sat up in bed, heart pounding. Sweat made my flesh clammy. Every dream is a metaphor, and the meaning of that one was all too obvious.

No more sleep for me; it was already four-nineteen in the morning.

I got up, went to the kitchen, looked in the fridge. Half a bottle of sauvignon blanc. I'd drunk the other half with the deli sandwich that had passed for dinner. If I sucked down the rest of it now, I'd be useless all day. I could take a bath, but I didn't feel like it. I had some sleeping pills my doctor had prescribed after a particularly personal case that had threatened both my livelihood and my life itself. But the pills would make me even more groggy tomorrow than alcohol.

So what else to make the night pass?

Work.

I went to the dining room table, where my laptop was set up, and began my own search into the life and times of Richard Tyne, MD.

I was fascinated by what I found. Hy had barely scratched the surface.

Tyne was described by various sources as a brilliant surgeon with something of a God complex. His bedside manner left a great deal to be desired: he was abrupt and cold with his patients, totally lacking in empathy. Personally, he was a risk-taker, enjoying dangerous sports. His parents were wealthy and had established a large trust fund for him; after his residency he could have set up his own practice, but instead he enlisted in the navy.

Why? Certainly not a desire to see the world. He could've done that on his own.

I dug deeper. And found a possible reason.

Shortly before Tyne enlisted, he was involved in a felony hit-and-run accident in his home town of Indianapolis. The passengers in the other car were not severely injured and got the make and license plate number of his car; when he was apprehended at his parents' house, Tyne's blood-alcohol level was high, and charges were filed. Later the charges were dropped. The influence of the wealthy parents?

Or had agreeing to put in time serving his country been part of the deal? No way to tell.

In the Philippines, Tyne at first was reported to be a model officer and physician. He partied heavily, but that was not uncommon on the naval base and in the wide-open town that surrounded it. However, by the time he was designated lead surgeon on the operation to restore Dan Kessell's shattered leg, Tyne's professional life was not going well: he'd been put on notice when a nurse reported that he'd been intoxicated on rounds. Three weeks after he operated on Kessell, he made errors resulting in the death of a patient during another procedure—also while intoxicated.

Relieved of duty and facing a court-martial, loss of his medical license, and a lawsuit by the patient's family, Tyne went AWOL, first cashing out his trust fund at a Manila brokerage house. And there the trail stopped.

Another disappearance. Coincidence? I didn't think so.

I'd exhausted my research skills. First thing Monday, I'd put Mick on this and see if he could produce further results.

But Hy—what was his interest in Dr. Richard Tyne?

I supposed I would have to ask him. And I dreaded it.

"Gage is probably gone for good," I said on the phone to Hy, and explained what I'd found out.

"God. That leaves me stuck with the whole company, and I'm not sure I want it."

"I think you should check with your bank, make sure he hasn't made off with corporate funds."

"I already have. He didn't."

"Too bad. If he had we could involve the authorities in looking for him." The moment I'd been dreading had arrived. "Ripinsky," I said, "what's your interest in Dr. Richard Tyne?"

Silence.

"The Tyne file was one that was deleted on your iMac."

"Oh, that. It was a name I came across in Dan's office one day when I went in there to get a document he'd signed for me. It was scrawled over and over on a legal pad. So I searched to see who the guy was."

"Why didn't you just ask him about it?"

"You think I could ever get a straight answer from Dan? He'd've accused me of invading his privacy—which I had. But I was concerned that he had a serious health problem he was hiding from Gage and me, so I Googled the guy. I guess he was Dan's doc in the Philippines."

Relief coursed through me. "Did you delete the file yourself?"

"No. I thought I'd noodle with it again, next time we were up at Touchstone."

"So whoever broke in there deleted it."

"Had to've been. But who would care?"

I'd need Mick's results from a deeper search on Tyne before I could hazard a guess.

I said, "I'll get back to you on that. But here's another matter: Paulina Morales."

"Gage's girlfriend?"

"Right. She's just eighteen, quit her job when she moved in with him, and now he's left her with no money and is selling the house out from under her. She's scared and doesn't know what to do."

"And you want to help her."

"Yes. Is there something wrong with that?"

"God, no. I'll go over there, see what she needs."

"Thanks, I'd appreciate it."

"That's one of the things I love about you, McCone. You care."

For a moment I couldn't speak. I cared about a relative stranger, but I couldn't unbend and give my husband the reassurance he needed at this crisis point. What did that say about the quality of my caring?

Finally I said, "That's one of the things I love about you, too."

Although it was Saturday, I went to the pier around noon and put in a few hours clearing paperwork. When I left around three, the sky had turned dark gray; I could smell a storm brewing.

Saturday afternoon. Nothing to do, no leads to follow. I didn't want to call any of my friends; they'd be too quick to sense something was wrong, and I couldn't bear to field their questions. I didn't want to go back to the safe house—while it was a large apartment, it made me claustrophobic. I didn't want to drive all the way to Touchstone, where memories of good times—such as the post-wedding party that our friends had thrown for us last August—would only haunt and sadden me. Finally I went to a movie, a hot new comedy that only made me feel worse. It passed the time, however, and on the way home I was hungry enough to pick up Chinese food.

As soon as I stepped into the apartment, I felt something was wrong. It held the same violated atmosphere I'd sensed at Touchstone.

I put the takeout on the kitchen counter, did a quick walk-through. This time the intruder hadn't been so subtle; things were moved, a drawer left partially open. My laptop's screen was raised, yet I always lowered it when it wasn't in use.

But how the hell had anyone gotten in here? Even though

Hy had ordered security only as far as the door, it was impossible—

I went downstairs to the command center. Jason Ng was on duty.

"Someone's gotten into my apartment," I told him.

"No way."

"Don't tell me no way. He left signs all over the place."

"I've been monitoring the cameras since two. And, believe me, Ms. McCone, I've been very vigilant."

"Who was on before you?"

"Todd Williams."

"Get him over here, please."

"It's Saturday night. I'll try, but Todd's a party animal."

Ng picked up the phone and dialed a couple of numbers without result.

"I'm sorry, Ms. McCone. I'll keep trying."

"Thanks. And I'm sorry I was so abrupt with you."

"Well, it's an upsetting situation." Then he frowned.

"What?" I asked.

"When I came on shift, Todd told me one of the surveillance cameras had gone out a while back. One that monitors the hallway on your floor. He said he'd tried to get it back on, but nothing worked, and he didn't want to leave the rest of the monitors untended. So I went up there and took a look. Loose wire. I fixed it."

Ng swiveled one of the monitors around, pointed at the image on it. "With that camera out, it would create a blind spot at your apartment door. But whoever unlocked the door would've had to have a coded key card, and only you and Mr. Ripinsky have those."

"There isn't a spare, in case someone, say you, needed to get in?"

"Sure, but they're locked in the wall safe."

"And the cameras on the stairway and the other unit were functioning the whole time?"

"Todd didn't mention having any trouble with them."

"Well, keep trying to get hold of him. I'll be upstairs."

I went back to the apartment and paced, the violated feeling strong upon me.

Same intruder as at Touchstone? He had detailed knowledge of security systems. Someone else? His search had left signs, unlike at the coast. Maybe he wanted *to leave signs? A warning that he could get to me—anyplace, anytime?*

I went to the laptop, booted it up. The new operating system I used allowed me to check the last time any of the files had been opened. All of those whose labels indicated they pertained to the RKI investigation had been viewed between twelve-fifteen and one o'clock. The intruder had spent a fair amount of time finding out what I knew. Nothing was deleted, however, and he hadn't bothered with the Dr. Richard Tyne file.

I drummed my fingers on the edge of the table for a few minutes, shut the computer down, and went to the kitchen, where my purse rested next to the containers of cooling Chinese food. Took out my cellular—in order to keep the landline open in case Jason Ng reached Todd Williams—and called Hy's phone. He answered after four rings, sounding groggy.

"I was planning to call you, but I fell asleep watching a movie," he said. "What time is it?"

"After seven." I explained about the break-in and asked, "Do you have your key card to this apartment?"

"I'll check." He set the phone down, came back in a few moments. "I must've misplaced it. You'd better get the code changed."

"How can you misplace something like that?"

He sighed. "You must remember, I haven't needed to use it, and it's been a . . . tumultuous time since I was last there."

"Yeah, it has. Where did you keep the card?"

"My wallet. In the slot above my driver's license."

"Who might've had access to your wallet?"

"Nobody."

"Think."

"I can't imagine who."

"Well, whoever it is knows security systems, knows the way RKI operates. Can come and go as he pleases. He could be in this building right now."

"McCone, get out of there. I'll have our people make an immediate sweep for explosives, but till then—"

"I don't think I'm in any danger. This was just curiosity on his part. Or a warning. If he's inside the building, he's not going to blow the place up. I'll get the key-card code changed right away."

"Please, for my sake, just get *out* of there."

"Okay," I said, "I'll go."

"Where will you be?"

I thought. Hotels and motels—even the best of them—weren't secure. I said, "I'll go to Rae and Ricky's. They've got the best security of anybody I know." Ricky had more than once been the victim of celebrity stalking.

"Good idea. I'll call them, tell them you're coming—and that I'm putting an additional man on their place."

"You don't need to—"

"I do, McCone. I'm not going to lose you—not that way. Not *any* way."

* * *

Rae said, "Ricky, why don't you go . . . do something so Shar and I can indulge in girl talk?"

He folded his arms across his chest and shook his head.

My former brother-in-law's handsome face had aged some in recent years, but the lines had only given it character; he'd let some gray strands weave their way into his chestnut hair, but I suspected their spread was controlled by an expensive colorist.

"I'm not going anywhere," he said. "Something's wrong in Shar's life, and I want to be here for her. Like she was for me way back when, even though the trouble was between her own sister and me."

"Sometimes things like this are better discussed with another woman."

"Sometimes things like this are better discussed when a man can contribute his insight."

Rae glared at him, her freckled face flushing. "Can't you see she's exhausted and miserable?"

"If she's exhausted and miserable, let her alone. Let her go to bed."

"At eight-thirty?"

"What's wrong with going to bed at eight-thirty? She looks like hell—"

I cut short the argument. "Stop talking about me as if I weren't here!"

They stared.

I added, "I want a glass of that great chardonnay you keep in your wine cellar. And then some privacy. I need to call Hy."

Hy said, "Our best man up there is sweeping the safe house."

"How do you know you can trust him?"

"He's been with us forever. I know him personally. Believe me, I can trust him."

"God, I'm getting paranoid. Were you able to do anything for Paulina Morales?"

"Yeah, but it wasn't easy. She was in bad shape when I got to Gage's house—drunk, and she'd smashed a fair amount of glassware. I pried the name and address of a friend out of her and took her over there. Gave the friend some money and said I'd check in tomorrow." He paused. "I'm thinking I might find something for her to do here at headquarters, so she can get back on her feet."

"That would be great. I don't know what skills she has—"

"What I'm thinking of doesn't take great skills. Anyone can file and answer phones."

"You're a good man, Ripinsky."

"Yeah, well, I've got a lot to atone for." Another pause. "I don't suppose you've changed your mind about talking about . . . this thing between us?"

"Not tonight. I'm too tired, and so are you."

Rae and Ricky were waiting for me when I came back to the living room. Cheese and crackers and salami were laid out on a plate on the raised brick wall of the pit fireplace that Hy and I had used as a model for ours at Touchstone. Ricky poured me more wine, and Rae heaped my plate. To my surprise, I was ravenous.

"So come clean," Rae said. "What's happened between you and Hy?"

"Why do you think there's something wrong with us?"

"Because I can smell man trouble. I've had enough of it

myself." She smiled at Ricky. "Even this guy's given me a hassle or two."

Ricky feigned an innocent look.

What the hell, I thought. They were the closest thing to family I had in the city. Closer in some ways than most of my relatives.

Between bites and sips, I explained the situation with Hy.

When I finished, they were both silent for a moment. Then Ricky said, "What he did—if he did it—is bad. But I don't understand: it was a long time ago. He's admitted to you that he did a lot of other equally bad things during his time with K Air. And he's changed completely. Why can't you accept and forgive this?"

"It's not the arms dealing per se. It's the fact that I thought he'd come clean about all of it, and now I find out he hasn't."

"You think he withheld it from you because it might've been too much for you to handle?"

"Possibly. And it worries me that there may be even more he withheld."

Ricky exchanged glances with Rae.

He said, "When Rae and I hooked up, I came clean about a lot of the bad shit that I'd done. And there was plenty of it—so much that there're things I've forgotten. Every now and then something pops to the surface, but I don't find it necessary to confess it to her, because I'm a different man now, and she knows that."

"But those things were woman-related."

"And drug-related. To say nothing of unethical business practices, letting myself go along with things I knew were wrong because I wanted so damn bad to be a star."

"Not the same."

"Maybe not. But the point is, Shar, trust in the present. The man you married is not the man who flew arms into the Middle East—if he did. The man you married is someone who is totally committed and wants to spend the rest of his life with you."

"How do you know that?"

"About the lifetime commitment? He told me. We're friends, remember?"

Again, rational advice from a man who—like my brother John—had turned his life around.

"So what am I supposed to do?" I asked. "Just let this go?"

"Certainly not. Listen to Hy, and if you still don't believe him, go after the truth. Nobody could stop you; you're a fanatic about truth. But until you know what actually happened, don't agonize. And in the meantime, don't make his life hell."

I looked at Rae. "How'd he get to be so wise?"

She smiled. "Some of *my* wisdom must've rubbed off on him."

Sunday

✦

MARCH 5

Rae and I had talked until almost midnight, while Ricky went downstairs to his studio to work on a new song. Then I slept in one of their guest rooms until my cellular woke me at nine. First good night's sleep I'd had in . . . I didn't know how long.

The caller was Gary Viner. "The body we released to the funeral home wasn't Dan Kessell's," he told me. "At least not the Dan Kessell who was related to Elise Carver."

"What!"

"She and her husband came down yesterday and viewed it. They were planning to meet with his lawyer at his condo later. Only they'd never seen the victim in their lives." He laughed—a harsh bark. "The sister cried with relief, but I could swear the husband was pissed. He'd probably been spending Dan's money in his dreams."

The wrong Dan Kessell . . . Owns a security company . . . Flies a beat-up old Piper . . . He's the same old Danny . . .

Dr. Richard Tyne . . .

Timber Cove . . . So close to Touchstone . . .

Ideas were tumbling about in my mind—unformed as yet.

I asked Gary, "You have anything else on the case?"

"Nada."

"Well, keep me posted."

The sky was overcast, but it was a high ceiling. I checked aviation weather, briefly stopped by the pier to make copies of Dan Kessell's photograph, then drove to Oakland's North Field and flew to Touchstone. The winter rains had not been kind to our airstrip; a bump had risen in the center, which made for a rough landing and would cause a pretty zippy takeoff—sort of like being launched into the air from a trampoline.

I'd come prepared to spend the night, so after I secured the plane, I went to the house and dropped off my laptop and briefcase. Then I went to the shed, got into our white Ford pickup, and drove north, toward Mendocino. Turned off Highway 1 south of there, on the road to Little River Airport.

We hadn't flown into there in a long time, since we'd graded the dirt strip on our property and then had it paved and—somewhat primitively—lighted, but we knew most of the airport personnel. Bob Gardner, the manager and author of several texts on flying, was behind the desk in the little terminal and welcomed me with some surprise. We did a bit of social chatting—How's the family? How's Hy?—and then I got down to business.

"I'd like to know if somebody landed at our strip between February eighth and twenty-second. He may have announced his position on your UNICOM if there were other aircraft in the vicinity, or someone may have seen a plane there."

Bob raised his eyebrows. "An unauthorized landing."

"Right."

"That's going to be tough to pin down."

"I know it's a long shot, but could you ask around?"

"Sure. You have trouble down there?"

"A break-in at the house. The perimeter security wasn't breached, so whoever did it either came by air or sea."

"You check the boat rental places?"

"That's my next order of business."

"Did this man rent a boat from you between February eighth and twenty-second?" I asked the clerk behind the counter at Bert's Boats.

He squinted at it and shook his head. "Never seen him. Maybe my wife has. Honey!" he called out.

A woman came through a door behind him, wiping her hands on an oil-stained rag.

"You seen this guy?" her husband asked.

She studied the photo. "Never."

I said, "It would've been a small boat, one that could be beached at Bootlegger's Cove at low tide."

"Sorry."

I sighed. I'd asked at every place on our stretch of the coast that offered rentals of boats that could navigate the shallows of the cove, and all the answers had been negative.

"You one of the folks who built that big house on the cliffs there, put in the airstrip?" the man asked.

"Yes."

"You're keeping that place damned nice, taking care of the land."

"Thank you. My husband's an environmentalist; we love

the property and planned the improvements so they wouldn't spoil it, or the views for people passing on the highway."

"You've done a good job." He turned to a coffeemaker on the counter behind him, poured into a foam cup, and handed it to me. "My treat. You give me your phone number, I'll call you if I see the guy around here."

"Thanks." I handed him my card, with the number at Touchstone written on the back. "May I leave a copy of the photograph for you to show to people in the area?" I'd been peppering the coast with them.

"Sure. There's a big crab feed at the volunteer fire department tonight. I'll pass it around."

Dusk was falling when I got back to Touchstone, where I found a message from Bob Gardner, asking me to call him. He wasn't at the airport, but the woman who answered gave me his home number.

"I got lucky," he said. "One of the guys who parks his plane here spotted a Piper Cub on the strip at your place on the fifteenth. Better yet, he knows whose it is—Dan Kessell from down at Timber Cove. Says he's seen it there before, figured he was checking the security. Kessell runs a one-man private patrol, although he doesn't have any clients this far north."

"Was he sure it was Kessell's plane?"

"Yep. There isn't a plane on the coast—or maybe in the entire state—that looks that scabrous."

"Where does he park it?"

"Ocean Ridge, in Gualala."

I'd have to be careful, I thought. If the man I'd encountered in Timber Cove had searched this house, looking for information on Hy's computer, he was dangerous and, as a security patrolman, probably armed.

I wasn't. I don't like to carry my .357 Magnum, even though I have a permit. Most of the time it resides in the safe at the pier.

Hy kept a .45 here, though, locked in the drawer of his nightstand, and I had a key. I went to the bedroom, unlocked the drawer, and checked the load. Carried it out to the kitchen counter and put it in my purse.

Not that I intended to confront the other Kessell immediately. There were inquiries I'd make first. But I was better off armed, since I now felt insecure in a place where I'd always felt safe.

I was so tense that when the phone rang, I flinched.

"Is this Sharon McCone?"

"Yes."

"Bert from Bert's Boats. I've got some information for you. One of the small-charter guys from Fort Bragg came down for the crab feed, and when I showed him the picture you left with me, he told me he'd taken the guy down to your cove on the tenth, waited around for about an hour, then took him back."

"He's sure of his identification?"

"I'll let you talk to him."

A deep male voice came onto the line. "Ms. McCone? Syd Garvey here. I'm sure the guy in the picture's your man. He had me bring him as far into the cove as I was able to go, then waded the rest of the way and climbed up those stairs to the top of the cliff. Stayed for about half an hour, then climbed down and waded back out."

"Did he say what he was doing up there?"

"He didn't, and I didn't ask. He waved a wad of money at me, and I took it. I don't know if you realize, but times are tough here on the north coast." A pause. "I hope you won't go to the sheriff's department with this. I've got a family to support."

"No, I won't. I know times are tough."

In more ways than one.

So now I had two potential intruders. One dead, one alive. Had the two Kessells been joined in some sort of conspiracy?

Time to further check out the living one.

Hy and I sometimes flew into Ocean Ridge Airport, when we were meeting friends in the Gualala area for lunch or dinner, and we'd gotten friendly with the manager, Walter Waggoner. I called his home—he lived on the premises—and said I needed to talk with him in person. He told me he'd be home all evening.

"You thinking of flying down?" he asked. "Because if you are, I wouldn't advise it. Fog's in thick, even on the ridge."

I glanced at the coastward windows; it was clear here, the sky peppered with stars. A reverse of the typical weather pattern. The Gualala area is what they call the Banana Coast, an unusually temperate clime for Northern California; at Touchstone we have frequent heavy mists.

"I'll drive," I said. "If you see someone wandering around in the tie-downs in about forty minutes, it's only me."

"Now you've got me intrigued."

"I'll explain later."

Distances always seem longer than they really are on Highway 1, because of its twists and turns and switchbacks. At night, they stretch out even more, because of the darkness. No streetlights in this rural territory, and in most places the lights from houses are far off the road. The towns and hamlets spring up suddenly—welcome oases—and then you're just as quickly plunged back into an obscure landscape. But when you reach your destination, you find the trip hasn't taken as long as you thought.

I arrived at Ocean Ridge in only thirty-five minutes. The fog was indeed thick, and the security lights in the tie-down area were faint. I left the truck by Walter's house, which also served as a small terminal, and walked over to the rows of planes. Beyond them was a parking area for local pilots and people who flew in to their second homes. The vehicles' shapes were obscured by the misty darkness.

I moved along the rows until I found the beat-up Piper Cub. As Bob Gardner had said, it was scabrous. I walked around it, trying to peer through the windows, but not touching it—you don't touch other people's aircraft, particularly a stranger's. What I could see of the interior was as bad as the exterior, but I knew that appearances could be deceiving; with regular mechanical maintenance, a plane can have a long, safe life span, even though it looks like it's ready to fall apart. I noted its number and went back to Walter's house.

He opened the door before I could ring the bell. Thin, with longish brown hair, about six-four—what Hy would call a "long, tall drink of water."

"Find what you were looking for?" he asked.

"Yes."

He motioned me through a room that was furnished with shabby old chairs, a counter, and the UNICOM, into a cozy living room with a much better decor.

"Want a drink?" he asked. "Some coffee?"

"Coffee, please. Black. I think I'm going to have a long night."

He left the room, returned with two white mugs. "And

what were you looking for?" he asked, sitting down on the opposite end of the sofa.

"A Piper Cub belonging to Dan Kessell."

"Ah, Danny Boy."

"He fly a lot?"

"Most every day, around the area. He's a security guy—home patrols—and uses the plane for surveillance on a few of his clients' properties. And he likes to do touch-and-goes at private airstrips when the owners're away. I know for a fact that that strip of yours on the cliff is one of his favorites."

Maybe that explained his plane being sighted there. Maybe.

I sipped some coffee. Tasty and strong, just what I needed. "He ever take longer trips?"

"A few times a year. I think he has relatives in Fresno that he visits."

"Does he file a flight plan?"

"Danny Boy? Shit, no. Not ever. Strikes me as unwise, at his age and with that bad leg, but he's seat-of-the-pants, old-school."

That bad leg. The ever-running man limps . . .

"Anyplace else he goes?"

"The occasional fishing trip. And once a year to Harris Ranch—that resort near Coalinga, belongs to the people who raise Harris beef—for a big steak dinner. Stays overnight. Pricey, but he saves up for it."

"He go any long distances lately?"

Walter frowned. "Now that you mention it, yes. On a Saturday, the twenty-fifth. I was checking out the planes in the tie-downs, and I found him with a sectional spread out on the wing."

Sectionals—aviation maps. "Which one?"

"Los Angeles. I asked him if he'd be gone for long. His answer struck me as strange: 'Long enough,' he said. 'I'm taking care of some old business.' And then he laughed, sounded kind of nasty."

That particular sectional covered San Diego. And the day that this Kessell had been studying it was the same day the other Kessell was shot.

My cellular would work here on top of the coastal ridge, so I went back to the truck, got Elise Carver's number in Fresno from information, and called her. She remembered me immediately and asked if I'd located her brother.

"Not yet. I have a question: does he walk with a limp?"

"Yes, he does. When he was in Vietnam, his unit came under enemy fire, and his tibia was shattered. They did surgery and therapy in a hospital in the Philippines, and for a long time it was hardly noticeable, but as he's gotten older, it's more pronounced." She paused. "Does this mean you've seen Danny?"

"I think so."

"Where is he? I'd like to talk to him. We had quite a scare last week when a man in San Diego with the same name was shot. We actually flew down there, but when we viewed the body it turned out to be a stranger. Thank God."

"I'm not sure where your brother is living, but when I see him, I'll ask him to get in touch with you."

After I ended the call with Elise Carver, I sat in the truck, imagining the scenario.

Dan Kessell—the living one—undergoes surgery in the Philippines by a doctor whose career is in serious trouble.

The surgeon, Richard Tyne, comes up with a plan to cash out his trust fund and flee, assuming Kessell's identity.

How?

Well, for one familiar with the hospital, it probably wouldn't have been difficult for Tyne to get his hands on Kessell's wallet and any other identification. Military records as well. Tyne already had a lot of cash, so it was easy enough to vanish, buy an aviation business, and build a life based on the theft of another man's identity.

Aviation business. Tyne was a doctor. Had he also possessed a pilot's license? Or learned to fly later?

I thought of the backgrounding I'd done on Tyne. He had indulged in risky sports. Some people—insurance companies, in particular—consider flying to be one. I'd ask Derek to check with the FAA in the morning.

Okay, the real Dan Kessell finds out that Tyne is a rich owner of a security firm, masquerading under his name. How?

They were both in the same field, although at opposite ends of the spectrum. Kessell/Tyne stayed out of the limelight, allowing Renshaw to front for him, but a year or so ago he'd granted an interview to a trade journal. I wasn't sure when it had come out, but Dan had expressed displeasure that they'd used a photograph of him without his permission. What if the real Kessell had seen it and become enraged? Started a vendetta against RKI? Flown to San Diego and shot Tyne? And then found no satisfaction in Tyne's destruction and gone on to bomb the Chicago office?

Would he continue destroying and maiming and killing?

I thought of the peculiar, limping gait of the man I'd seen in the San Francisco alley and on the Chicago street. Thought of Kessell's bad leg.

If I was right, the real Dan Kessell was even more dangerous than I'd previously thought. So why was I going to drive down to Timber Cove and spy on him? Why not call Gary Viner and explain what I suspected?

The problem was, what I had was mere conjecture. There was no proof that Kessell knew about Tyne, much less had flown to San Diego and shot him. The sectional he'd been studying covered a huge area.

I needed evidence, hard evidence.

The fog was even thicker in the little enclave at Timber Cove. I was about to park in a turnoff on the highway and walk in, when I spotted headlights coming out. It was Kessell's big truck and it turned north. Probably going for his nighttime rounds. I made a U and followed him.

First stop was a big oceanside home with an iron gate flanked by tall pillars. Kessell activated the gate by a keypad and drove through. I turned off the truck's lights, drifted to the shoulder. Took out the binoculars we keep in the glove box for whale-watching, found the house number, and noted it. I could see Kessell's lights shining through the trees as he checked the property. After a few minutes, the gates swung open, then closed behind him.

I waited a moment before I turned on my lights and followed.

Another oceanside stop: no gates, but I knew the house because it was way out on a point and impressive even from a distance. Kessell spent more time there, allowing me the opportunity to jot down the number posted on the grapestake fence. Once again he drove north.

When he turned onto a road on the east side of the highway, I decided not to follow. Too much chance of him noticing my headlights, trapping me in a dead end. There were only two house numbers tacked to a post, which I duly noted. Fifteen minutes later, Kessell's truck came back down the road, turned north again.

Small oceanside cabin. Large oceanside estate. House set up on the ridge, but visible from the highway. House set close to the road on a curve; that would have unnerved me, since a motorist's miscalculation would probably land his vehicle in the living room. Odd oceanside place whose turrets mimicked those at Fort Ross.

Finally, after checking out a modest but attractive A-frame on the eastern side of the highway, Kessell headed south. I turned north. It was late, and the information I'd gathered would be the basis for tomorrow's inquiries.

Monday

✦

MARCH 6

I was up and dressed at seven o'clock, drinking coffee and chafing at the thought that I really shouldn't bother anybody till at least eight. At eight on the dot I called the office. Ted sounded cheerful when he answered and put me through to Derek. Mick, whom I'd originally asked for, hadn't come in yet. He was probably in bed celebrating his engagement to Charlotte.

I asked Derek to query the FAA about a pilot's license issued to Richard Tyne, then read him the list of addresses Kessell had visited on his patrol last night, asked for names and phone numbers of their owners—both in the Timber Cove area and at their primary residences. He said he'd get right on it, and I settled in to wait. But then another idea occurred to me, and I phoned Garland Romanowski, our security man here at Touchstone.

"Hey, I'm sorry I didn't get back to you yet about that estimate for wiring the platform," he said. "I did go down there and checked to see if we can connect it with the system on the stone cottage, and it's a go. Save you a lot of money."

"Thanks, but that's not why I'm calling. When we talked

before you said you don't know Dan Kessell, that private patrol guy at Timber Cove, but can you think of anybody who might?"

"Not offhand, but I can check around."

"Would you, please?"

"For a good client like you? No problem."

"And if you do find somebody, would you also ask about who Kessell would hire to make his rounds if he was out of town for a while? And try to find out if he has an alarm system on his house."

"Can do. I've got three appointments today—one in Anchor Bay, the others south of Fort Bragg. Plenty of time in between to do some phoning on the old cell."

I waited. And waited. Around noon I microwaved a packaged burrito that I found in the freezer. It was horrible, and I threw most of it out.

By two, there were still no calls. I took the cordless phone with me and went for a walk, inspecting the property, assessing the winter weather's damage to our runway. It wasn't all that bad; some patching, and it would be as good as new.

No one called.

At three Derek phoned to say a Richard Tyne of Indianapolis had received his private pilot's license two years after Dan Kessell had received his. Derek was e-mailing me the other information I'd asked for. I got on the computer and checked the list of owners whose property Kessell had visited last night; none of them was familiar to me, but I hadn't expected them to be. Two appeared to be permanent residents—locals who employed Kessell on a temporary basis while they went on vacations. I'd hold off on contacting anyone; with Garland's help, it might not be necessary.

More waiting. Waiting makes me hungry, so I microwaved some popcorn, doused it liberally with melted butter, and gobbled most of it up while sitting by the seaward windows.

At three-thirty, Garland called.

"The guy who subs for Kessell is Jerry Leader," he said, and gave me an address and phone number. "This about your break-in?"

"Could be. What about Kessell's alarm system?"

"Negative. In fact, a lot of his pals razz him about not having one. Physician, heal thyself—that sort of thing."

"This is Jerry Leader," the nasal voice said in answer to my inquiry.

"This is Linnea Carraway"—an old friend from high school whose name had popped into my head a second before. "I've recently been hired by Dan Kessell as his bookkeeper. His records are . . . well, incomplete. I wonder if you could fill me in on the dates you've subbed for him in the past couple of years."

"Sure. I sub for a lot of the patrol guys here. Keep a log so I can be sure I've been paid. Just a sec."

Sounds of a drawer being opened and closed, pages being turned. "Yeah, here it is." He proceeded to reel off a list of dates and whatever reasons he could recall for Kessell's absences.

"He's used you a lot," I said when I finished making notes.

"Well, my buddy Danny's not much for work."

"Really? He seems pretty professional to me."

"Oh, he's a pro, all right. But he also likes to fly and fish."

"I see. Thank you, Mr. Leader. I'd appreciate it if you didn't tell my employer about my call. I don't want him to think I'm questioning his business practices."

"Wouldn't think of it. I don't want him to know I've been telling tales out of school."

I said good-bye to Jerry Leader and broke the connection. Then I began comparing the dates he'd given me with the dates of the RKI bombings.

January 17 of last year, when the Detroit office was bombed and the manager killed: Leader didn't recall the circumstances under which he'd been asked to take over the patrols for two days. February 21, the date of the attack in Houston: Leader hadn't worked for Kessell, but that didn't mean he hadn't hired someone else or simply neglected his patrols. August 18, Kansas City: abalone season, off harvesting the potentially endangered species. February 15 of this year, Mexico City bombing: Kessell had flown to Harris Ranch for three days, but Walter Waggoner had told me Kessell only stayed there one night, and had to save up for it. Miami, May 10: he hadn't hired Leader. August 1, the training camp: again, Leader had been hired but didn't recall the circumstances. February 20, Green Street: Leader hadn't subbed. The twenty-fifth, when Tyne/Kessell was killed: the same. The twenty-eighth, date of the Chicago bombing: away four days, business unspecified.

None of the reasons Kessell had given Jerry Leader for hiring him were verifiable, except Harris Ranch.

I got the resort's number from information and called it. There was no record of a Dan Kessell staying there at any time in February.

What now? Kessell couldn't have flown that Piper of his to Detroit, Kansas City, Mexico City, or Chicago; it didn't have the range to make it there and back in the allowed time. How long did airlines keep passenger lists?

I called Toni.

"This is a tough one," she said, "but United's hub is Chicago. I might be able to get you something from them."

"Would you please? I promise, I'll go to Moorea."

"First class?"

I winced. "Deal."

While I was waiting for Toni to call back, I considered Kessell's trip on the day the usurper of his identity had been killed. He'd left Ocean Ridge early in the morning, and probably flown to Lindbergh Field—also known as San Diego International Airport. There were other airports he could have chosen in the area, but they were smaller and farther from downtown. Given the number of movements—takeoffs and landings—at Lindbergh, he would have been relatively anonymous, and could take advantage of a variety of car rentals.

Whenever Hy and I flew Two-Seven-Tango to San Diego, we parked in the tie-downs at Lindbergh. There was a charge, and when you paid, your name and plane number were put into the log. I got the phone number of the airport from airnav.com, called, and asked for the office at the general aviation tie-downs. A woman answered, and I gave my own name and occupation. I was working on a deadbeat dad case, I told her, and had reason to think he'd flown his private plane to San Diego on February 25. The deadbeat dad excuse worked—it usually does with women and a surprising number of men—and she confirmed that Kessell's plane had been in the tie-downs overnight. Okay, he'd have needed a rental car—

The phone rang. Toni.

"No record of a Dan Kessell on any of United's flights to Chicago around the date you mentioned," she said.

Damn! "Thanks. One more favor?"

"You're going to love Moorea. What is it?"

"Car rentals in San Diego. Same person, this time on the twenty-fifth. Probably one of the less expensive outfits."

"I'll get back to you."

More waiting, during which I began to wonder how Kessell—if he really was the ever-running man—had gotten the materials for the bombs onto the commercial flights he'd taken. Ever since the arrest of twenty-some terrorists in a plot to bomb British airliners bound for the United States in 2006, security had been rigorous. Well, there were still ways to disguise potentially lethal devices, particularly when broken down into their components; risky, to be sure, but the ever-running man seemed to thrive on risk. Or maybe he didn't transport the materials with him. The Internet gave sources for the makings of bombs; he could have purchased them locally.

Frustrating that Kessell hadn't been on any of the United flights Toni was able to check. Of course, he could have taken a different airline or flown to Midway. Or to an airport in a nearby state and driven. No way Toni could access that kind of information, but maybe my nephew the genius could—

Phone. Toni again.

"He rented from Econocar." She gave me the details. "Returned it the next morning."

"He leave a contact number where he was staying?"

"Yes." She read it off to me.

"Thanks. If you ever want a job as an investigator—"

"All I want is a commission on your Moorea trip."

I hung up, dialed the phone number she'd given me. It belonged to Spike's Bar. Probably a number Kessell had made up at random.

Did I have enough to give to Gary Viner? Yes. If they

brought Kessell in, they might be able to connect him with the RKI bombings as well as Tyne's murder. I dialed the SDPD. Gary was out of the office. I left a message.

What about the FBI? No. With the exception of the agent I'd met in Chicago, the others on the case had been cold and dismissive to everyone. Besides, if I contacted them, I'd alienate Gary. I had a connection with him because of Joey's death that I didn't want to lose.

In the end I settled for e-mailing him a brief message outlining what I'd found out, as well as the Dr. Richard Tyne file.

Phone again. Walter Waggoner at Ocean Ridge.

"I thought you'd like to know, Dan Kessell just flew out, said he'd be gone overnight," he told me.

"No indication of where he's going?"

"None."

"Well, thanks for keeping me posted."

Kessell would be gone overnight. That left me a large window of opportunity.

There was still a thin line of pink and gold on the horizon when I arrived at Timber Cove. I parked on a wide, graveled place east of the highway, the truck camouflaged from traffic by the encroaching vegetation. There I waited, munching on the cold, greasy remainders of my microwaved popcorn and sipping bottled water, till full dark. Then, equipped with flashlight, surgical gloves, lock picks, and Hy's .45, I slipped across the road and walked swiftly toward Kessell's house. It looked the same as the first time I'd seen it—down to the light in the kitchen window—except that the Doberman was in its run.

As I approached, the dog began barking, so I sprinted past toward the larger house at the dead end, waited, and then doubled back. By the time I reached the rear of Kessell's house, the barking had ceased. I went up on my toes and peered through the kitchen window. A few dirty dishes were stacked in the sink, but otherwise nothing was changed.

Okay. Garland Romanowski had said Kessell shunned security systems.He'd better have the right information.

Years ago, one of my informants had given me the set of handmade lock picks and lessons in how to use them. I rarely did, but every now and then necessity overwhelmed my good sense. And in this situation, the risks of being caught were minimal. I put on the surgical gloves and went to work on the door next to the kitchen window. It took longer than I thought, but eventually I was inside.

I went hunting. The house was only five rooms—kitchen, living room, two bedrooms, and a bath. The smaller bedroom was set up as an office, so I started there.

Kessell was more careful about the security of his computer than his home; I couldn't get into any of his files without a password. The computer was set up on a plank balanced on two filing cabinets; most of the papers in them were client invoices going back many years. No personal correspondence, but there were other files holding home, vehicle, and airplane titles and insurance policies, as well as a twenty-five-thousand-dollar whole life policy whose beneficiary was his sister, Elise Carver. Another folder contained a will, leaving everything to her. I noted down the name of the attorney in Santa Rosa who had drawn it up.

The room's closet contained a few wire hangers and three boxes on the shelf above the clothes pole. I pulled one of them down, found canceled checks dating back at least a decade. Another held old income tax returns. But the third was full of mementoes.

A picture of a young, slender Kessell leaning against a Cessna and grinning widely—the kind of photo the instructor takes after your first solo flight. A second showed him by the same plane with a man who looked remarkably like Hy: Joe Ripinsky, Hy's father and Kessell's flight instructor. I studied the man who, had he lived, would have been my father-in-law, and glimpsed in his eyes and set of jaw the same strength that I saw in my husband.

Another photograph: Gina Kessell, later Hines. Kessell had his arms around her, smiled at the camera over the top of her head. Gina's expression was more complex and guarded.

Cards from Gina: birthday, Valentine's Day, wedding anniversary.

Divorce decree. Military discharge papers. Old pilot's logs.

And at the bottom, an envelope with Gina's first name on it. No address, no stamp. It was dated the year he had run into her in Oakland.

Gina, honey—

I'm sorry. I didn't mean to scare you yesterday. I was blown away by seeing you, and then when you didn't recognize me, all the bad feelings came back. What I said was real bullshit. I'd never hurt you or your family. I've put all that behind me, and I've got a good life now. Well, maybe not so good, but it suits me. Please forgive me. Jesus, what am I saying? I'm never going to get to mail this. I don't even know your married name or address. But at least I've gotten it down, and I'll put this letter where somebody might find it after I'm gone and take the trouble to find you. Then you'll know that your Danny never meant to hurt you. Not ever again.

It was signed with a big, sprawling letter *D*.

No wonder Gina Hines had been afraid after her encounter with her former husband.

Too late, Danny. She went to her grave without ever reading your apology.

I put the mementoes back in the box, except for the letter to Gina Hines, which I stuffed into my jacket pocket. Returned all three boxes to the shelf in approximately the same places I'd found them. Odds were Kessell seldom looked at the closet shelf, or if he did, wouldn't notice if the boxes' positions were a little different. Then I turned off the desk lamp and felt my way toward the living room.

A truck's engine growled past the house. A big pickup, running without its lights. The dog didn't bark. I froze.

The dog wasn't barking because the truck belonged to his owner.

A trap.

He'd found out I was asking around about him; word carries fast in sparsely populated areas like the north coast. He'd fed Walter Waggoner the story about an overnight trip, hoping Walter would alert me. Then he'd flown around for a couple of hours, possibly reconnoitering Touchstone for the truck, and returned to Ocean Ridge. Now he was outside. I heard his footsteps approaching from where he'd left the pickup, and then a key turned in the front door lock . . .

I slipped down the hall into the kitchen. Yanked the door open. And ran.

The bluff was barren, except for a stand of trees around the dark house at the dead end. It was a clear night and the moon shone brightly. I was thankful that the jacket I kept at Touchstone was black.

To get back to the highway, I'd have to pass Kessell's house and the dog run. Impossible, without alerting him. Besides, Kessell had probably located my truck—it was an obvious hiding place if you knew its owner wanted to escape detection—and soon would realize I'd been inside his home. The back door hadn't completely shut behind me, and there were scratches on its lock from my pick. I moved toward the dark house and slipped into the shadows. Peered back along the road.

No one. He probably hadn't yet figured out I'd broken into his house.

I moved deeper into the shadows, feeling my way, not daring to use my flash. A couple of times my feet slipped on the uneven ground, but finally I came to the wall of the house—shingled, rough to the touch—and paused, listening.

Silence, except for the lapping of the waves below.

I began moving around the eastern side of the house, deeper into the trees where the scents of pine and eucalyptus blended. The ground was thick with needles, muffling my footfalls. I couldn't see more than a yard ahead, so I kept one hand on the house's wall; the ground began to slope, and I slid on the needles, one foot going out from under me, and landed with my butt on a rock.

Gritting my teeth against the pain, I stood and took stock of my surroundings. Through the trees ahead I could see moonlit waves breaking in one of the many coves that scalloped this part of the coast. In the distance to my left a truck boomed while gearing down for a curve on the highway.

What now? Make my way through uncertain terrain toward the highway? Risk falling into a ravine cut by a creek on its way to the sea? Even if I did make it, the highway was a dangerous place to walk at night—or even in daylight. And then I might find Kessell and his dog waiting at my truck.

No, stay here till morning. It would be a cold, unpleasant night, but I'd had plenty of those.

I followed the wall of the house toward the bluff's edge, looking for shelter. There was a lower story cut into the cliff, with a large deck jutting out from it; part of the deck was protected from the wind by Plexiglas panels and covered by the balcony above. I found a stack of lounge chairs stored under the overhang, pulled one down, and sat there, Hy's .45 at my side, waiting for first light.

Falling, falling, falling . . .

I know this is a dream.

Plane's in an uncontrolled spin. Falling . . .

I can't wake up from this, even though it's just a dream. Or maybe it isn't—

Sudden bright light in my face.

I came awake in an instant, reached for the .45, but it was gone.

A voice that I recognized as Kessell's said, "Well, Nancy Estrada, aka Sharon McCone."

I shaded my eyes with my hand and sat up. Dammit, why had I fallen asleep? Why had I sat here instead of moving around? I should have known he'd search the area.

"Surprised?" he added. "You've got your contacts up and down the coast, but so do I. First you come here, showing me a fake driver's license and saying you're looking for a street that doesn't exist. Then you're asking around at Little River and Ocean Ridge. What the hell do you want?"

So he didn't suspect that I'd connected him with the other Kessell's murder and the bombings.

"A couple of pilots I know spotted your plane making unauthorized landings at my airstrip. I want to know why."

"You've never made an unauthorized landing anyplace?"

"No."

"Come on, lady."

"Well, only in an emergency."

"Bullshit."

"Okay, whatever you say. But would you get that goddamn light out of my eyes?"

He lowered the flashlight, and I could see Hy's .45, trained on me in his other hand. He also wore a shoulder holster.

"You have a carry permit for that?" I motioned at the holster.

"You got one for this?" He nodded at the .45.

I didn't answer.

"What I'm wondering," he added, "is why all this sneaking around, just because I've been using your runway for touch-and-goes. Why break into my house?"

"I didn't—"

"Yeah, you did. You think I'm stupid? You left the back door open."

"Not me." I sat up, swung my legs off the chair.

He moved the .45 higher.

I judged the distance between us. He was taller and heavier than I, but he had a bad leg. Maybe—

"I don't know who you are," he said. "Just that you must be rich, owning that big property with an airstrip. Frankly, I don't pay much attention to second-homers unless they hire me to patrol. But tomorrow I'm gonna find out. And then we'll settle this one way or the other. I don't want to hurt you, but I will if I have to. Stand up."

"Where are we going?"

"Stand up."

I stood.

"Turn around."

I turned.

Kessell set the flashlight on the lounge chair, pulled my arms behind me and handcuffed my wrists.

"False imprisonment, Dan," I said. "Maybe even kidnapping."

"Breaking and entering. Trespassing on my clients' property."

"Unauthorized landings at a private strip."

"Shut up." He pushed me toward the glass door to the house. Slid it open and shoved me inside. The interior smelled musty and damp.

"Owners aren't due here for a month," Kessell said, "so don't get your hopes up. They hire me to patrol, air it out, and set up the cushions on the deck furniture before they come."

He turned on lights, guided me through what looked to be a family room and down a hallway to a closed door. Keyed the lock, opened it, and pushed me inside.

"Have a good night, Ms. McCone," he said. "I'll get back to you after I do some asking around of my own."

The door shut, and the lock turned.

Tuesday

✦

MARCH 7

I was in a storage room. I could tell by touch: cardboard cartons, cushions for the outdoor furniture, a kettle barbecue that I backed into and nearly tipped over. It was totally black in what must be a windowless space.

I'd become disoriented, and it took a moment to locate the door Kessell had pushed me through. There ought to be a light switch to one side or the other. I rubbed my upper arm along the wall, located it, and pushed at it with my shoulder. A bare overhead bulb came on. A storage room, all right; a lot of second-homers rented out their places when they weren't in residence and kept possessions they didn't want the tenants to use under lock and key.

Kessell's handcuffs were tight around my wrists but loosely linked. I moved them to my left side, twisted around, and craned my neck so I could see my watch.

Five after midnight. Horrible start to a new day.

I had time, though; there was no need to panic. Kessell probably wouldn't make any inquiries about me at this hour. He'd said he didn't know who I was, just that I must be rich because I owned the Touchstone property. So he didn't know

I was an investigator, let alone that my husband was a partner in RKI. He'd also said he didn't want to hurt me—which was natural, because anything that happened to a "rich" property owner would trigger a serious inquiry by the Mendocino and Sonoma County authorities—but once he made the connection with RKI, my life wouldn't be worth two cents. The bluff here was high, the house invisible from the highway, the ocean currents wicked. One shove, and I'd disappear without a trace, become fodder for sharks.

So get moving.

I slid down onto the concrete floor, lay on my back. The cuffs chafed my wrists, sent a sharp pain up my spine. I raised my hips and slid my cuffed hands under them. Then I pulled my knees to my chest, bent my calves down, and pointed my feet toward the ceiling. The cuffs caught on my heels, and I strained to free them; then they were over my feet and in front of me.

I lay on my back for a minute, wrists throbbing, heart pounding. Thank God for the stretching exercises I did most days and the frequent swims in the health club pool. Finally I struggled to a sitting position.

Even though he knew I'd been in his house, Kessell hadn't searched me. I still had the lock picks in my jacket pocket.

Not bright, Danny Boy.

I went to work.

The lock on the cuffs was a piece of cake. They were so poorly manufactured I could have broken them with a pair of pliers. Kessell had probably purchased the least expensive set he could find, against the rare instance when he had to roust a squatter from one of the properties he patrolled.

The door lock proved trickier. I tried a variety of picks and techniques, none of which worked.

My watch showed three-fifteen when I selected my favorite pick, in terms of aesthetics. The Serpentine, my informant had called it—an elegant, long, snakelike piece of flexible metal. Unfortunately, it had limited use and was seldom effective. But this time: a gentle probe, a careful positioning, a swift upward motion, and I was free.

I shut off the storage room light and stepped into the hallway. Listened for a moment. Empty-house sound and feel. Kessell had left. I crossed the family room to the deck where I'd earlier fallen asleep. Kessell wasn't there, and he'd replaced the lounge chair on its stack. It was still dark, not a trace of light showing above the ridgeline.

I stood there, considering my options.

Kessell was probably in bed asleep. But what if he'd left the Doberman on guard? Or positioned himself outside, in the event I'd somehow escape? If I opened the sliding door, it might alert one of them. I didn't have my flashlight anymore, and even if I did, using it to get to the highway would also give me away. But staying here was an unacceptable risk—

Idiot!

My cellular wouldn't work here, but there had to be a phone in the house. Second-homers—even those who use their places less frequently than Hy and I—don't have the service disconnected when they aren't in residence; it's too much trouble, and expensive.

I found a phone on a table between two chairs facing a big-screen TV. Picked up the receiver and got a dial tone. And then sat there, trying to decide whom to call.

The county sheriff? God, no. I'd have to file charges against Kessell, and then he'd file countercharges against me, and even if I'd left no evidence that I'd been in his house, it would trigger an inquiry by the state department of consumer affairs that would put my license in jeopardy. I'd already gone that route once, through no fault of my own, and I wasn't about to travel it again.

I'd have called Hy, but he was far away in San Diego. No help there.

There were any number of friends on the coast I could wake up and ask for assistance, but their driving along the road to this house might alert Kessell. One of the rules of my profession is not to involve friends and family in a potentially dangerous situation.

How to get myself out of here?

No. Get Kessell *out of here.*

I called the San Diego PD. Gary Viner was off duty. I tried information. Fortunately, he was listed. I dialed his number, and he answered after two rings—homicide cops are used to early-morning calls.

"Did you get that file I e-mailed?" I asked.

"And a good morning to you, too."

"The file?"

"Yeah. Promising information."

"More than promising." I told him what I'd found out up here, omitting the fact that Kessell had me trapped in a stranger's house. "I need you to issue a pickup order on Kessell to the Sonoma County Sheriff's Department, effective immediately."

"Why immediately?"

"I think he's about to commit murder again."

"Who's the potential victim?"

"Me."

"Jesus, McCone, what makes you think that?"

"He's figured out I'm on to him." When Gary still hesitated,

I added, "He's trespassed on my property up here before, and he knows how to breach the security system."

"Okay, I guess we've got enough to ask Sonoma County to pick up and hold."

"Great. I think he's at the home address in the file I sent you. And, Gary, can you leave me out of it for now?"

"Why?"

"I can't say."

"What have you done?"

"Nothing. But I don't need the publicity."

". . . Okay, I understand. For now, you're out of it. I can't guarantee that indefinitely, though. Now, hang up so I can get this thing in motion."

A faint pink line had appeared above the coastal ridge by the time a sheriff's department cruiser pulled up in Kessell's driveway. I watched from the front window on the upper level of the house where he'd trapped me as two officers went to his door and were admitted. Five minutes later, they came out with Kessell, who was yelling, although I couldn't make out his words, and gesturing toward this house. On the other side of his cottage, the dog barked wildly. The deputies ignored Kessell's protests, put him in the backseat of the cruiser, and drove away.

The tension that had been building as I waited ebbed. God, I was tired. Still, I checked around the house for any evidence of my presence. My fingerprints weren't on any of the surfaces I'd touched, as I hadn't removed the surgical gloves I'd used to search Kessell's place. There was nothing I could do about locking the storage room door, but the owners would probably consider that an oversight on their own part. They'd probably complain to the phone company about the calls to

San Diego and have them removed from their bill. I climbed to the upper level again, and left by way of the front door.

Okay, Kessell was gone and wouldn't be returning for some time, if ever, but now I had another problem: what had he done with Hy's .45? If the case against him proved strong enough for the authorities to get a search warrant for his house, they'd most likely find the gun, and its registration would lead directly to Hy—and me. Its presence there would be difficult to explain.

I moved along the road toward the green cottage. Both the front and back doors were locked, but not the deadbolt on the front. I went to work with my picks on the snap lock and was inside within a minute. After a quick sweep of all the rooms, I found the .45 under a pile of dish towels in a kitchen drawer next to the back door. I took it and left the way I'd come.

The light above the ridgeline intensified as I trudged along the road toward the highway and my truck. Kessell's Doberman yammered a good-bye.

Back at Touchstone, I locked the .45 in Hy's nightstand and then called Gary Viner; his voice mail message said he would be out of town today on official business. When he got on to something, he got on to it right away.

The light on the machine was blinking. I depressed the play button. Walter Waggoner, at ten-forty p.m.: "Sharon? Are you there? Kessell came back, said he was having problems with the plane's radio. He's on his way home."

Second message: Hy's voice, recorded at 2:51 this morning.

"McCone, if you're there, pick up." A pause, then a sigh. "Oh, hell. Call me when you get this—it's important."

I dialed his cellular; he answered immediately. "What's wrong?" I asked.

"The ever-running man's been at it again. This time he took a shot at me in the parking lot."

"Are you okay?"

"Yeah. I sensed a motion in the shadows, ducked, and the shots—two of them—broke the windows in the company car I've been using. Then the night crew came running out of the building, and he disappeared."

I sank onto the chair next to the phone. "What time was this?"

"Around two-thirty."

No way Kessell could have made it to La Jolla in two hours after he'd imprisoned me, much less back by the time the sheriff's deputies took him away. He couldn't have been the shooter.

Was I wrong about him being the ever-running man?

"McCone?"

"You sure you're okay?"

"Yeah. More pissed off than anything else."

"You call the police?"

"They came out, took a report. I told them to get in touch with Viner at SDPD." La Jolla was a separate jurisdiction, with a police force of its own.

"You tell them why?"

"Yeah. They'll pass the information along to Viner."

"Gary's on his way up here." I explained what had happened last night, omitting nothing.

Hy was silent when I finished. Then: "So Dan really was this Dr. Richard Tyne. He took over Kessell's identity, Kessell found out years after the fact, and killed him."

"Apparently. He left a fairly clear trail to San Diego and back."

"But he's not our ever-running man."

"Not unless he was working with someone else. I suppose he could've contacted a partner after he imprisoned me and ordered a hit on you."

"That doesn't feel right."

"No, it doesn't."

After a pause, Hy said, "What I don't understand is which Kessell broke into the house and deleted the Tyne file from my iMac. Ours, who came by boat, or the one up there, who came by air?"

"I suspect it was our Kessell. The other just liked to do touch-and-goes at our strip. Our Dan—Tyne, whatever—must've realized you'd been in his office and seen the pad where he scribbled Tyne's name. He knew that would make you curious, that you'd probably Google Tyne, but you wouldn't do it on your office computer. And he knew about the iMac from the time he stopped by Touchstone and you showed him something on it."

"The Tyne file was on the desktop, easy for him to access. But I keep a computer at the ranch as well; why didn't he go there?"

"Had he ever been to the ranch?"

"No. I don't think he even knew where it is."

"There's your answer."

"So what's next on your agenda?"

"Sleep—if possible. Then I'll get hold of Gary, ask if they've gotten anything out of Kessell. And then back to the city. I want to go over this information with my staff, help Patrick coordinate his flow charts, see if anything new comes out of that."

"Everything okay at Touchstone?"

"Now it is."

When I broke the connection, I realized that this had been the most normal conversation—if talk of a shooting attempt can be considered normal—that I'd had with Hy since last week's unpleasant revelations. Somehow, maybe, we were making our way back to each other.

Air traffic was heavy at Oakland, freeway and bridge traffic even heavier into San Francisco. I'd slept till two in the afternoon and was hitting the Bay Area at a busy time of day. I tapped my fingers on the steering wheel of the MG, watched its temperature gauge rise. I loved this car, had gifted it with a new engine, extensive body and interior work, and a new convertible top. Now the paint was blistered from the explosion at Green Street, and something else was about to go wrong. Minor, but still . . .

Maybe I should buy a new car. Something like Rae's BMW Z4. Bells and whistles—

No. This little gem was a classic that car lovers like me would kill for. I'd keep it, and if I bought a second vehicle, I'd get something inexpensive, sensible, and nondescript—the perfect car for stakeouts. Like my investigator friend Wolf's car: it was so nondescript I wasn't even sure of its make, and he'd driven it forever. But, come to think of it, Bill—Wolf was my nickname for him—didn't do many stakeouts anymore since he and his partner, Tamara Corbin, had hired a couple of new operatives. Neither did I.

The hell with it. I'd keep the MG, and use the agency van when I needed to be inconspicuous. A second, inexpensive, sensible, and nondescript car be damned.

I pulled into my parking space on the floor of the pier at

quarter to five. Patrick's car and Mick's motorcycle were in their spaces, but everybody else's vehicles were gone.

I hurried up the catwalk, thrust my head into Ted's office. Kendra Williams, who took the MUNI to work, smiled up at me. "You're back! Ted'll be relieved. You know how he worries when you fly."

"Do I ever." I smiled back at Kendra. She was a petite woman in her mid-twenties with a milk-chocolate complexion and cornrows; she was also the perfect assistant office manager for the agency—unflappable, and so efficient that even Ted was in awe of her.

"He go home early?" I asked.

"No, the dentist. Between his twitchiness over having his teeth cleaned and you flying, he's been wringing his hands like Butterfly McQueen. He said to tell you that all's on an even keel here. And I can testify to that." She handed me a few message slips. "Nothing important, I don't think."

"Thanks." I went along the catwalk to my office, amused by the reference to the *Gone With the Wind* character who had performed her histrionics long before Kendra—or even her mother—was born.

Once I'd hung up my jacket and used the restroom, I glanced through the message slips. Hy, of course, from the early hours of the morning. Ma, twice—God, I'd have to remember to phone her tonight! A client, thanking us for a job well done and particularly praising Julia Rafael's work. Jim Keys, the contractor at Church Street, asking if I wanted to check the progress on the house. A couple of new clients whom Ted noted he had referred to Charlotte and Craig.

I picked up the receiver and called the Sonoma County Sheriff's Department in Santa Rosa, where I knew they would have taken Kessell. Gary Viner was there, but conducting an interview and couldn't be interrupted. I left a message for him to call me. Then I buzzed Mick and asked him to come to my office.

As soon as he stepped through the door, I could see he was depressed: his shoulders slumped, and he shuffled his feet. He didn't look me in the eye.

Oh, God, the romantic weekend in Carmel and the marriage proposal must not have gone as planned.

"How are you?" I asked.

"If you really want to know, I feel like shit." He flopped into one of the clients' chairs.

"Not a good weekend?"

"No. Well, it was fine till Saturday night when I sprung the engagement ring on her. She turned me down flat. Said she's felt pressured by me lately. She thinks she needs more space." He laughed, with a bitterness I hadn't heard from him since his parents' divorce. "She's moving out. Temporarily, she says. I suspect it's permanent."

Damn! He was so happy when he showed me the ring.

"Shar, I don't know if I can work here anymore." His face reminded me of when he was a confused little boy contending with a badly dysfunctional family. But he wasn't a little boy anymore; he was a grown man who'd already suffered more than his fair share of life's disappointments.

I said, "You can, and you will."

"But she doesn't want to quit her job, and I honestly can't ask you to fire her."

"I wouldn't, under any circumstances. What's between the two of you is your private business."

"But how can I—"

"Let me tell you a story," I said. And explained exactly what had gone on between Hy and me since Mick had revealed his information about Hy's past.

"If you're strong about this," I finished, "if you're professional, Charlotte will respect you. She may not come back, you may never even be friends again, but she'll respect you, and you'll respect yourself."

"But you said you and Hy might be coming together again."

"I said we *might*. There's no certainty."

He bent his head, his longish blond hair falling over his forehead, and remained in that pose for a moment. Then he looked up at me and said with a half smile, "If you can live with that kind of situation, so can I. I always told Mom and Dad that when I grew up, I wanted to be just like you."

"Thanks for the compliment. Now let's call Patrick in and fill in some of the gaps on his flow charts."

The more gaps on the flow charts that we filled in, the more we realized we didn't know. Unless Dan Kessell broke down under Gary Viner's questioning and admitted to being the bomber—something that seemed unlikely—we would have to assume the ever-running man was still out there. When Gary called at around six-thirty, what he had to report confirmed that line of thinking.

"We've got a strong case against Kessell in the San Diego murder," he told me. "We've already confirmed the vic as Richard Tyne. A search of Kessell's plane turned up a thirty-eight police special in the cargo space, and I'm sure ballistics'll make a match. The other evidence you gave us is circumstantial, but with the weapon, the prosecutor can build a case that'll stick."

"Is Kessell talking?"

"He says he went down to San Diego to ask Tyne for 'compensation' for using his identity all these years, but Tyne refused, so he went to a motel and flew back north in the morning. When I questioned him about the thirty-eight we found in the plane, he said he didn't know how it got there. And then he lawyered up. We'll be bringing him down to San Diego for arraignment tomorrow morning. Hold on a second."

Muted voices in the background. Gary came back on the line. "Here's something interesting: the thirty-eight was registered to Dan Kessell—the one in San Diego."

"To me, that sounds like they argued, Tyne pulled the gun on him, and Kessell shot him in the course of a struggle."

"Sounds like that to me, too." Gary yawned. "His lawyer'll probably plead him self-defense, but that's the DA's problem. Now, on these other allegations—the bombings—Kessell's lawyer gave us a list of his alibis for those dates. Most of them check out."

"But not all?"

"No. We've turned the information over to the feds, and they'll do a more thorough investigation, but I'd say there's a good chance he isn't the bomber."

"Or was working with an accomplice."

"Possibly. But my instincts tell me that the Tyne shootings and the bombings don't mesh. This guy isn't bright enough to engineer those, and he doesn't really strike me as a premeditated killer."

"I think you're right. Unfortunately."

"McCone," Gary spoke in a lowered tone, "Kessell told the deputies who brought him in a story about you breaking into his house and then hiding in the vacant place next door that belongs to one of his clients."

"What? He's crazy. He just wants to make trouble for me because he heard I was asking questions that put him in San Diego at the time of the murder."

"That's what the general consensus here is; you've got a good rep. And I've reinforced it, told them I've known you most of my life, and you would never break and enter. He's stopped talking about it since his lawyer got here. But . . ."

"Yes?"

"Don't ever do anything like that again. At least not down in my jurisdiction."

"I wouldn't dream of it. Did you get the report on someone shooting at Hy in the RKI parking lot?"

"It came from La Jolla this morning, and headquarters faxed it to me here because of the connection with this case."

"What d'you think?"

"Sounds as if this ever-running man is trying to throw everybody off track, tie in the bombings with the Tyne murder. Your husband told La Jolla the shots didn't even come close to him."

"Anywhere near him is too damn close."

"Back to square one," I told Mick and Patrick when I finished talking with Gary. "We'll need to keep working tonight."

Mick said, "Fine with me. I'm in no mood to go home and watch Charlotte packing."

Patrick shot him a sympathetic look—been there, done that. "How about if I redo these charts?" he said. "Remove the element of Tyne's murder. They'll be cleaner, and maybe we can see something that all this clutter is concealing."

"How long will that take?"

"An hour or so."

"Okay, while you're doing that I think I'll take care of some personal stuff. When you're ready, we can start again."

Once Mick and Patrick had left my office, I called Jim Keys's cellular and told him I couldn't possibly come over to Church Street and view his progress until the final walk-through. He said that was fine; all was going as planned.

Michelle Curley wasn't home, but her mother told me the cats were doing well. Allie had screamed all the way to and from her annual appointment with the vet, and afterward had turned her back every time she caught a glimpse of 'Chelle. No surprise there.

Ma and Melvin weren't home, thank God. I left a long, reassuring message.

Rae told me she and Ricky would be in all evening. She insisted I again make use of their guest room, and I took her up on it.

Hy answered his cellular, and I brought him up to speed.

"Now what?" His tone was flat.

"Patrick and Mick and I brainstorm. We wait to hear what the FBI comes up with on Kessell's alibis."

"More like we wait till this maniac strikes again."

"Listen, I know how discouraged you feel. I've felt that way at this point in every major case I've worked. But then something makes it all come together."

"McCone, I hope that something comes soon."

"So do I." I thought of telling him about Mick and Charlotte's breakup, but changed my mind. When your own relationship's on rocky ground, the worst thing you can discuss is the failure of someone else's.

* * *

Mick, Patrick, and I brainstormed for hours. The charts looked less cluttered, but nothing significant stood out. Finally we took a break and opened a bottle of wine that was stashed in the little fridge in Ted's office. We hadn't ordered in any food, and on empty stomachs the wine soon made us feel mellow.

"You know," I said, "we need to look at the bigger picture."

"What d'you mean?" Patrick asked.

"Our assumption all along has been that this is a vendetta against RKI. What if it goes back farther than that?"

Mick said, "To Thailand. And K Air."

"Right. All three partners were there at the same time. Renshaw didn't work for the company, but Kessell—Tyne—had a lot of illicit dealings with him."

"I don't know, Shar. That was a long time ago. A long time for someone to harbor a grudge. Why didn't he act on it years ago?"

"Maybe he couldn't, for some reason. Or he didn't know where to find them till recently."

"Which brings us back to the real Dan Kessell," Patrick said. "Maybe he *is* the bomber."

"No, I agree with Gary Viner's instincts. Kessell only wanted to extort money from the man who stole his identity, and his attempt turned fatal. These bombings feel . . . I don't know. Different."

"How?"

"They're methodical, well planned. There's a coldness to them, but it's a coldness that masks a great heat. Does that make any sense?"

"No," Mick said, and poured us more wine.

"Maybe I don't mean heat. Try hatred. Controlled rage.

And he's covered his movements well; Kessell didn't. The bomber is very smart; Kessell's kind of dim."

"Okay, but whatever it was would've happened way back when, in a foreign country."

"Hy once told me that most of K Air's pilots and employees were Americans. If the pilots are alive and still hold licenses, the FAA will have records. I'll call him, ask him to send you the names of anybody he recalls who was employed there. We'll locate those that we can; maybe one of them will remember an incident that might've triggered this vendetta."

Mick said, "As soon as you get the list from Hy, Derek and I'll get on it."

"And I'll be standing by," Patrick added.

When I got to Rae and Ricky's house at eleven-thirty, I made a call to Hy and told him of the new approach Mick, Patrick, and I had come up with. He liked it, said he could remember the names of at least five other pilots, as well as mechanics and office personnel. He'd have the list to Mick by the start of business tomorrow.

"Also consider anything you might not've told me," I told him, "even if it doesn't seem important."

"Will do."

No resistance to the suggestion. No denial of withholding any information. And I sensed he wasn't employing his skill at silence. Maybe . . .

Set it aside, McCone. Set it aside until this nightmare's over.

I said, "I'll talk to you tomorrow."

I went to the kitchen, where Rae was heating up leftover lasagna and Ricky was opening some red wine. While I ate like a pig—Rae makes great lasagna—I told them about the previous night's experiences. Ricky looked horrified. Rae looked as if she was taking mental notes for a new novel.

Then I went to the guest room and fell asleep while repeating my new mantra: *A break in the case. Soon. Anything . . .*

Wednesday

✦

MARCH 8

My cellular rang as I was getting into my car to drive to the pier the next morning. A male voice identified himself as Todd Williams.

"What's this in regard to?" I asked.

"You wanted me to call you. I work security at the RKI safe house in San Francisco."

The man who'd been on duty when our apartment there was broken into. I'd forgotten all about him.

He went on, "Jason Ng said you wanted to talk to me about my shift last Saturday. Sorry it took so long to get back to you; I had a few days off, so I took a trip to Vegas and didn't check my messages."

"Oh, right. Thanks for calling. I'm interested in the malfunction of the camera outside the apartment Mr. Ripinsky and I are occupying. Can you pinpoint when it happened?"

Pause. "Could've been as early as noon."

"You see anyone approaching the blind spot on the other monitors?"

". . . Not that I recall."

"Were you paying attention?"

"What's that supposed to mean?"

"Your job is to check those monitors constantly, Mr. Williams."

"Well, excuse me, but we were understaffed on the weekend. Plus there were all these people from headquarters who used to work at Green Street in the building. I thought it was okay to leave the monitors to take a leak."

Hy really needs to look at the quality of the staff in all of RKI's facilities.

"Okay, Mr. Williams. You saw the camera was out. Why didn't you contact one of the on-call technicians and ask him or her to check it?"

"I did try. But 'on-call' doesn't mean much to them, I guess. The only one I could reach couldn't get there for an hour. By then, Jason would be on shift and could check while I watched the monitors."

Why can't people do their jobs these days?

"Ms. McCone? You're not gonna report me for taking a leak, are you?"

"No, don't worry about that."

I'm going to report you for being an idiot.

When I got to the pier, the first thing I did was put Kessell's unmailed letter to Gina Hines as well as a brief note of explanation into an envelope and address it to her daughter. She and her father deserved an explanation of why Gina had been so frightened toward the end of her life. Then I buzzed Mick and asked him to come to my office.

He looked dreadful: red-eyed, rumpled, unshaven.

"You sleep here last night?" I asked.

"On that air bed Ted keeps in the supply room closet. It didn't inflate all the way, and I felt like I was on one of those old-fashioned waterbeds. But I couldn't've slept well anyway."

"I'm so sorry you have to go through this."

"I'll survive. But I'm trying to avoid Charlotte. She's in her office, business as usual, Patrick tells me."

Not a harmonious situation, in an agency where people had always related well. As I'd told Mick yesterday, I couldn't in good conscience fire Charlotte. But there must be some solution . . .

"You get that list of names from Hy?" I asked him.

He frowned at what he must have perceived as my lack of compassion, but said, "Yeah. So far I've located one pilot, Edward Biggs, currently living in Cedar Rapids, Iowa."

"You have a phone number for him?"

"Uh-huh." He slid a piece of scratch paper across the desk to me.

"Okay," I said. "I'll call him. And you keep on it."

As he left my office, I added, "And tough it out as far as Keim goes, kid."

"Don't call me kid, old lady."

Cedar Rapids, Iowa. Central time zone, two hours later there. I dialed the phone number Mick had given me. Edward Biggs, the woman who answered informed me, had died two months ago. "Would you like to speak with his wife?"

"Please."

A pause. Muffled conversation. Then, "This is Nan Biggs."

I identified myself and said I was looking into an insurance matter concerning K Air. "I understand your late husband flew for them in Bangkok."

"An insurance matter? That company went bankrupt years ago."

Bankrupt? That was something new. "Perhaps I have the wrong information. When did it go bankrupt?"

"Sometime in the late eighties or early nineties. I forget. An accountant embezzled most of their funds and disappeared."

That was after Hy had left the charter service and moved back to his ranch; he wouldn't have known about the bankruptcy. And I was willing to bet it wasn't an accountant, but the owner who had cleared out and used the funds to re-establish himself in California.

"Was your husband still working for K Air then?" I asked Nan Biggs.

"Oh, no. He was only with them a couple of years. He quit and came back to the States, got a job flying for Federal Express."

"I see. Mrs. Biggs, how did your husband die?"

"The engine failed on his homebuilt plane. What does this have to do with an insurance matter?"

"Nothing. I'm sorry, Mrs. Biggs. Forgive me for intruding."

I hung up. I hadn't given the woman my phone number, and she probably hadn't internalized my name. She'd wonder about the conversation, then put my questions down as nosiness.

One lead gone.

I did some paperwork, conferred with Ted. Stopped in at Mick and Derek's shared office space; they were both busy and shooed me away. Julia and Craig were out in the field. I glanced toward Patrick and Charlotte's office, then went back to my own. I wasn't sure I was up to facing Keim yet.

Patrick appeared in my doorway to ask if I had anything to add to his flow charts.

No. But it was nearly noon, so why didn't we go to lunch?

We walked down the Embarcadero to the Ferry Building and ate at Hog Island Oyster Company. On the way back, I asked him how his meeting with Hank had gone.

"He thinks I've got grounds for full custody."

"You going for it?"

"Yeah. I know it'll be hard, working full time and raising my kids by myself, but it's better than them being exposed to addicts and God knows what else. My mom and sisters've said they'll help."

"Good for you." A lot of men in his position would have shrunk from the burden of parenthood, but not Patrick.

Mick came to my office at quarter to two. "I've located another former K Air pilot," he said. "This one's here in the city."

I took the sheet of scratch paper he held out: Kurt Wilhelm, address on the Great Highway.

He added, "That's in the condos across from Ocean Beach."

The ones on the former site of Playland. I remembered the controversy when a developer bought the fabled amusement park by the sea and tore it down; San Franciscans love their institutions, no matter how tattered and out-of-date they become. To add insult to injury, the developer then went bankrupt and the site became a gaping scar on the city's landscape until someone else finally built there years later.

"No phone number?" I asked Mick.

"Unlisted."

"Well, that's not a problem. I think it's better to pay him a surprise visit. Given the nature of K Air's business, many of their former people aren't going to want to make an appointment to discuss it."

At the pier, the sun had been shining; at the beach, fog was sweeping inland. The gray sea looked forbidding, the rolling waves dangerous, but people were still walking on the sand. I parked in one of the spaces by the seawall, took the crosswalk—dodging a Ford Expedition whose driver apparently hadn't heard of the pedestrian's right of way—and entered the stucco complex, whose units were painted in various innocuous shades. Most of the windows that faced the Pacific were covered with blinds or curtains; a direct westerly view often is not as charming as it might seem—particularly on warm days when the sun glares on all that glass, or a day like today when gloom threatens to invade your home. Kurt Wilhelm's unit was on the ocean side in the middle of the complex. I rang the bell and after a moment heard footsteps within. The door opened, and a tall man with a head of thick white hair looked out at me.

"Mr. Wilhelm?"

"Yes?"

I identified myself, handed him my card. "I'd like to talk with you about K Air. I believe you worked for them in Bangkok."

His features went very still, eyes watchful.

"You *did* fly for K Air?"

"Why do you want to know?"

"My husband, Hy Ripinsky, was also one of their pilots. He gave me your name."

His guarded expression disappeared, and he smiled. "The Ripster! How the hell did he get a good-looking woman like you?"

Soon I was seated on Kurt Wilhelm's big leather sofa, a glass of single-malt Scotch in hand. I don't often drink hard liquor, and I don't like Scotch—the result of a disgraceful episode during college where I spent most of an evening hugging a toilet bowl—but I can tolerate single-malt, and I sensed it was important to Wilhelm that I join him in a drink. Important because I'd interrupted him in what was probably not his first of the day.

"The Ripster," he said, sitting down opposite me in a matching leather chair. "He was one stand-up guy. Fearless pilot. Fearless man. Absolutely."

"He still is."

"So he sent you to talk with me about the old days?"

"In a sense. He wanted you to know that Dan Kessell has died."

"Kessell? Too bad. A good man. What happened?"

"Heart attack. Did you know him well?"

"Dan and me were buddies, yeah. Where's he been all these years?"

"San Diego. He was a partner with Hy and Gage Renshaw in an international security firm."

"Renshaw. Jesus Christ. What a character."

"He certainly is. If you could tell me what you remember about those days in Bangkok, Hy and I would appreciate it." I took my tape recorder out. "We're planning a memorial service, and we'd like to have statements from Dan's friends to read."

"I'll come to the service. When is it?"

"We haven't scheduled it yet, but we'll be sure to let you know."

"I'll be there. Now turn that thing on, and we'll talk about Dan."

* * *

Dan had a reputation as a loner, and maybe he was. He didn't say much about his personal life. But the flying life, that man could hangar-fly with the best of them. A bunch of us—the insiders who knew about the operation—used to get together at a bar near the airstrip. Sadie's, it was called. We'd go on and on for hours.

The insiders? Well, we knew what cargo some of those planes were carrying. We knew the side of the operation that wasn't legit, and we were free to talk about it among ourselves.

No, the Ripster wasn't part of that group. He knew, sure, but I always thought he didn't want *to know. He went his own way.*

Yeah, Dan was quiet about his personal life. I didn't even know where he lived. I did know there was a woman . . . A Thai woman . . . Funny name . . . Sorry, I can't recall it.

Let's see . . . Who else was in that group? Charlie Madsen. He died in a crash in Cambodia. Ralph Levinger. Don't know what happened to him. Oh, right, somebody you should talk to—Lex Richards. He was closest to Dan of any of us. He and I still exchange Christmas cards; I've got his address in Healdsburg on my computer.

I listened to the tape as I drove back to the pier. One sentence stood out: *No, the Ripster wasn't part of that group.*

Hy wasn't an insider; he knew, but he didn't want to know. That was how he'd always portrayed himself.

Lex Richards, the pilot who had known Kessell better than any of them, lived some seventy miles north of the city in Healdsburg, a small town in the Sonoma County wine country. Kurt Wilhelm had called him and put me on the line; Richards had agreed to talk with me. I was to meet him at a brewpub off the town square at eight. When I got to the pier, I asked Ted if he knew of a place to stay there, and he recommended a small hotel that he and Neal liked; the rates were surprisingly inexpensive. I asked him to make a reservation for me. Then I tidied up a few loose ends, left the pier, and headed for the Golden Gate Bridge and Highway 101.

Healdsburg is a charming town, but I wouldn't want to live there. Well, maybe if I lived in the surrounding countryside, which is among the most beautiful in California. But it's also vineyard land, and prohibitively expensive. Besides, when I'd go into town I'd have to contend with the tourists and cute shops and overpriced—although excellent—restaurants.

Since it was March, the town wasn't too crowded with those seeking souvenirs and gourmet meals and the wine-tasting experience. The Healdsburg Inn on the Plaza was a pleasant surprise, too: friendly service, a comfortable and well-decorated room, and the promise of a full breakfast in the morning. As I freshened up, I decided Hy and I could use a getaway other than the coast or the ranch; we would stay here—

My God, I'm planning a future for us! In a way, that seems premature. But in another way, it doesn't.

The Bear Republic Brewing Company was a block off the plaza, between two new buildings, one of which housed a very chichi hotel. Toni the travel agent had stayed there last year—the cost comped, of course—and had told me it was "a place that doesn't know what it wants to be." Well, I could understand that: my earthquake cottage hadn't decided what it wanted to be since it was constructed in 1906.

Lex Richards had told me he'd arrive early and take a table in the outdoor seating area of the brewpub, since the weather was beautiful there today. Actually, he'd said, "My table."

When his friend Kurt Wilhelm handed the phone to me that afternoon, the voice that spoke held a measure of authority that told me that the man would command his own table wherever he chose to go.

The restaurant wasn't at all pretentious, and the patio was pleasant, heaters having been turned on to counter the evening chill. Richards was seated at a table by the outer railing, and when he rose to greet me, he towered over me—another long, tall drink of water, with curly red hair and a full beard that was showing streaks of white. He pulled out my chair, asked what I wanted to drink, and motioned for the waiter, who took the order and said, "Right away, Mr. Richards."

I smiled at Richards and said, "You certainly get good service."

It was the right opening comment; he grinned like a pleased child.

"I come here a lot; the waitstaff and the chef know me."

"You live in town?"

"No, I own a vineyard up Alexander Valley way. You know the area?"

"Not very well."

"My property"—he took a pen from the pocket of his blue shirt and began drawing on a paper napkin—"is here. Near Hanna and Field Stone. I don't make wine—too much work—but I grow grapes for a lot of prime vintners. It's a nice life."

"After flying for K Air, I'd say so."

He capped the pen and replaced it in his pocket. "So you married Ripinsky."

"Right."

"Well, you're a pretty lady and he's an ugly mutt, but you couldn't've done better."

I considered the insult to my handsome husband, decided it was a guy thing.

"So Dan's dead," he added.

"Heart attack, a couple of weeks ago."

"Where the hell's he been all these years?"

I explained about RKI.

"Dan had to *work* for a living? Jesus, I thought he would've retired after he made off with K Air's funds."

So I'd been right about the "bankruptcy."

"I think he liked keeping his hand in at intrigue and subterfuge," I said. "RKI isn't the most ethical of the multinational security firms."

Richards smiled. "That's a good way of putting it. I'm surprised Ripinsky went in with him, though."

My wine arrived. I sipped and asked, "Oh, why?"

"Because he was royally pissed at Dan when he left Thailand."

"Really?"

"Yeah. Probably pissed at himself, too. Seems Dan misrepresented the cargo they were carrying on a flight to Kuwait. Ripinsky didn't check it out, like he should've done, since he was flying left seat."

So maybe he didn't *know about what Dan and Gage were into.*

"He quit a couple of weeks after that," Richards added.

I recalled a former K Air pilot named Cam Connors telling me about the night when Hy had decided to leave Thailand. They'd been drinking in a sleazy Bangkok bar when Hy announced, "Man, I've got to get out of this life and back to the high desert where I can feel clean again."

I've misjudged him—horribly.

"Ms. McCone?"

"Sorry, just thinking. In answer to why Hy became partners with Kessell—Dan had changed. They became good friends, which is why we're planning a memorial service for him. We're collecting comments from the people who knew him well, and I'd like to hear yours." As I'd done with Kurt Wilhelm, I took out my recorder. Like Kurt Wilhelm, Lex Richards didn't protest.

I was closer to Dan than anybody else in Bangkok. Don't know why he let me into his life, but he did. Maybe it was because we both had unhappy childhoods and unrealized dreams. He wanted to be a doctor, I wanted to be a lawyer. But we both ended up flying. I don't mean that we didn't like being pilots, but it fell so short . . .

Yes, Dan had a woman. Lalita Gatip. She was lovely. She had a child, a little boy, and I always assumed Dan was the father, although I never asked. That would've been overstepping the boundaries of our friendship. But Dan called the kid Chad—short for Chadwick; that was his father's name.

What happened to Lalita Gatip and Chad? Well, I know about her. She was in an accident—a car hit her crossing the street—and was in chronic pain for a couple of years. She got dependent on meds, and when the docs tried to wean her off them, she went to Gage Renshaw. He gave her bad drugs, and she died. The boy, I don't know about him, but I doubt Dan brought him stateside. Dan wasn't father material; he acted indifferent around the kid.

I played the tape three times before I turned out the light in my hotel room. Something important there, but I wasn't sure what.

Thursday

✦

MARCH 9

As I drove back to the city the following morning, I tried to come up with a method of locating the son of a woman who had died in Thailand all those years ago. So many children—particularly the illegitimate offspring of Americans—had been abandoned in southeast Asia, left to fend for themselves or rely on the kindness of extended families who didn't really want them. Lalita Gatip's son could have died before he reached adulthood; if not he would be a man in his late twenties or early thirties now—and might be anywhere in the world.

Well, maybe my genius nephew would come up with a solution. God knew he needed something difficult to sink his teeth into, after the breakup with Charlotte.

The pier was bustling with activity when I arrived: deliveries were being made, vehicles were coming and going. I went to Ted and Kendra's office; they were huddled over the copy machine with a repairman. Ted threw me an exasperated glance and said, "This thing's all fucked up again. We really need a new one."

"Not in the budget."

"The repairs and parts for this—"

"If they're getting out of hand, we'll talk about our options later. Anything else going on here that I need to know about?"

He moved away from Kendra and the repairman, lowered his voice. "Mick and Charlotte got into it over the coffeepot in the conference room about an hour ago. I had to tell them to keep it down."

Dammit! I supposed I'd have to deal with that situation soon—but now wasn't the time. "Otherwise?" I asked.

"Everything under control. Except for that." He glared at the copy machine.

"Good." I left before he could continue to lobby for better-quality equipment.

There were message slips on my desk: Hy, Gary Viner, Ma, a couple of clients to whom we'd sent final reports thanking us for good service. I called Hy back first.

"Ted told me you were in Healdsburg overnight," he said.

I summarized my conversations with the former K Air pilots. "Did you know Dan's woman?" I asked.

"I met her once, I think."

"Was her son his?"

"Everybody thought so, but no one ever knew for sure."

"What about the dose of bad drugs Gage supplied her?"

"I heard she died of an overdose, but I didn't know Gage was involved."

"And the son?"

"I never even saw him. When I reconnected with Dan over here, I assumed he didn't bring him back with him. Maybe he placed him with a family there, made support payments."

"Or maybe he just abandoned him."

A pause. "I hate to say it, but that would be more Dan's style."

"Well, I'll get Mick on it right away, and call you with a report in the evening. What's going on down there?"

"It's quiet. Too quiet. I feel like one of the pioneers in a wagon train—the attackers are right over the rise, hiding behind the rocks. I'm heading over to the training camp tomorrow. No problems there, but I want to check anyway."

"Well, why don't I meet you. I've been meaning to get down there, but things just keep coming up."

He agreed, and we set a time to meet before ending the call. "There's a guard in the UNICOM shack," he told me. "He'll come out to meet you and give you a visitor's badge."

Ma's message I set aside. The clients' didn't require a response. Gary Viner's gave his number at SDPD.

"Viner."

"Hi, Gary. Sharon. What's the story on Kessell?"

"He's being arraigned this afternoon. The feds haven't gotten back to me on the alibis we couldn't verify, but I suspect there won't be enough evidence to charge him with the bombings."

"He isn't the bomber."

"So who is?"

"I don't know, but I'm working on it."

"Keep me posted."

Mick said, "This is one tough assignment."

"And perfectly suited for your talents."

We were at a table in the outdoor dining area at Gordon Biersch, the brewpub across the Embarcadero in Hills Brothers Plaza. I'd decided that, given his stressful circumstances, he needed a pleasant lunch.

He wasn't enjoying it, though. He ate a garlic fry, picked up his sandwich, set it back on his plate. His eyes kept moving toward the pier, as if he were afraid Charlotte would follow us over here and begin berating him.

"I'm not working too well these days, Shar."

"So focus on this project. Get your mind off your problems. Did you sleep at the pier again last night?"

He shook his head. "At the condo. She's gone, along with all her stuff. I remembered to take the office air bed home with me. She paid for our bed, so it's hers."

"At least it's your condo."

"No, it's Dad's condo. He bought it for me."

"It was a gift. Your dad has enough real estate; I doubt he'll begrudge you yours. Have you told Rae and him about the breakup yet?"

"Nope."

"Well, you should—and soon. You need support from your family."

"Yeah, I do. You hear about the fight Charlotte and I had in the conference room this morning?"

"Yes."

"Well, I guess it was really the fight *I* had. At least, I did most of the yelling."

"About what?"

"Her inability to commit. The fact that she left all the framed photos of us. God, I'd've yelled at her for taking the last of the Stilton cheese from the fridge, if I'd thought to. And while I was venting, she was calm, in that smug, superior, older-woman way she has."

Keim was seven years older than Mick; at first the age difference hadn't mattered, but apparently now it did.

I said, "A scene like that can't happen again, you know. Not at the agency."

"I know."

"Look, you've got a tough assignment here. Leap into it and forget Charlotte's just down the catwalk."

"I'll try. But that's like forgetting giraffes, when you've just been ordered not to think about them." It was an old game Ricky and Charlene had played with their kids—a variant on the don't-think-about-elephants game my parents had played with us.

"Okay, don't think about your tough assignment."

"Well, now you've got me fixated on it."

It was a slow afternoon. I met with a couple of new clients, opened case files, then assigned them to the appropriate operatives. Approved Julia's and Craig's reports on cases they'd been working and ordered them delivered. In my absence, Mick had come up with a few addresses and phone numbers for former K Air employees. I began calling them, learning little, until I connected with Heidi Schmidt in Kona, Hawaii.

"Yes," she said in answer to my inquiry, "I worked for K Air. My boyfriend at the time was an engineer assigned to a project in Bangkok, and I went along. He worked so much that after I'd done the tourist thing, I got bored, and a friend whose husband was a K Air pilot recommended me for a gal Friday job there."

That was a term I hadn't heard in many years; you'd never get away now with such a job description—thank God.

"Did you know Dan Kessell?" I asked.

"Not well. He wasn't friendly with the office staff, just a small group of the pilots."

"What about the woman he lived with, Lalita Gatip?"

"I saw her a couple of times. She was beautiful."

"She and Dan had a son, Chad. Did you know him?"

"I never knew there was a child— Did you say Chad?"

"Yes."

"Now, that's strange. There was a Eurasian boy named Chad. He must've been nine or ten. Mr. Kessell asked me to accompany him on a flight to LA. He said he was an orphan and was being adopted by a wealthy family there."

"And did you?"

"Yes. Chad cried when Mr. Kessell turned him over to me, but on the plane he became very silent—an angry kind of silence. By the time we got to LA, the anger was still there but under control. I'd describe him as . . . resolute. He was in this situation, and he was going to cope with it, like it or not. Of course my impressions are filtered by time and limited by a lack of knowledge and perspective; I'm now a child psychologist, but back then I didn't have the training or expertise to fully evaluate Chad's emotional state."

"I see. When you got to LA, did you turn him over to an adoption agency?"

"No, the couple was there to meet him. He was stiff with them, but they appeared to be caring people who would be able to forge a good relationship in time."

"Do you recall their names?"

"Yes. Merkel. Donald and Elizabeth Merkel."

"Where did they live?"

"I never knew. But it must've been in an affluent area not far from Los Angeles International. When they put Chad into their Jaguar sedan, I heard Elizabeth tell him that it wouldn't be long before they were home."

After I concluded my call to Heidi Schmidt, I hurried down the catwalk to Mick and Derek's office. Mick was alone. As I stepped inside, he swiveled away from his computer and spread his hands in frustration.

"I'm getting nowhere on this, Shar."

"Quit that angle. Try Donald and Elizabeth Merkel, in an affluent area not far from LAX."

He swiveled back, fingers poised on the keyboard. As he typed, he asked, "Who are these people?"

"Adoptive parents of Dan Kessell's kid." I explained about the mother and the bad drugs Renshaw had given her.

"Have a seat. This shouldn't take long. Compared to what you gave me before, it's—as Hy would say—a piece of cake."

I sat down in Derek's chair, chafing at even a minute's delay.

As he searched, Mick said, "You're thinking that this kid knew about Renshaw giving his mother the fatal overdose, and was pissed at him. Then his father shipped him off to an adoptive home in LA, and he got pissed at him, too. And as an adult he set out to get even."

"I think 'pissed' is too mild a word."

"Yeah. You're right. Pissed is what I was when I ran away at Christmastime because Mom and Dad wouldn't buy me a moped."

"And it cost me all of Christmas Eve trying to find you."

Tap, tap, tap . . .

"You ever going to forgive me for that?" he asked.

"I did the next day, when you helped me fix Christmas dinner. Your idea of adding cranberries to my turkey stuffing was a huge success with my guests, and I've done it every year since."

Tap, tap, tap . . .

"Anything?" I asked.

"Not yet."

I sighed.

"You need to learn to be patient, Shar."

"I know."

Tap, tap, tap . . .

"Got something. Donald Merkel, financial consultant with offices in Beverly Hills, and homes in Bel-Air and Tahoe, died four years ago. Survived by his wife, Elizabeth, and son, Chad."

"Damn!"

"I'm checking now on Elizabeth and Chad."

I waited, trying to be patient. But I had little patience under these kinds of circumstances. I tapped my fingers on Derek's desk, rocked back and forth in his chair, which squeaked.

"Stop that!" Mick exclaimed.

I pressed my hands to my knees, sat still.

After a moment Mick said, "Elizabeth lives in Santa Barbara now."

"And Chad?"

"Give me a minute, will you?"

"Sorry."

Tap, double tap, tap . . .

"He graduated with an MBA from USC eight years ago. Was with a Merrill Lynch brokerage branch in LA for two years, then at their Santa Barbara branch until two years ago. No current address. "

"You have an address for Elizabeth?"

"Address, but no phone number. You going down there?"

"Yes. Will you print me out a map from the airport to her house?"

"You taking your plane?"

"If the weather forecast's good—and it should be."

"I'm coming with you."

"What about your work here?"

"Caseload's light; Derek can handle it. And I can't handle being around the office right now."

We arrived in Santa Barbara after dark. I rented a car and we drove to the twisty, narrow street high in the hills where Elizabeth Merkel lived. The house was large, Spanish-style, and no lights showed in any of the windows.

"Not home," Mick said.

"Or sleeping. If she is, we don't want to disturb her. Nothing makes people more resistant to talking with you than being woken up."

"What now?"

"First food, then a motel. Tomorrow we'll pay a visit to Mrs. Merkel."

Friday

✦

MARCH 10

I woke up the next morning on one of the hardest beds I'd ever encountered, my muscles aching. Normally when working for RKI I'd have splurged on one of Santa Barbara's luxury hotels, but given the trouble that Hy's company was in, I'd decided to keep expenses down and opted for a chain motel near the freeway. Besides, I didn't want Mick to get ideas about what the old expense account would bear. He and I had had a mediocre dinner in the attached restaurant, but neither of us was very hungry: Mick because of his emotional upset, me because I sensed my investigation was coming together.

I did a few stretching exercises, showered, and dressed. Then I went next door to Mick's room and knocked. He was wearing only sweatpants; I'd awakened him. His reddened eyes and the puffy circles under them told me he'd had another bad night. I said to take his time, I'd meet him in the coffee shop.

He looked better when he slid into the booth opposite me. I was pleased to hear him order the country special—fried eggs, bacon, hash browns, and toast. I asked for the same.

After the server had departed, Mick asked, "So what's the plan?"

"I pay a visit to Mrs. Merkel. You can come along, but only to observe. I'll introduce you as my assistant. If there's anything you notice or think I should ask, write it down and hand it to me."

"This sounds like the field training you gave Patrick. Maybe we could do more of it, and I could get out of the office and away from Charlotte."

I considered that; it might be a viable solution to the problem between Keim and him. Then I dismissed it. "You're much too valuable to the agency heading up computer forensics—which, I remind you, was your idea."

He nodded. "And it's what I really like to do."

"We'll come up with another solution to your problem, Mick. I promise."

I promise, but I don't have a clue as to what.

Sprinklers were throwing spray onto the lawn fronting Elizabeth Merkel's house. The lawn was impossibly green—was there dye in that water?—and each blade of grass looked to be the same height as the others. We went up the brick walkway to the front door, avoiding stray droplets; the bell chimed softly when I pressed it.

After a moment, the door opened and an attractive dark-haired woman who could have been in her early fifties looked out at us. "Oh," she said, "I thought you were the postman with a package."

"Are you Elizabeth Merkel?" I asked.

"Yes."

"I'm Sharon McCone, and this is my assistant, Mick Savage." I handed her one of my cards.

She studied it. "Private investigator? From San Francisco? Is it about Chad?"

This was going to be too easy. "Yes, it is. May we come in?"

"Certainly."

She led us into a tiled entryway with a wrought-iron chandelier and sconces and a wide staircase rising at its rear. Paintings of old western scenes that looked like original Charles Russells hung on the walls. Several archways opened off the entry, and Mrs. Merkel took us through one, into a living room furnished in southwest style. She indicated we should sit on a sofa upholstered in a peach-colored fabric, and took a cushioned chair made of rustic wood.

"Are you working in cooperation with the Andreeson Agency?" she asked. "Do you know where Chad is?"

I ignored the first question. "I don't know his exact whereabouts, but I have a lead on some of his recent activities."

Her fingers, which were clasped around the knees of her beautifully tailored gabardine slacks, tightened. "What has he been doing?"

"Before I answer that, I'd like you to fill me in on his disappearance. My reports aren't all that detailed."

"Of course." She glanced around, distracted, as if she was trying to shape the facts in some logical manner. "Would either of you care for coffee? Or tea?"

"No, we're fine."

"Well," she said, "I don't know where to begin."

"Why not from the date you adopted Chad. I understand a woman named Heidi Schmidt delivered him to you at LAX on a K Air flight from Bangkok."

She smiled at the memory. "He was ten years old, and frightened, but trying so hard to be brave. Ms. Schmidt led him up to us, and he actually shook our hands."

"Was the adoption through an agency?"

"No, it was private, through an attorney friend of my husband's in Bangkok. Although I was relatively young at the time, I couldn't have children—the reason isn't important. The waiting lists with the agencies here were long, and my husband and I had a commitment to helping out children in difficult circumstances. When the attorney contacted us about Chad, we jumped at the chance."

"What did he tell you about Chad's background?"

"The father was an American vacationing in Thailand. He took no responsibility for Chad. The mother had died of a drug overdose."

"That's all?"

"That was all we needed to know. From the time he came to us Chad's past was erased."

Maybe for you, but not for him.

Beside me, Mick moved restlessly, as if he shared my thought.

"What kind of a child was Chad?"

She considered. "Quiet. Sometimes too quiet. Reserved. He didn't like to be hugged or kissed, but he expressed his affection for us verbally and in other ways, such as small gifts on no special occasion. He was studious, made all A's in school and straight through college. If anything, I'd describe him as determined. Sometimes too determined."

"Did he ever seem angry?"

"All children get angry."

"But what specifically would set him off?"

"He had a certain mechanical aptitude, but when things didn't go his way—working on his model trains, for instance—he became enraged, rather than normally frustrated. Then he'd smash them. One time he built a beautiful model airplane, then took it out on our second-floor balcony and crashed it on the flagstones around the pool. He hated anything to do with planes—probably a result of the trauma of flying away from his native country."

"I wonder why he bothered to build the model plane, then?"

"I've always suspected it was so he could destroy it."

"Did Chad ever use drugs?"

"Never. When he was in college, he would rail about people who did. Sometimes I wondered if that was normal. Most college students experiment with one substance or another. His father and I did."

Mick wrote something down, but didn't pass it to me. I knew what it was: Chad's attitude toward drugs *was* normal, because his mother had died of an overdose.

"Does Chad limp? I believe someone mentioned that to me."

"Yes, but only when he runs or he's tired or stressed. He had a bad football injury in his senior year of high school. I was opposed to him playing at all, but my husband said to let the boy be a boy. Well, that idea cost Chad."

"Let's fast-forward to Chad's college days. He went to USC . . ."

"And received an MBA with honors."

"And then?"

"My husband became ill—a rare form of cancer—Chad helped me care for him for a year before he died. After that, he took a job with a brokerage firm in LA, and when I decided to move up here, he transferred to their Santa Barbara office."

"Did he live at home the whole time?"

"In Bel-Air, yes. But when we came here, I bought him a

condominium. But he came to see me frequently, until he vanished two years ago."

Vanished.

Mick made a surprised sound, and I frowned at him.

"And what was that date?"

Elizabeth Merkel frowned. "The Andreeson Agency certainly hasn't provided you with much information."

"Sometimes in the investigative process, we ask questions we already know the answers to, in order to verify the facts."

"Oh, I see. Well, no one knows for certain, but the police assumed it was New Year's Day. He'd spent the night before at a party—and I assume in bed—with his fiancée, Veronica Wylie. She was the last person to see him, at around eight the next morning."

"Did he take any of his possessions with him?"

"None, except for some clothing, his shaving kit, and his computer."

"Did his fiancée have any ideas about why Chad disappeared?"

"None at all. Or at least, none that she would share with anyone. She was adamant that there had been no trouble between them, and no trouble for Chad at the brokerage. His supervisor confirmed that."

"Are you still in touch with Ms. Wylie?"

"She calls every week or so to see if the detectives have found out anything. I expect that will stop soon; over two years is a long time for a young, attractive woman to wait."

"May I have a current phone number and address for her?" I asked.

"Certainly." She took a pad from the table beside her and wrote them down. "Now, what can you tell me about Chad's current activities?"

"One of my operatives may have sighted him in San Francisco. I have him working on it, and this background material you've given me will help. I'll talk with Ms. Wylie, and be in touch with any results."

Elizabeth Merkel's brow creased. "Your operative *may have* seen Chad? That's all? God, you private investigators are useless! The Andreeson Agency has been on this case nearly a year and a half, and they haven't found out anything."

"I'm sorry, Mrs. Merkel, but missing-person situations are the most difficult we encounter, particularly when it's a voluntary disappearance and the individual doesn't want to be found."

She scowled, as if she didn't want to acknowledge that her son had deliberately vanished, then showed us to the door.

As we got into the rental car, Mick said, "You were kind of rough with her there at the end—and you lied about somebody spotting Chad in the city."

"I know."

"Doesn't that bother you?"

"Yes."

"Then why did you do it?"

"Means to an end. And this is exactly why you don't belong in the field."

He was silent for a long moment. Then: "What now?"

"We try to talk to Veronica Wylie before Elizabeth Merkel warns her we're on our way."

Veronica Wylie lived in an old-fashioned bungalow court two blocks from the beach. Little stucco units arranged in a U around a grassy courtyard. Well kept up, with tall palms and colorful plantings. The effect was simple, even humble, but the rents would be astronomical. Californians will pay big bucks for nostalgia.

Wylie wasn't home, but a talkative male neighbor told us she worked at an insurance company downtown on Anacapa Street. "An executive, she is. Young woman, doing well. Of course, she'd be doing better if that boyfriend of hers hadn't disappeared."

I wanted to ask him more, but I was also in a hurry to contact Veronica Wylie before Mrs. Merkel did. As a compromise, I left Mick to chat the man up and headed for Wylie's office. The interview would go better without Mick's distracting presence.

Santa Barbara is an attractive town, the Spanish influence everywhere. Stucco buildings, tiled roofs, mosaics, and brilliant flowers abound. Veronica Wylie's insurance company occupied the lower level of a two-story structure on Anacapa Street. I entered by way of a courtyard where a fountain splashed softly.

The interior of the office didn't fit with the building; it was starkly modern, deeply carpeted, with African masks and other artifacts on the walls of the reception room. While I waited for Wylie—the receptionist said she would be in a meeting for another fifteen minutes—I paged through a coffee table book on African art. Most of it was beautiful but disturbing; I wouldn't have wanted to live with it on a daily basis.

Finally Veronica Wylie came up to me. She was petite and very slender, with shoulder-length dark hair styled similarly to mine. I'd expected a tailored business suit, but her bright pink sweater and flowing flowered skirt spoke more of a vintage clothing store than the designer department at Nordstrom. Her handshake was firm, her gaze forthcoming.

"Ms. McCone," she said, "Elizabeth Merkel called to say you wanted to talk with me. She was upset that she hadn't given you my office number."

No, she called to warn you about me; she was upset because I'd pumped her for information and then given her no satisfaction.

I said, "Can we talk someplace other than your office?" Once Mrs. Merkel starting rethinking our conversation, she'd call the Andreeson Agency and find out they'd had no dealings with me. And then she'd call Wylie back.

"There's a coffee shop a couple of doors down," she said. "I could do with a latte."

Soon we were seated at an outdoor table, coffees in hand. I commented on the good weather and Wylie shrugged. "I guess I take it for granted. This is God's country."

"What can you tell me about Chad's disappearance?"

"What do you need to know?"

"As part of my investigative process, I like to familiarize myself with the subject. Get inside his head, so to speak. Chad is something of an enigma to most people, including his mother."

Veronica Wylie sipped her latte, gaze focused on something over my shoulder. She set the coffee down and said, "Enigma. That's a good term for him. I was with him three years. We were planning to be married last July. And I guess I didn't really know him, because I never thought he was a man who would just walk away without an explanation."

"He disappeared on New Year's Day."

"Yes. We'd gone to a party and spent the night together at his condo. We'd had a good time, everything was perfect. I had to get up early to visit my family in Ojai for the day. While I was driving back, I tried to call Chad on both his home and cell phones, but he didn't answer. When I got home, it was too late to bother him, and then I couldn't reach him the next day. After work I went over to his condo. His cell was on the coffee table and Chad was gone."

"Do you recall anything unusual about him in the time before he disappeared?"

"Don't you think the police and the other detectives have asked me that?"

"Of course they have. But think again."

She closed her eyes, sighed. "Okay. The time before. It's always divided between before and after, isn't it?"

I didn't reply.

"The time before . . . He'd been moody for months. He made a lot more computer searches than he usually did, but was vague about what he was after. Then, around November, his mood broke. He was cheerful, looking forward to the holidays. But he still spent a lot of time away from me. I put it down to an extra-heavy workload. Toward Christmas, I sensed a change in him, but I'm not sure I can explain it."

"Try."

She kept her eyes closed for a moment, then opened them. "I could feel an edgy energy in him. It was like he . . . hummed with it."

"As if he was making plans?"

". . . Something like that."

"Did he seem excited?"

"No. He was more . . . purposeful."

"What about anger? I understand he had a problem with that as a child."

"So he told me. But, no. He wasn't angry."

"How was Christmas?"

"Wonderful. He gave me great presents, and I gave him an engraved Rolex. He took it with him when he left."

"What did the engraving say?"

" 'To Chad. Love always, Veronica.' "

"I don't want to go back to San Francisco," Mick said. "Why can't I come down to the training camp with you?"

We'd dropped off the rental car and were in the terminal at KSBA. I'd just handed him his ticket on Southwest.

"Mick, it's time. Spend the weekend rearranging the condo. Buy a real bed. Get on with your life."

"But I found out something good from that neighbor of Wylie's. Maybe I could help you out at the training camp."

The chatty neighbor had told Mick that a dozen red roses came for Wylie three days after Chad disappeared; she'd been at work, and he'd taken them in and, he admitted, "peeked" at the card. The message was: "I'm sorry. Please forgive me. Love, Chad."

It made me wonder why Wylie hadn't told anyone about it. Was the message some kind of code? Was she still in touch with Chad? Did she know what he was doing?

To Mick I said, "You going down to the training camp would only make things awkward. Hy will be there."

Pause. "Oh, I get it."

"They've called your flight. Get going."

He hugged me, then got into the security line. Once he passed through, I headed for the private tie-downs.

I flew southeast toward El Centro, with the familiar feeling that bits and pieces of information were starting to form a recognizable pattern. I concentrated on piloting, not trying to force the connections.

Kessell/Tyne's son Chad was old enough at the time of his mother's death to know what had happened to her and who had supplied the drugs. Good reason to hate Gage Renshaw. When his father gave him up for adoption and sent him off to Los Angeles, the boy had been sad and angry. Good reason to hate Dan, too.

As a child, Chad had anger management problems and an aversion to anything having to do with airplanes. But he'd been a good son to his adoptive parents and an excellent student. And later an excellent employee and fiancé.

So what had sent him over the edge into a vendetta against the company his birth father had founded?

Veronica Wylie had noticed a change in him the November before he disappeared. Or so she said.

November, two years and some months ago . . .

Right. One of RKI's clients, a wealthy Montecito businessman and philanthropist, was kidnapped. Their operatives traced the kidnappers to a run-down house in rural Santa Barbara County. Kessell/Tyne made the decision to bypass ransom and hostage negotiations, and instead operatives had made a dramatic raid on the house, rescuing their client and killing the two men who had taken him. The incident had generated nationwide attention, as well as a debate over what limits should be placed on private protection firms. I recalled that Hy was angry because Kessell/Tyne had ignored his suggestion to negotiate with the kidnappers.

Gage Renshaw, one of the men Chad Merkel had reason to hate, had dealt with the press. The name Kessell would have alerted Merkel to the whereabouts of his birth father. Further research set off an old anger that tipped the scales in favor of vengeance.

The training camp looked strangely deserted as I approached its small airfield. Nothing moved, and there was only one aircraft parked there—a company helicopter. Hy must have flown it over from San Diego. A few years before, he'd renewed his chopper rating and now enjoyed flying machines that—as any pilot experienced in them will tell you—are composed of ten thousand movable parts, each one of them trying to do you serious bodily harm.

I landed and taxied over next to his dangerous bird.

As I got out of the plane, I immediately became aware of the intense heat and an eerie silence. I'd never been to the camp before, but Hy had told me it usually buzzed with activity. New operatives trained twelve hours a day—classroom work, evasionary driving tactics, firearms instruction and practice, self-defense disciplines, hand-to-hand combat.

But now, I heard nothing, saw no one. The guard who Hy had said would come out of the UNICOM shack to greet me didn't materialize. Neither did anybody else.

I tied down the plane, keeping a watchful eye, then took my .357 Magnum from my purse, where I'd stowed it before leaving San Francisco. Tucked it into the waistband of my pants, locked the plane, and walked toward the shack. No one there, but the UNICOM was on.

Something really wrong here.

I stood at the window on the other side of the building and surveyed the camp. Straight ahead stood a large two-story structure that probably was the dormitory and dining hall. The buildings to the right and left of it were equally large but single-story—classrooms, exercise facilities. The firing and evasionary driving ranges must be beyond them. As well as the administration building, which, Hy had said, was near the front gate and guardhouse.

That was most likely where I'd find him. Or not. More likely not.

I thought I knew what was wrong.

I stood very still, holding my breath as the pieces of information I possessed formed one perfect image.

There was a phone on the desk; I picked up the receiver. But there was no dial tone. Probably the camp's whole system was disabled.

The ever-running man was here. He'd somehow gotten everybody out of the camp, taken Hy hostage. He'd heard my plane, knew I was here, too. And he most assuredly had an explosive device.

What could I do? Hy had warned me my cellular wouldn't work here. I couldn't search the camp in daylight without the possibility of being seen and taken hostage or even shot.

I looked out the window again. Already the sun was sinking in the west. Not long before nightfall. I'd wait till then.

I moved out around six-thirty, under cover of darkness, the .357 in hand. The dormitory and classroom buildings were unlit. I slipped alongside the nearest one and peered around its front corner; a paved road led away to the left and the right. Beyond it I could make out little but the shapes of cacti and scrub vegetation; there was only a slice of moon—not enough to help me get my bearings. But also not enough to illuminate me to a watcher.

After a few moments' hesitation I went right, walking along the edge of the road. Even in the sand, my footfalls sounded loud. I smelled sagebrush; now and then a branch brushed at my leg. The night was cooling; I wished I had my jacket, but I'd locked it in the plane. I walked faster, past three smaller outbuildings, and after about a hundred yards the road widened to a large paved area where at least two dozen cars were parked.

I moved slowly toward them, slipped between the first two rows. The vehicles looked as if they ought to be in an auto salvage yard: scrapes, dents, crushed hoods, missing bumpers, shattered windows, sprung trunks. The clunker fleet. On the other side of the parking area, several roads branched off: the evasionary driving range.

Back the way I'd come, past the outbuildings, dark dormitory, and classroom buildings. The road divided and, although it hadn't worked before, again I went to the right.

Bad choice. I'd seen enough firing ranges to know this was one, even though the targets weren't visible.

Back again, and straight ahead. Soon I could see the administration building and guardhouse; there were lights on in both, as well as along the perimeter fence.

Hy . . .

Careful, McCone. Don't go rushing in.

I moved to the side, crouched down next to a saguaro cactus, and studied the situation. It wasn't good. There was no one in the guardhouse and I couldn't see into the administration building.

A trap?

Yes. He's there, and he must've heard the plane. Why didn't he come after me? And what's he done with Hy?

I tried to put myself inside the ever-running man's head. He had no reason to kill Hy. But me . . . if he thought I was getting close to learning his identity he'd have to take me out. Hy was the live bait to reel me in, and then he'd kill both of us.

I extended the Magnum in both hands as I moved toward the lighted building. At its wall, I stopped, listening. Inside, someone coughed, and the sound drew me to a high window that was slightly open. I went up on my toes and peered over the bottom of the frame.

Brent Chavez—aka Chad Merkel—sat at a desk, his profile to the window. He was tinkering with what I recognized as the makings of a bomb. After a moment, he glanced at his watch—probably the Rolex Veronica Wylie had given him.

Had a warning phone call from Wylie triggered this situation? I didn't think so. The woman had seemed genuinely bewildered at Chad's defection. Just because she hadn't told me about his final gift of roses didn't mean they'd had any further contact.

I came down off my tiptoes, crouched, and put distance between myself and the building. Took refuge by the saguaro and ran the facts through my mind again. My conclusions were the same.

I didn't know where he'd come up with his new identity, but Brent Chavez and Chad Merkel were one and the same. He'd been in San Francisco the night the Green Street building blew, and probably at the safe house when our apartment was broken into. And when the Chicago building exploded, he'd supposedly been out sick.

I was willing to bet he'd been away from La Jolla on the dates of all the other bombings.

A childhood hatred, nurtured over the years but kept under control, had been unleashed when Merkel found out that both his birth father and the man who had supplied his mother with a fatal dose of drugs were living successful lives in San Diego. But he hadn't lost control; it was a skill he had learned over time. Instead, he'd made a careful plan, and now was about to carry it out to its conclusion.

But why hadn't he stopped when his birth father was killed and Renshaw vanished? He could have slipped away and gone back to his real life, claiming something as ridiculous but unverifiable as amnesia.

But that would be too rational. I suspected Merkel had become monomaniacal where RKI was concerned. Or perhaps once he'd tasted the ultimate power—to take or spare lives—he'd become addicted to it.

Well, he wasn't going to take Hy's life—or mine. No way.

Where are *you, Ripinsky?*

The psychic connection that Hy and I had shared until recently—a connection I'd at first found strange but now took for granted—gripped me. He was nearby, waiting for me to come free him. I moved away from the saguaro, into the darkness. Stopped and studied the large buildings.

No.

Merkel wanted to kill us with that bomb, but he didn't want to create an explosion that would be seen for miles and bring the county fire department and sheriff's deputies to the compound. If the admin building or any of the others blew, it would create a conflagration that would light up the desert sky and provoke an immediate emergency response. An explosion at one of the smaller outbuildings up the road toward the evasionary driving range probably wouldn't create a stir; after all, they were always firing guns and doing God knew what else out here.

I moved through the darkness alongside the road. Again, my footfalls on the sand seemed loud. I came to the first building; its door was padlocked. I said in a low voice, "Ripinsky?"

Nothing.

My God, what if Merkel's drugged him and he can't answer me?

Keep going.

The second building was a wellhouse, its interior illuminated by a low-wattage bulb, two big holding tanks taking up most of the space. Merkel could have drowned Hy . . .

No. Not possible: I feel the connection; he's alive.

The third building was the largest, and locked with a deadbolt. I pressed my face to the edge of the door, said Hy's name.

"McCone, what took you so long?"

I sagged against the door, weak with relief.

"Get me out of here," he added.

"I can do that— Shit!"

"What?"

"My lock picks—they're in my purse in the plane."

"Don't go back there. You'll be too exposed."

"He's in the administration building, assembling a bomb. He won't see me."

"No. Don't risk it."

"I have to."

I moved away through the darkness, heart pounding. Every few yards I stopped to listen for motion nearby. The airfield was deserted; white lights outlined the runway. The UNICOM crackled and a pilot's voice announced he was turning for final at some airport nearby that I'd never heard of. I ran for the Cessna. Ducked down and clutched the strut as I unlocked the door and grabbed the lock picks from the zippered compartment of my purse. Then I pushed the door shut till the latch barely clicked and began my return.

All was as quiet as before. In the brush small desert creatures scurried away as I passed. How long, I wondered, did it take to construct a bomb? And when did Merkel plan to detonate it? I moved as quickly as I could on the unfamiliar terrain.

"I'm here," I whispered when I got to the outbuilding. "And I've got the picks."

"Thank God. I was getting worried."

"Ripinsky, where're all the people?" I selected a pick, tried to insert it. That one wasn't going to work.

"Off-site exercise in survival skills. The notification of it never got to my desk. Chavez's doing, of course."

"But the staff and the guards—"

"The staffers're given time off during exercises. Whatever's happened to the guards isn't good."

Another pick that wasn't going to work. Damn! I told myself to go slow, keep my hands steady. "You know that Chavez is really Chad Merkel, Kessell's . . . Tyne's son?"

"Oh, yeah, he was determined to tell me the whole pitiful story of his life while he was wrapping me in duct tape. I've managed to work a lot of it loose."

"How come you brought him out here?"

"He asked to ride along, since he'd never been here. Turned out he had, when he blew up those clunker cars."

I rejected another pick.

"I don't understand why he went after you," I said. "His father's dead, Renshaw's vanished, the company's in plenty of trouble."

"Because of a remark I made in his hearing, attempting to reassure a couple of the employees at headquarters. I told them I was meeting you down here and you'd have the case solved by then."

The Serpentine, my last resort. I began maneuvering it gently.

"So he thought I was on to him, and decided to kill both of us. He try anything in the chopper?"

"Nope. He was so afraid of flying I thought he might puke. He didn't make his move till we were on the ground."

The Serpentine was doing its magic. I should've tried it first.

I asked Hy, "How'd he manage to get control of you?"

"I'm damned cooperative when facing down a forty-five."

Quick upward thrust, and the lock gave. Finally I opened the door and Hy, ankles still bound by the duct tape, fell into my arms.

"You're a woman of rare talents, McCone," he said into my hair as he rested his head on top of mine.

I pushed him back inside. "What is this place?"

"Storage building."

"Do the lights work?"

"Yes, but you don't want to use them."

". . . Right. What now?"

"There're plenty of phones in the camp."

"Plenty of nonfunctional phones. I think he's disabled the system."

"Dammit!"

"Let me get that duct tape off your ankles." I knelt down, began sawing at it with a sharp-pointed pick.

I asked, "How could Chavez have gotten on with RKI, considering the background checks you run on prospective employees?"

"Because Brent Chavez is a real person, with college and grad school transcripts, letters of recommendation—the whole thing. He was Merkel's roommate at USC when they were both working toward MBAs."

"Merkel told you that?"

"Sure. He was in a very confessional mood. People who're raised thinking they're the center of the universe constantly crave attention—even from somebody they're planning to kill."

"So Merkel's as talented at appropriating someone else's identity as his birth father." I sawed through the last of the tape, ripped it off, and Hy was free. "We've got to get out of here," I told him as he flexed his ankles.

"You say he was still building the bomb?"

"Half an hour ago, yes. I wonder why he didn't assemble it in San Diego."

"Turbulence on the chopper could've set it off. And I suspect he's biding his time. He may even figure to wait for morning when an explosion'll attract less attention."

"But he knows I'm here—"

"And he's not looking for you. He's probably counting on the explosion drawing you out, making you easy prey."

"Then we have to move now."

"Give me a minute, McCone. It's not easy getting over being trussed up for hours like the Thanksgiving turkey." There was a strain in his voice that told me he was in more pain than the ordinary type that being confined will cause.

Before I could ask what else was wrong, he said, "You know, this Merkel is a very weird mix. He's bright—ingenious, really—and he's made this plan and killed all those people. But while he was taping me up he lapsed back into little-boy mode, trying to convince me that he didn't really intend to kill anybody: he didn't know there would be anybody in the Detroit office; he placed the charges in the wrong places at

Green Street. But he didn't make any excuses for Chicago. I think by then he'd started getting off on the killing."

"He had a great upbringing, a promising future, but something inside him is warped, I guess."

"Heredity. Dan's contribution." Hy moved toward the door. "Let's head for the airfield."

We slipped out of the storage building and stood at its far side, looking around and listening. It was very dark and silent now, the lights of the administration building and guardhouse faint in the distance.

I whispered, "What if he's been there, disabled the plane and chopper? I didn't think to check when I was getting the picks."

"Well, that's possible. It doesn't take a rocket scientist to open the engine compartment and yank a few wires."

"Then it's too risky. Is the fence around this compound electrified?"

"Yes. We can't climb it and walk out, if that's what you're thinking."

"Well, what about that fleet of clunker cars? Let's find one with a lot of power and enough gas in it to get us to El Centro."

Over the sand, staying a safe distance from the road. Hy leading—he knew the terrain. We'd pause every now and then to listen.

Silence.

The parking area came into view. Hy's hand stopped me.

"What?" I whispered.

"I'm studying on which one is the best. They're all high-powered, but some're better than others." A pause. "Okay, I think that flashy Chevy, two cars back on the right."

"What if he's taken the keys out?"

"It would never occur to him. I know this guy. He's been clever and lucky so far, but in a lot of ways he doesn't think things through."

"Okay, let's go for the Chevy."

Practically crawling through the sand. At the edge of the parking area, Hy stopped me and pointed to the car. It was at least twenty years old, had caved-in side doors and a broken rear window. Scrapes and dents galore.

This was a flashy Chevy?

"You drive," he whispered. "Bastard dislocated my right shoulder."

"Why didn't you tell me—?"

"It's no big deal."

"How can you be in that kind of pain and not—?"

"Shut up, McCone. We're on our way out of here."

He nudged me forward and we moved low to the ground toward the Chevy. I went to the driver's side, reached up to open the door, and slipped in. The keys dangled from the ignition. Hy got in on the passenger side.

"We'll make a quick run for the front gate," he said. "Put your seat belt on tight."

"What about gas? I can't see the indicator."

"Switch the dash lights on, but not the headlights. We'll have to run dark."

"No problem. Together we've got a pretty good idea of the lay of the land." I switched the dash lights on; the gas indicator showed the Chevy's tank was half full.

"We're okay," I said, and started it up. The heavy-duty, reliable purr of its engine told me why Hy had chosen it.

"He'll hear us," I said.

"Not till we get close to the admin building; sound carries strangely out here. And by the time he realizes we're on the move, we'll be going so fast he won't be able to stop us."

I put the Chevy in forward gear, eased out of the parking space, and drove between the rows of cars to the road. Then I pressed down on the accelerator.

We were nearing the administration building, headlights still off, going at least seventy miles an hour on the straightaway.

"Brace yourself," Hy said. "That gate is one heavy mother."

I gripped the wheel to control its shuddering. Wondered if the car had been retrofitted with airbags.

"Christ!" Hy exclaimed. "Look out!"

A figure had leaped out of the darkness to the right, and was running diagonally toward us.

Merkel. He held a rectangular object in his upraised hand.

The bomb!

I jammed the accelerator to the floor. Merkel kept running toward the car, but in the darkness he misjudged the angle and our speed. Before he could hurl the bomb, we were upon him. The Chevy's bumper grazed his body, knocked him sideways. I controlled a potential skid and kept going.

The bomb detonated close behind us, the concussion shaking the car.

The ever-running man had finally stopped running.

I aimed straight for the gate, braced for the impact. When we burst through, metal shrieked and tore, the hood crumpled, the windshield cracked. I was thrown forward so hard I was afraid the seat belt would give.

No airbags. But we're out of there.

Hy was gasping; the impact had sucked the breath out of him. The car skidded, veering toward a ditch at the side of the access road. I reclaimed control of the wheel, wrestled with it, and got us out of the skid. Then I turned off the ignition and let the Chevy slow of its own accord.

The sky behind us, reflected in the rearview mirror, was bright with smoky firelight.

I laid my head on the wheel, closed my eyes, breathing heavily. Finally I sat up and turned to Hy. He had twisted around, was staring out the side window.

"Jesus, McCone," he said.

I released my seat belt and looked back through my window. The administration building and the guardhouse were both aflame.

"We could've been in there," he added.

"But we aren't. We made it."

"Yeah, we did. You've always been a good driver, but that was one spectacular run."

"To tell the truth, I didn't know I had it in me."

He turned to me, took my hands, and held them tightly in his. "I did," he said.

Saturday

✦

MARCH 11

It was three-fifteen in the afternoon before the Imperial County authorities, the FBI, and the ATF let us go. We'd made statements, promised to turn over investigative reports, and drunk entirely too much bad coffee. When we left, the sheriff's deputies and FBI and ATF agents had already begun to wrangle over jurisdiction. The FBI, of course, would prevail.

The county fire department had been able to control the flames before they spread to the airfield. The deputy who had driven Hy to the hospital for treatment of his dislocated shoulder and brought in food while we were making our statements agreed to drive us back to the compound and to wait till we checked both aircraft for flightworthiness.

The camp was a disaster area. Emergency crews still patrolled the twisted rubble of the administration building, dormitory, and one classroom building, looking for hot spots. The smell of smoke and ashes and chemicals was thick in the air.

I said to Hy, "I want to get out of here as soon as possible."

He squeezed my hand. "We will."

Neither the plane nor the chopper had been tampered with. We said good-bye to the deputy, and I went about pre-flighting Two-Seven-Tango. I'd pilot; Hy was on strong pain meds, his right arm in a sling.

"Will the chopper be okay here?" I asked.

"It'll be fine. I'll have somebody from headquarters pick it up soon." He turned, smiled, and added, "Ready to go, McCone?"

Wednesday

✦

MARCH 15

The Ides of March: inauspicious for Julius Caesar, auspicious for home owners. At three that afternoon Hy and I did the final walk-through at the Church Street house, and found everything to our liking. More than to our liking; it was perfect.

I wrote the last of many checks to Jim Keys, and he departed. He'd left a welcome-home bottle of champagne in the fridge, but no glasses, and ours were in storage in order to avoid the ravages of heavy construction. We opened it anyway, and passed it back and forth while sitting on the deck. Ralph and Allie alternated between brushing around our legs and running back to the fence to cast suspicious looks at the house. They wanted to think our presence was permanent, but still had their doubts.

Hy and I had spent Saturday night at Rae and Ricky's. They'd wanted to hear all about what had happened at the training camp, and we'd stayed up late talking with them, then gone to bed and fallen asleep immediately—miles apart on the king-size mattress. On Sunday, Hy was up by the time

I woke, and packed to fly down south. Since then, he'd either been in La Jolla or at the training camp, coping with the aftermath of the ever-running man's final rampage. I'd moved back into the RKI apartment, and had actually managed to get in some shopping on Tuesday, buying more items for a new wardrobe. The rest I'd order off the Internet on the weekend.

Hy said, "Imperial County sheriff's people discovered the bodies of two guards at the training camp; they were in the classroom building that didn't burn—both shot in the head. I've been dealing with their families. It's a job I don't look forward to doing again."

"I don't blame you. What else?"

"The FBI's established Merkel's presence in each city where our offices were hit. He didn't cover his tracks all that well."

"You were right about him: he didn't think things through."

"Well, it's over, thank God."

"Have you decided anything about RKI?"

He shook his head, passed me the champagne bottle. "It'll take a lot of thinking, a lot of time with our lawyers. No one knows where Gage is, or what his rights are."

"He shouldn't have any rights."

"I know that, but the lawyers might think differently, since he didn't make off with any company funds. In the meantime, I'm committed to servicing our current clients."

"When d'you go back to La Jolla?" He'd come up on Southwest, arriving at noon.

"I've got a seven o'clock flight."

I felt a stab of disappointment, followed by relief. Things were still awkward with us; we needed to talk, but right now too much was going on.

He asked, "You okay about dealing with the storage company alone?"

"No difficulty in that. I call, they deliver. There's no hurry about unpacking the breakables, and they'll put the furniture where I want it."

"Good."

"Ripinsky, I need to ask you a favor."

"Anything."

"Remember when I hired Charlotte Keim away from RKI? I want you to rehire her."

He looked surprised, but said, "No problem with that. She was one of the best financial experts we had. But why?"

I explained about her breakup with Mick and the disharmony it was creating at the agency.

"Too bad. But what'll you do without her?"

"There's no shortage of young, hungry MBAs who would love a job like hers. I bet I can find somebody within two weeks. In the meantime, Patrick can handle what jobs come in. And I have a feeling Keim will jump at the chance of a change of scene."

"It's gonna cost me plenty; Keim never came cheap." A pause. "McCone, when I get a break from La Jolla, I'm going to fly up to the ranch."

"Oh?"

"Just overnight. There's some stuff I need to get. What d'you say to meeting at Touchstone a week from Saturday?"

"What stuff?" I asked.

"You'll see. Is it a date?"

"It's a date."

Saturday

✦

MARCH 25

The Pacific was a brilliant turquoise, the sky cloudless, the breeze warm—one of those rare early-spring days we get on the Mendocino Coast, when you erroneously think that the fog will never again appear on the horizon, much less creep in.

I took it as a good omen.

I'd driven up the night before, and Hy wasn't due till around noon, so I took a morning walk in the cove. There had been a recent heavy storm that had brought in some interesting driftwood. I collected a couple of the better pieces, poked around in the sea caves where bootleggers had once hidden their illegal Canadian whiskey, and did a bit of thinking.

I thought about the value of a long-term relationship, and how it should be nurtured. Thought about the importance of truthfulness, and the betrayal of trust. Thought about love. And forgiving.

Thought about Hy—and me.

When I heard the drone of the plane, I dropped the driftwood—we had too much in the house already—and hurried up the stairway to the platform. By the time I got to our airstrip, he was already tying down. I grabbed one of the chains and helped him.

"Great day," he said, and hugged me as one would a party hostess. "Let's get my gear."

He opened the plane's right door, handed me a small flight bag, hefted a cardboard carton. "That's it."

We walked toward the house.

I asked, "You have a good flight?"

"Very good."

"How's the ranch?"

"Looking better than ever. How's the Church Street house?"

"I've actually unpacked everything."

"Good for you. The cats okay with it?"

"They love it. All those new carpets and paint smells to sniff."

"No more glaring from the fence?"

"Nope."

We lapsed into silence until we reached the house. I took Hy's bag to the bedroom. When I came back, I found him in the kitchen opening a bottle of Deer Hill chardonnay—my favorite.

"Let's go out on the platform," he said. "Can you handle the bottle and glasses?"

"When have you known me not to handle bottles and glasses?"

"Never." He picked up the carton that he'd set on the counter.

We crossed the gopher-mounded excuse for a lawn—if you're a lawn fanatic, it's best to stay away from our part of the coast—and sat down on one of the benches on the platform. Earlier I'd taken the cushions from their storage box and set them out. Hy put the cardboard carton on the floor at my feet and poured the wine. Toasted me and said, "Here's to great escapes."

"Amen."

We drank, and then he said, "We need to talk."

"I know."

"But first open the box."

I reached down, pulled the flaps loose, and looked inside. "Pilot's logs?"

"Mine. From the time I worked for K Air. You can read them. They show that I only flew into the Middle East twice—one time with Dan, to rescue that idiot Ralston. And I swear to you, the cargo was pipe fittings for the oilfields in Kuwait. The other time, Dan claimed he'd checked the cargo, and I was fool enough to believe him and neglect my responsibility. When I found out we'd illegally imported arms, I stewed about it for a couple of weeks and quit. All of a sudden, the business seemed so ugly, and I felt so dirty. I'd had enough."

"I know."

"You do?"

"One of your fellow pilots told me."

"And you believed him? If he knew, he was as crooked as Dan."

"He made no bones about that, but what he said about you—that was the man I know and love." I reached down again and closed the box. "I don't need to read these."

"I'm offering them—"

"I know. As proof. But it's totally unnecessary."

"McCone—"

"Let's close the books on this past month and move on."

He smiled, brushed a lock of hair from my cheek, where the sea wind had blown it.

"Okay," he said, "but to where?"

"I don't know. There've been a lot of unpleasant scenes between us, mostly of my doing."

"There're always unpleasant scenes in any marriage."

"Even in your first marriage—even with Julie?"

"God, yes."

"I thought she was a saint."

"Nobody's a saint."

I felt an easing inside me, even though I still didn't know the answer to his question of where we'd move on to.

After a moment I laid my head on his shoulder and we watched the play of the light on the water—together.